God Bless the Trappers 3

Lock Down Publications and Ca$h
Presents
God Bless the Trappers 3
A Novel by *Tranay Adams*

Lock Down Publications

P.O. Box 870494
Mesquite, Tx 75187

Visit our website @
www.lockdownpublications.com

Lock Down Publications
Like our page on Facebook: Lock Down Publications
@
www.facebook.com/lockdownpublications.ldp
Cover design and layout by: **Dynasty Cover Me**
Book interior design by: **Shawn Walker**

Stay Connected with Us!

Text **LOCKDOWN** to 22828 to stay up-to-date with new
releases, sneak peaks, contests and more…
Thank you.

Submission Guideline.

Submit the first three chapters of your completed manuscript to ldpsubmissions@gmail.com, subject line: Your book's title. The manuscript must be in a .doc file and sent as an attachment. Document should be in Times New Roman, double spaced and in size 12 font. Also, provide your synopsis and full contact information. If sending multiple submissions, they must each be in a separate email.

Have a story but no way to send it electronically? You can still submit to LDP/Ca$h Presents. Send in the first three chapters, written or typed, of your completed manuscript to:

LDP: Submissions Dept
Po Box 870494
Mesquite, Tx 75187

DO NOT send original manuscript. Must be a duplicate.

Provide your synopsis and a cover letter containing your full contact information.

Thanks for considering LDP and Ca$h Presents.

Tranay Adams

CHAPTER ONE

Odette pulled into her driveway. She and Marquise hopped out of the car and made their way around her vehicle, headed for the steps. Odette stopped and grabbed her son's hand when she reached the bottom step, seeing the shadows upon the porch moving. Her eyes grew big and she gasped. Taking off in the direction that she'd come from with her son in tow, she'd gotten about five feet away when she heard a familiar voice call after her. She stopped cold in her tracks and slowly turned around. That's when the man that had spoken with the familiar voice came walking down the short steps, casually. The closer he got to her, the more of him appeared out of the shadowy area of the steps. It wasn't long before he was standing over her with a smile that stretched across his face. The New Era Angels fitted cap he was wearing was so big all she could make out of his face was his huge lips and thick nappy beard.

"Donald? What are you doing here?" Odette frowned and looked around as she awaited his response.

A frowning Marquise looked back and forth between his mother and the man she knew as Donald.

"I'm in town, on tour," Donald told her. "Listen, shorty, this isn't a social call. I'm here on family matters, yo. I know you said you already checked for ya self, but I gotta know myself if lil' dude is mine or not." his eyes darted to Marquise, who was still trying to figure out what the exchange was between him and his mother, "Shit's been fuckin' with me tough, I don't want my seed out here bein' fathered by anotha man. If lil' dude is mine, then I'ma step up. You feel me?" he spoke in a hushed tone that only the two of them could hear.

"Momma, who is this man and what is he talkin' about?" Marquise asked curiously.

"It's momma's friend, baby. We're just talking about a friend of ours." She lied smoothly, and then addressed Donald. "You shouldn't have just shown up here like that, Donald. I gotta man now, if he found out you were here he'd have a fucking fit! You gotta leave now, we'll discuss this some other time." She said as she tried to move past him and head into the house. She'd just brushed against his shoulder on her way around him when he grabbed her by her arm. She looked over her shoulder at him, and then at his hand on her arm, and then back again. When he saw that she was hitting him with the *get your hands the fuck off me* face, he took a step back with his hands held up.

"Please? It's only gonna take a minute," Donald claimed as he held up a home paternity test before her eyes. Before now she hadn't even noticed that he had something in his hand. She figured that by it being so dark out she couldn't make out the paternity test box in his hand at first.

Odette took a deep breath as she looked away and thought about what Donald was asking of her. When she turned back around to him, she nodded her head and said, "Alright, let's get this over with, but as soon as it's done you gots ta go, nigga. I'm not finna jeopardize what me and my man have over some bullshit. Is that clear?" she stated sternly while pointing her finger in his face.

"I got chu, ma, no funny business." Donald said with a broad smile. "Ain't chu gone introduce me to your son?" he looked between Marquise and her.

Odette made the introductions and Donald dapped up Marquise. The little dude smiled. He didn't know what it was about Donald but he kind of liked him.

"Come on, you gotta be quick 'cause I know he'll be back soon," she waved for him to follower her and he fell in step behind her and her son. Donald licked his lips and bit down on his bottom one as he shook his head, thinking of how he had her big chocolate ass tooted up in the air the last time he was fucking her doggy style.

"Lord, have mercy." He shook his head as he followed Odette and Marquise up the steps of her house.

***

Donald walked into the kitchen and took a glass down from out of the cupboard. Opening the freezer door, he reached inside and grabbed a fist full of ice cubes, dropping them down inside of the glass. He then stepped over to the faucet and filled his glass with faucet water. Leaning back against the kitchen counter, he took a sip of his water and watched Odette where she was at inside of the living room. As soon as Odette had gotten little man asleep, she took the time to swab his mouth as well as Donald's for the home paternity test. With the task done, all they had to do now was send it off and wait for the results to come back.

Donald was suppose to have left once he'd gotten what he'd came for, but he decided to kick it for a little while in hopes of getting some pussy. Now, he'd knocked a few chicks off since he'd been on the road, but he still hadn't met a piece that compared to Odette. She had the best pussy he'd ever had in his life.

Watching Odette from where she was on the telephone, Donald couldn't help thinking about all of their sexual encounters from back in the day. He had her in every position known to men, tearing her little thick, short ass up. What he really liked about her was, she was willing to bust it wide open for him where ever and whenever he wanted her to. Rarely did she turn him down when he cracked for the ass.

Feeling a pair of eyes on her, Odette looked over her shoulder and found Donald molesting her with his eyes. She already knew what he was thinking and it wasn't about to happen. Little momma wasn't thinking about his ass. The only nigga she had any holler for was her baby Kreon. She loved that nigga'z dirty drawers. He was perfect to her in every way. Since they gotten together she couldn't even fathom the thought of being intimate with anyone else. In fact, the idea of marrying him and baring his children had come to mind several times. There was absolutely no doubt in her mind that he was the man for him.

Odette flashed Donald a half hearted smile and thought, *I'm gonna have to hurry up and get this motha-fucka up from out of here. If Kreon was to pop up now, he'd shoot both of our asses dead. Let me hurry up and get sis up off the jack so I can put a rush on this fool.*

Odette had gotten home about 30 minutes ago from the incident down at The Bar Fly between her, Kreon and Carlos. She didn't waste any time putting Marquise to bed and hopping on the telephone to tell her sister what happened. Now she was pacing the floor, frantically while cradling her telephone to her ear. Every five minutes, she found herself peeking through the blinds to see if Kreon had made it to her house. She was terribly worried that he may have gotten caught up with the police for pistol whipping her son's father. If he did, she was ready to rustle up the few dollars that she'd saved and pawn all of her jewelry, including her wedding ring to get him out if she had to. He was her man and she would do any and everything thing in her power for him. That's just how little momma was, ride or die.

"For real?" Shonda asked. She couldn't believe what her sister had just told her. "Yeah."

"Gon', brotha in law, 'cause, God knows that nigga Carlos needed a good ass whopping."

"I agree. But now I'm worried that's something has happened to him."

"You think the police may have snatched him up?"

"Yes. And there's no telling how that will go."

"You don't think he's fool enough to shoot it out with the police, do you?" Now Shonda was sounding worried about Kreon's safety.

"Kreon's unpredictable, there's no telling, especially with his condition."

"Condition?"

"His mental illness," She peered out between the blinds.

"Mental illness? Wait a minute. You mean to tell me that…"

"Love you, gotta go." She disconnected the call and hurriedly unlocked the door. Forgetting that Donald was still there just that fast, she turned back around to him. "Look, Donald, my man is here now. Do me a favor, just so I can avoid all of the drama, go on and head out the back door, please. I've had one hell of a night, and I ain't tryna get in no more static, especially not with my boo."

"Alright. I'ma leave the box unda the kitchen sink though. Just send off the test and lemme know what's up later. Cool?"

"Cool," she replied holding the door cracked open.

"Aiight then," he drunk the last of his water, dumped the ice inside of the sink and sat the empty glass down in it. He then made his way towards the back door of the house.

***

Kreon pulled up four cars down from Odette's house and hopped out of the Nissan. He walked down the sidewalk, looking at the dry blood that covered his hands and the sleeves of his hoodie. As soon as he got into Odette's house, he was going to wash up and have her stash his pistol. Although his boo claimed her man was a street nigga, he wasn't taking any chances on him, abiding by the unwritten codes of the streets. For all he knew, the police were combing the streets looking for him at that very moment.

Kreon's cellular was inside of his pocket and set on silent, so he didn't know Odette had been blowing him up and trying to find out exactly where he was. He had programmed his cell this way so he wouldn't hear her calling him on his way to handle her husband. The last thing he needed was his cell ringing, disturbing his thinking. See, he needed to conclude exactly what he was going to do. He had it in mind to get him to sign the divorce papers and slump his ass, or just slump his ass. That's when he thought about what Odette said back at her house, about not wanting Marquise to grow up without his father.

Kreon knew the struggle growing up without his father, too well. He didn't meet the man he was told was his father until he was ten years old. He was around until he was fifteen, and those five years were the worse of his life, hands down. It was because of this reason and this reason only, that he allowed that punk ass nigga, Carlos, to keep his life. If it hadn't been for little Marquise, he would have peeled that nigga'z cap back.

Kreon was so caught up in the examining of his blood stained hands, he was ignorant to the presence of danger. An Envoy truck with it headlights out, was creeping up the street. From the movements of the silhouettes inside, you could tell that they were retrieving their weapons and making sure that they were locked and fully loaded. The back passenger side window descended and a large man appeared in it.

"Slow up, slow up!" Carlos said to Royce, from the front passenger seat of the Envoy truck. He'd just spotted Kreon walking up the block, en route to Odette's house. The hulk of a man scowled and smiled behind the bandana he was wearing on the lower half of his face and gripped his AK-47 in his hands firmly.

That's him?" Royce asked, wanting to be sure.

"Yeah, that's that mothafucka." he nodded, eyes stuck on his mortal enemy.

"Alright," He flicked the roach end of a blunt out of the window, sending embers flying. He then pulled his red bandana up over the lower half of his face, sitting his Desert Eagle in his lap. He murdered the headlights of the truck and brought that bitch to a crawl up the block. The SUV blended into the night, making it hard to see to the naked eye.

Carlos let his window down and the night's cool air rushed inside, ruffling his clothing. He could hear his heart pounding inside of his chest as well as inside of his ears. The moment of truth was near. He had to deliver on his threat to Kreon and show his cousin that he was about that life, just like he was. The closer he drew to Kreon, the more two sounds grew to him. That was his breathing and the beating of his heart as his adrenaline rushed the blood throughout his veins. Slowly, he inched himself out of the window and made to take aim at the nigga he planned on smoking. As soon as he met the surprised look on his face, he was pointing the dangerous end of his AK at him.

"Mothafucka, you and yo' homies jumped my relative and you thought chu were gonna get away with it?" Royce talked that shit behind his bandana. His eyes were threatening and his body language displayed hostility. Hearing this chilling voice, Kreon whipped his head around.

"Yeah, nigga, pop that shit now!" Carlos' menacing eyes bored into his enemy's and his finger curled around the trigger.

Kreon's eyelids snapped open and he gasped.

Odette came running outside to the front porch, hands to her face, she screamed, "Krrrreeeeeoooooon!"

Fuck, niggaz, caught me out here slippin', Kreon thought to himself, seeing the barrel of Carlos' assault rifle spitting flames.

"Noooooooooooo!" Odette called out as she came running across the yard. She as well as everything else seemed to be moving in slow motion to Kreon, who glanced over his shoulder to see her running at him. At any moment then, he was expecting the piping hot, jacketed bullets to come ripping through his flesh and his blood to be misting the air. But fortunately for him, God sent him his guardian angel. She was the most beautiful angel there ever was and she had the most amazing set of feathered wings.

When she ran it appeared as if she was flying at him full speed ahead. And just like the Lord, she may not have been there when you wanted her, but she was always right on time.

"Oof!" Kreon winced as he was tackled to the lawn out of the line of fire of the AK-47. He landed on his back hard and when he peeled his eyelids open, he found Odette with her arms wrapped around him. Her fearful eyes looked up at him as she wondered if he was okay and if she got him out of the way before he'd felt the onslaught of the gunman's choppa. There wasn't any time for her to ask though. Nah, because the tires of the enormous GMC truck squealed loudly in the night, and when the couple looked up the block, that big mothafucka was turning around.

The SUV swerved as its driver struggled to regain control of it. It sped up the street just as Odette had pulled her man back upon his feet. That nigga Carlos stuck his ski-masked head out of the window and out came that big ass choppa right behind him. His pupils looked like twins suns as they burned like balls of fire. He gritted and pointed his weapon just as Odette and Kreon retreated towards the house. They appeared to be growing closer and closer in his eyes the faster the GMC flew up the residential block. By this time, the giant didn't give a mad as fuck that his baby momma was out there. The way he saw it since that bitch wanted to ride for her 'new' man then she could die with his ass too.

Carlos pulled his ski-mask off because he wanted his enemy to see exactly who it was that was about to close the curtains on his life. He then called out to Kreon and he turned around, whilst still running towards the house. Once he saw that he had his attention, he smiled devilishly and pointed his AK right at him. His chubby finger went to pull back on the trigger when gunfire rang out in the night.

Blocka! Blocka! Blocka!

The first shot slammed into the backdoor of the SUV, the second shattered its window while the third struck him in the arm. He howled in pain and nearly dropped his AK-47. Fighting back the pain in his arm, he hoisted the choppa back up and tried to leave the gunman flat-line, but the fire kept on coming and he eventually dropped the choppa out into the street. The assault rifle tumbled a bit and then skidded down the asphalt to a complete stop.

Kreon and Odette looked back and found Donald on the porch with a smoking Glock .40. He kept on down the steps firing at the truck, with flames spitting from his weapon's barrel.

Fuck is this nigga? Kreon thought as he scrambled to his feet, looking up the block at the truck toting the niggaz that had just got at him. He then drew his pistol from his waistline and told Odette to stay down. Right after, he got down on one knee, gripping his small revolver with both hands and taking aim. He squeezed one eyelid shut and hugging the trigger of his .38.

Bop!

The shot he'd taken burst the back tire of the truck and it swerved out of control. He rose to his feet and Donald came to stand beside him. Together, they let loose on the enormous vehicle, shattering its back window and loading the rear of it with holes. Kreon and Donald watched as the truck fishtailed and slammed into a tree on the curb, mashing the front end of it up. Its rear brake lights glowed in the night as Royce backed it up from the tree, its fender dragging on the street. The enormous vehicle dropped off of the curb on its back tires and drove away making a funny ass noise.

"Yo' you aiight, son?" Donald gave Kreon the once over.

Kreon was about to say something when Odette interjected, "Oh my God, babe, were you hit?"

Kreon looked to the blood on his sleeves and said, "Nah, this ain't my blood…it's someone else's."

"Who's?" she asked with a wrinkled forehead.

"Carlos." He told her while looking her dead in her eyes.

At that moment, Odette wrapped her arms around him, kissing him all over his face and then checking him for wounds.

"Jesus, I thought you were for sure dead when I saw that stick spitting like that." She spoke of the assault rifle in slang terminology.

"Nah, I'm straight, slim." He replied as he looked Donald up and down, wondering who he was. He was about to ask who the fuck he was when Odette interjected once again.

"Do you know who that was shooting at chu?" she inquired.

"Yo' punk ass baby daddy." He scowled.

"My baby daddy?" her brows furrowed and she leaned closer.

"Yeah, that was that big ass Mexican, Dominican nigga, or whateva the fuck he's suppose to be." he stated with glassy eyes as he looked her in the face.

The audacity of that hoe ass nigga tryna get at me, I got somethin' for that ass though. Best believe that bitch-boy.

"Damn, he came back like that?" Odette looked away then turned back around to him. "If Carlos got at chu like that then that was his cousin Royce riding with him. He's the only nigga that he trusts to bust a move like that with him."

"Oh yeah? He a killa?" Kreon asked.

"From what I hear, bae, yes. He bang too, he's from Piru."

"I Griff you, but don't none of that mean nothin'. A hot one will put an end to all of that gangsta shit."

"Aye," she said as she held up her hands in surrender. "I'm not holding the nigga's dick, I'm just telling you his get down is all. Don't shoot the messenger."

Kreon looked up at Donald, but spoke to Odette, "O, who is…"

"Y'all come on, we needa stash these burners and I needa get chu outta these clothes, bae." Once again Odette interjected, not knowing she was interrupting what Kreon was trying to ask.

"Aahhhhhhhhh!" All of their heads snapped in the direction of the house hearing Marquise crying out. Odette and Donald took off running inside of the house, leaving Kreon behind.

Standing where he was, Kreon found himself steaming mad and confused. He wasn't for sure, but he believed that homeboy that came outside busting his gun for him was that nigga Donald that Odette had fucked behind her baby's daddy's back. If so, she was a scandalous ass bitch that couldn't be trusted as far as he was concerned.

CHAPTER TWO

"You okay, my nigga?" Royce's head whipped back and forth between Carlos and the windshield, seeing him wince from his gunshot wound.

"Hell naw, I'm not fuckin' okay?" Carlos's bugged eyes looked down at the bleeding black hole in his arm as he clenched it, blood slicking his fingers. "That bitch ass nigga shot me." He threw his head back and squeezed his eyelids shut, gritting his teeth to fight back the fire in his limb.

"Lemme see, Blood," a frowning Royce grabbed his cousin's arm and turned it from left to right, seeing that the bullet was still in him. "It's still in there, but I'm sure we can get it out. We just gotta get chu some medical attention and you'll be good."

Nigga, I can't fade no hospital, The Ones will be all over the place askin' questions about this shit." He looked to the hole in his arm as it ran with blood.

"You think I don't know that? I grew up in these streets. I ain't new to this I'm true to this…" he lifted up his shirt and showed off the old staple wounds and gunshot wounds going up his torso. Once he'd let his relative see them, he let his shirt fall over him. He'd gotten them courtesy of a shootout with a rival gang when he was just a young nigga trying to make a name for himself in the streets. "My man's girl took care of me."

"She's a doctor?"

"Nah, a veterinarian, but she knew enough to help a nigga out. I'ma hit her up for you," he whipped out his cellular and placed a call to homegirl that could take care of his kinfolk's gunshot wound. "Yo, Vanessa, what chu doin' right now?" he spoke into the receiver as soon as he heard his homeboy's fiancée pick up the telephone.

"Ahhhhh, fuck, shiiiiiit, Grrrrr," Carlos had his head tilted back, eyelids squeezed shut and teeth gritted. He was sitting at the kitchen table with Royce gripping his hand tightly. In fact, he was gripping his hand so tight that the veins showed up both their arms and wrists. While Royce was giving him support, he was taking the occasional swig from the bottle of Jack Daniel's to help him combat the fire in his wounded arm.

"Fuuuuck, man, this shit hurt's!" Carlos continued to complain as the blonde haired, baby blue eyed Veterinarian known as, Vanessa, struggled to pull the bullet out of his arm with a medical tool. Her face was shiny from sweat and her eyes were focused on the hole in Carlos's arm as she tried to dig the metal slug out of it. She had a face masked with dedication and determination. Feeling she'd grasp the metal slug with her tool, she smiled triumphantly and pulled it out. The small hunk of metal was mashed up and stained crimson.

"There's the little fella that's been giving my friend Carlos all that trouble."

Vanessa dropped the ruined slug into a tin bowl which was sitting on the table. Afterwards, she cleaned up Carlos's wound and bandaged it up. She placed gauze and medical tape on the kitchen table and suggested that his wound be changed twice a day. Next, she prescribed him a pain killer, which she'd gotten through her plug that worked at a CVS pharmacy.

"There's about sixty of those in there. You should take no more than three a day. Anymore than that and you're looking to overdose." Vanessa packed her things away inside of her worn black leather bag and closed it. She then picked it up from off the kitchen table and looked at Royce as he counted out the money he was suppose to give her for her services.

Once he came up with her quota, he passed her the money and she stuffed it inside of her bra.

"You guys take it easy." Vanessa shook Royce's hand and patted Carlos on his back on her way out of the door.

20

Royce shut the door behind Vanessa and locked it. When he turned around he found Carlos on his feet. He was standing beside the stove with the bottle of Jack turned up guzzling it. Bringing the bottle down from his lips, he hissed and squeezed his eyelids shut. Next, he wiped his mouth with the back of his fist and looked up at his cousin.

"You needa take it easy on that liquor, Blood. You not 'pose to mix that shit with them pain killaz." Royce warned his first cousin.

"I'm already numb to the pain, cousin. This drank got me faded for real, for real. Know what I'm sayin'?"

"Fa' sho'."

"Yo' I'ma crash here tonight if you don't mind, and then in the a.m I'm outta here. Cool?"

"Bool," he dapped him up. "Look, don't worry about nothing. We gone find that bitch-ass nigga and we gone split his mothafucking onion. Straight like that, Bleed. We ain't letting shit ride."

"That's love, cousin." Carlos gave him a one armed hug and pulled back, taking the Jack to his head again.

"I'ma get chu a pillow and some blankets and shit, G. The couch is all yours, homie." Royce went off down the hallway to get the shit he told him he was going to give him.

***

"Shhhhh, it's gone be okay, lil' man, everything is going to be alright." Donald tried to calm a crying Marquise. Hearing all of the shooting outside had awoken him from his sleep. He ran up into the living room, just in time to see Carlos hanging out of the window with the stick, shooting at Kreon and exchanging gunfire with Donald. He'd never seen a live shootout before and it terrified him. He was afraid that Kreon, Donald and his mother would be killed.

Kreon appeared to be even angrier when he entered the house and heard Donald's voice coming from Marquise's bedroom.

"Who the fuck is this nigga?" Kreon asked Odette as he entered Marquise's bedroom and flipped the light switch on. He found Donald sitting on the side of Marquise trying to comfort him as he lay in bed crying. As soon as Donald heard the hostility in Kreon's voice, he whipped his head around and wondered what was going on. For the first time Kreon could see his face clearly. Homeboy was a brown-skinned dude that stood about five foot ten. He had a muscular build and light brown eyes that appeared to glow. He had a wide, flat nose and lips twice the size of Kreon's lips. The beard surrounding the lower half of his face was thick and plentiful, but it was well trimmed and aligned his face perfectly.

"The friend of mine I told you about...Donald." Odette hurried up and said it. She knew that Kreon was about to blow his fucking top and she was afraid of what the aftermath was going to be. Her heart thudded and her palms began to clam up.

"Donald?" His brows furrowed further and he went to approach Donald. Odette jumped in front of him trying to explain the situation, but he shoved her aside.

"Kreon," Marquise sprung from his bed and ran over to his mother's boyfriend, leaping into his arms. The boy kissed him on his cheek and pressed his head against him, holding him tight. "You're alive, you're okay. I thought that bad man hangin' outta the window of that big car had killed you."

"Nah, lil' homie, Kreon is hard to kill." Kreon said with his eyes glued on Donald as he mean mugged him. "O, take lil' man into yo' bedroom."

"Wait, what are you about to do?" she asked, taking her son away from him.

"Just do like I said." he replied as he continued to mean mug Donald. Without uttering another word, Odette went to oblige her man's orders. Once she was gone, Kreon addressed Mr. Rap star. "Fuck is you doin' at my girl's house, homeboy?" He spat rapid fire at him.

"You should ask yo' girl that." Donald responded as he rose to his feet. He was in a blue thermal and puff vest. A pair of unlaced construction Timberland boots was on his feet. A gold and diamond chain hung loosely around his neck with the DMK (Dope Money Klique) logo on it, which was D.M.K set against black onyx with two syringes crossing one another to form an X.

Old boy dressed, moved, talked and acted like a nigga straight off Connecticut soil.

"Nigga, you don't tell me what the fuck to do!" Kreon spoke in a tone laced with animosity as he pointed his .38 at Donald. Donald had gone to pull his gun, but the young man was just a little too fast for him. He had about two bullets left and he was dying to put them all in his chest.

When Donald saw the revolver, he froze up and slowly lifted his hands up in the air, palms showing. He was scared but he wasn't trying to show it.

"This how you treat the nigga that just saved yo' life, yo?" Donald asked in his Connecticut drawl.

"Nigga, save these nuts!" Kreon capped back with his trigger finger itching, he cocked the hammer on his revolver with his thumb.

"Yo' homie, be easy," Donald tensed up, his heart racing.

"Shut cho hoe ass up 'fore yo' label mates be makin' a rest in peace song! You was up in here fuckin' my bitch, wasn't chu? Wasn't chu, nigga? You thought chu was gone come up in here and make me look like a mothafuckin' fool like you did her baby daddy, didn't chu? Well, I'ma 'bouta make you look like the fuckin' fool."

"Man, it ain't even like that, I came over here 'cause..."

Swhack!

Kreon cracked him across the face with his .38 and he bowed at the waist, holding his face with both hands. When he rose back up there was a nasty gash over his eyebrow and it was oozing blood. The blood had gotten into his eye so he squeezed his eyelid shut to stop any more from getting in there. He stood before Kreon, pistol pointed in his face, wincing and wishing he'd never came by Odette's house, but it was far too late now. Kreon ordered the nigga to slowly pull out his banga and toss it onto Marquise's bed, and he obliged him.

"Now, you talk when I tell you to, nigga, run me all yo' shit!"

"Aww, naw, dawg, I can't go out like da..." Another crack in the face cut his words short and he grabbed his face again. This time when he removed his hands there were a few cuts on it, which were red and threatening to trickle blood.

"There goes that mouth again! Now, un-ass yo' shit!" Holding the pistol on Donald, Kreon watched as he relieved himself of all his jewelry and laid it on the bed. He then pulled out the money in his pockets and tossed it on the bed. "Now, strip!" Donald frowned and looked at him like he couldn't be serious.

This pissed Kreon off and he threw his hand into the air, firing a shot into the ceiling and causing debris to fall. The gunshot startled Donald and he took off his Angels fitted cap and exposed his receding hairline. The nigga had a hairline like George Jefferson's.

Odette walked back into Marquise's bedroom to see what was happening. "What's going on in here? Oh my God, bae, what're you doing? I told you it's not even like..."

"Shut up! Shut the fuck up! This all yo' fuckin' fault, I'm not even tryna hear that noise!" Kreon barked over his shoulder heatedly.

He was so angry that the vein on his temple was twitching and his nostrils were pulsating. When he turned back around, he found Donald in his boxer briefs and socks. "Yo' draws too, homeboy, hurry that ass up!" he wagged his .38 at him.

Donald looked like he wanted to protest but decided against it. He could tell that Kreon wouldn't hesitate to put something blazing hot in his ass and he didn't want to agitate him any further.

"Mommy, is everything okay?" Everyone heard Marquise from inside of his mother's bedroom. He was standing at the door with it cracked open.

"Ev...everything is fine, baby boy. I want chu to climb in bed and turn the TV up as loud as you can get it. Can mommy's big boy do that for her, huh?"

"Okay." The boy shut the door.

Donald took off his boxer briefs and kicked them to the side. Now, he was standing in the bedroom holding himself. He was frowned up and his jaws were clenched so tight that his muscles shown in them. He looked like he wanted to spit threats, but something inside of his head told him he'd do better keeping his mouth shut.

"Get cho lil' boyfriend's phone," Kreon ordered Odette, still holding his pistol on Donald. "I want chu to film this shit."

Odette did exactly what she was told and started filming Donald.

"Alright, Donnie Boy, here's what I want chu to say..." Kreon went on to tell dude what to say on camera. When he bucked, he threatened to shoot his balls off and he complied.

"'Sup y'all, dis dat bitch ass nigga D. Dot from the Dope Money Klique, I just wanted to say fuck dem niggaz from my squad. EZ Money Bagz, Too Fly, Fowl Language, Strategy and that nigga, Khaos. All dem niggaz can suck my dick, straight up! All you niggaz some bitch-ass niggaz and I'm King of the bitch- ass niggaz, word to mine, son!"

"Good. Now walk, pussy!"Kreon kicked Donald in his ass and pitched him forward. He nearly fell but kept on walking to the living room like he'd been ordered. Once he'd gotten to the front door, Kreon told the nigga to open it and step out onto the porch. As soon as he did, Kreon kicked him in the ass and he fell down the steps. He then scrambled to his feet and took off running down the block, butt ass naked.

Slam!

Kreon slammed the door shut and turned around to Odette. His pupils danced with fire and his nostrils flared. He was gripping his .38 so tight that his knuckles turned white.

At this point, Odette was terrified of Kreon. He was madder than he was that night in the parking lot when he'd gotten into it with the white dude in the Trans Am. With how angry he was now, she pondered whether he was going to harm her or not.

"Gemme this fuckin' cell phone," Kreon snatched Donald's cellular from her and slid it into his pocket. He then tucked his .38 on his waistline. This put Odette at ease some, but he still had his fist to thrash her with, so she was still cautious of him.

"Kreon, the only reason Donald came over here was because he wanted..."

"I don't give a fuck what reason he had to come ova here! I said, no mothafuckin' exes, and you agreed to it! You lied to me so you can't be trusted!" He barked on her and his spit clung to her face.

At that moment, she was in the corner of the living room, looking as scared as a mouse, quivering. "You can't be trussstteeedddddd!" Kreon blacked out and started slamming his fists into the wall on the side of her, and knocking several holes into it. Plaster and debris went flying everywhere and falling to the floor. Odette ducked under him and ran over to the couch. Standing where she was, she watched in horror with her hands to her bosom.

Kreon turned around to Odette. His eyebrows were arched and his nose was scrunched up. His arms were hanging at his sides and his fists were clenched tightly, veins shown in his hands. There was plaster residue on his fists and some of it dropped to the floor. Kreon's eyes were red and he was seething. His jaws were locked so tight that they throbbed.

"Kreon, you need to stop, you're scaring me!" Odette cried. Her tears were cascading down her cheeks.

"You ain't gotta be scared of me no mo', O. We done!" he made to walk out the door and she rushed over and grabbed him by his arm. He looked down at her hand like it was covered in vomit.

"Wait a minute, what do you mean we're done?"

"Like I said, nigga, we through, I ain't fuckin' witcho scandalous ass no mo', real shit."

"Kreon, I swear to God, I wasn't fucking with Donald. Look, bae, just sit down and lemme explain."

"Nah, ain't shit to explain. Even if you wasn't fucking that nigga ova here, you had 'em up in here. I told yo' black ass no exes and you still disrespected me by having some nigga up in the house. And not just any nigga, the same mothafucka that chu crept on yo' baby's daddy with." Kreon became silent as if he'd just came to the realization of something. "Awww, man, the same nigga, Mocha? You tryna play me for real, huh?"

"Bae, I..."Kreon hushed her with his finger to her lips and said, "Nah, lil' momma, you ain't gotta say nothin' else. What's done is done." He took his finger from her lips and continued, "As soon as I walk outta that door, you dead to me. I'ma forget that you ever existed. In fact, I'ma have your funeral in my head before I make it outta yo' yard."

Kreon turned his back on Odette and opened the front door. As she watched him shut the door behind him, she began to cry. She stood where she was in the living room trying to imagine what life would be like without him and she couldn't see herself without him...ever. If she wasn't sure of anything else she was sure that she was in love with him. There hadn't been a man yet that touched her heart the way that he had, and she wasn't about to let her foolish pride stop her from going after him.

With that in mind, Odette opened the door and ran out onto the porch. She made it outside just in time to see Kreon jumping behind the wheel of his vehicle and cranking it up. Acknowledging this, she hurried down the steps and to the gate of her home. By the time she'd made it to the gate, Kreon was driving off past her.

"Kreon! Kreonnn! Kreonnnnn!" Odette called out after her lover over and over again, but he kept on going as if he didn't even hear her, which he didn't. Not one to give up easily, Odette darted back inside of the house to get Marquise ready; she was going after her man. She'd be damned if she lost the best thing that had ever happened to her when she'd just gotten it.

CHAPTER THREE

Newport wedged between her fingers, Ella zipped up the last of her duffle bags and dropped it on the floor beside the other duffle bag. Stepping before the mirror of the dresser, she took one last pull from her square and sat it down in the ashtray. Smoke wafted from it and disappeared in the air. Picking up a beige rubber band, she stared at her reflection and pulled her graying hair back into a ponytail, tangling the rubber band around it. Her eyelids had swollen from crying for so long and her eyes were pink and glassy. Her cheeks were slicked wet, having shed so many tears.

Ella couldn't believe her son blamed her for his mental illness. She couldn't see how she was solely responsible for his condition. Sure, she housed the man that harassed and abused him, but there were other incidents that contributed to him being emotionally disturbed. She refused to hold all of the weight herself. Sure, she wasn't the ideal parent, but who was? Ella did the best she could raising her son. She did everything in her power to give him a better life than she had. So even if she failed, she could sleep at night knowing that she tried.

Ella took another pull from the end of her cancer stick, pulling smoke into her lungs. Allowing the intoxicating fog to roll around inside of her chest, she blew it back out with the other smoke lingering around her. Afterwards, she mashed the cigarette out inside of the ashtray, leaving a black smear behind. Next, she threw on her corduroy jacket with the wool around the collar and jotted down something on a slip of paper. She folded the paper up and stuck it inside of an envelope, licking it closed. Having signed her son's name on the front of the envelope, she grabbed her duffle bags and headed for the living room. Coming across the portrait of herself and a younger Kreon, she stopped where she was and turned around.

Dropping her duffle bags on the floor, she picked up the portrait and admired it. A smile etched across her face

"My baby boy, my sweet, sweet baby boy," She kissed her hands and placed it to the glass of the portrait, sliding her fingers down the center of it. Next, she tucked the portrait inside of her jacket, grabbed her duffle bags, and headed out of the door. Holding the door open, she took one last look at the apartment before taking her leave.

Ella came down the stairs and made her way to the back of the apartment complex were the parking lot was located. She opened the trunk of her vehicle and tossed in her luggage, slamming it shut. Now that that was out of the way, she jumped in behind the wheel of her '96 Mercury Mystique and peeled out of the parking lot. Her first stop was at the gas station on Manchester and Hoover. She pulled up to pump 4 and headed up to the bulletproof window to purchase some gas.

"Yeah, lemme get twenty on number four and a pack of Newport 100s..." Ella told the stubby Mexican clerk, with the short hairstyle. Ella's face frowned up when she saw the clerk grabbing the wrong kind of smokes. "Noooo, not shorts, 100s. Yeah, yeah," she nodded her head once she saw the woman grabbing the pack of cigarettes she wanted. "Thank you." She grabbed her pack of smokes and her change. She shoved the money inside of her pocket and cracked open the pack of smokes. Pulling a cigarette out of the pack, she stuck it between her lips and sifted through her purse for a lighter. She triggered the bluish orange flame of the Bic lighter. She was startled by the sudden bellow of a voice that caused her to drop the cigarette from her lips, which deflected off the tip of her sneaker.

"Gemme all of your money, all of it, now goddamn it!" an older white man ordered. He had sunken in, baggy eyes and pronounced cheek bones. He had long stringy, dirty blond hair and a shaggy beard that made him look like Charles Mason. He was in a wrinkled ass grape juice stained shirt and tattered jeans that were torn at the left kneecap. He looked around paranoid with bulging eyes and thin ashy lips. He was nervous as hell that the cops may pop up. This was his first time robbing someone. He was jonesing for some meth, but he was flat broke and this was the only way he knew how to get some fast cash. "Hurry the fuck up!" he spat angrily and spit leaped off of his lips. Ella hurriedly searched through her purse trying to give him the money out of it. Frustrated, the meth head snatched the purse and ran off into the night.

A terrified Ella looked to her hands and they were trembling uncontrollably. The robbery had her shaken up. As soon as old boy pulled out on her she thought that her life was over. She could literally see all of the most important events of her life flashing before her eyes like a movie trailer.

***

Drennen was gangsta leaning in Kreon's Pontiac, gripping the steering wheel with one hand. He nodded his head, listening to George Clinton's *Atomic Dog*, spitting the lyrics along with him. If any of the cars in the lanes beside him knew his current situation, they'd think he'd lost his mothafucking mind. And who could blame them? He was cruising through the streets without a care in the world with a dead body in his trunk.

Sometime later, Drennen's forehead creased with lines. This was because he saw orange cones in the street that was leading traffic to one side of the road, as well as a lit up sign that read, *check point ahead*. Drennen's heart quickened in his chest. It was at this time that he thought about Jaekwon's body in the trunk and the gun that he'd used to kill him, which was underneath his seat. Before he knew it, he was being forced to drive in one lane by cones. The palms of his hands had grown moist, idling in the lane and seeing that there were only three vehicles ahead of him. Drennen believed that he was fucked with a capital F. The police usually asked for your driver's license and checked to see if you were under the influence. He didn't drink or smoke, so he was good as far as being under the influence, but he didn't have any L's. Hell, he had been locked up for the past few years, so it wasn't any way that he could provide proof of that.

Fuck that. I'ma hold court in these streets before I go back to the pen, he removed The Ghost Gun from underneath his seat, tucking it in between the seat and console. As soon as the cop asked for his driver's license, he was going to blow his wig back. Drennen pulled to a stop and a burly officer with a bushy mustache approached his window, knocking on it. Smiling, the ex-con let the window down and greeted the law enforcer.

"Hey, how are you doing there, partner? May I see your license and registration please."

"Sure. I got it right here, sir." Drennen smiled at the officer. Turning his head away from him, he scowled and went to pull his weapon. Gripping his gun, he went to turn around and shoot him when the unthinkable happened.

Boom!

The cop went flying like a rag doll when a Toyota pickup truck slammed into him. The driver of the vehicle tried to mash on the brakes but it was too late, he went crashing into one of the police cruisers parked alongside the curb. As soon as it happened, the other officers that were present went running towards the cop that had been hit. One of them radioed in for an ambulance as he ran amongst the other, en route to the injured officer, who was lying bloody and twisted in the street. Blood was pouring out of his nostrils and mouth. He gargled on the blood in his grill as he struggled to breathe, his pupils moved around aimlessly between his narrowed eyelids. Seeing that the rest of the cops were busy taking care of their own, Drennen knew he'd better take advantage of the situation. That's when he drove off. On his way past the wrecked Toyota pickup, he glanced over at the driver who was getting yanked out of the vehicle by irate officers. Drennen could tell by the look on his face that he was indeed drunk.

"Hmmph, betta his ass than mine," Drennen told himself as he drove on, and stashed his gun where he'd drawn it from.

Drennen sighed with relief since he'd avoided a possible shoot out with the cops. He was sure the law would have eventually gunned him down, had he decided to take that route, but he sure as hell wasn't going out without taking at least a handful of those mothafuckaz with him. Drennen slid his gun in between the seat and the console. He left the window open and allowed himself to feel the cool breeze that drafted inside, ruffling the collar of his suit.

That shit was a close call right there, boy. A nigga thought that was the end to his story, but God shined light on a G, for real, for real. After I get rid of this punk ass nigga in the trunk, I'm takin' my black ass home to lay it down. Straight up.

***

The headlights of the vehicle looked like two bright orbs as he drove through the woods. Its headlights illuminated the many creatures that inhabited the grounds and cast their shadows at the backs of them. The brittle leaves and twigs that covered the surface crunched and snapped under the pressure of the car's Goodyear tires. Drennen made it one mile inside of the woods before he found his headlights shining on a pre-dug grave and a pile of dirt with a shovel sticking straight up out of it. Beside the dirt pile was a big ass bag of lye that he was going to use to cover the body with to help dispose of Jaekwon's corpse.

Drennen hopped out of the Pontiac and removed his suit's jacket and the button-down he wore underneath it. As of now, he was left in his wife beater and slacks. He pulled his gloves from his back pocket and slid them on his hands, flexing his fingers in them. Afterwards, he reached inside of the window of the car and popped the trunk. Walking around to the rear of the Grand Am, he pulled out Jaekwon's dead body and dragged him over to the hole he'd dug. He then removed his clothing until he was naked. Next, he kicked his body over to the grave and it fell inside. Jaekwon's body lay inside of the grave with his arms and legs lying at funny angles.

Ol' weak-ass nigga, couldn't hold his own when them Jakes applied that pressure to his hoe ass, Drennen shook his head pitifully as he stared down into the grave he'd thrown Jaekwon inside of. He then tore open the bag of lye and hoisted it up, grunting. Cradling it in his arms, he poured its contents out onto Jaekwon's corpse until he'd completely covered it. Next, he tossed the empty bag aside and went about the task of shoveling dirt into the grave. Once he was done, he smoothed the dirt over the grave and stabbed the shovel into the ground.

Drennen pulled a garbage bag from out of his back pocket and opened it. He stuffed Jaekwon's blood stained clothing into the bag and tied it tight. He then snatched his shovel from out of the ground and headed back to the trunk of the Pontiac. He tossed the shovel and the bag of bloody clothes inside of trunk, and slammed it shut. Jumping behind the wheel of the Grand Am, he cranked it up and drove from out of the woods.

Drennen drove the Pontiac into an alley. He pulled out the bloody interior inside of the trunk and sat it down beside a trash bin alongside the bag of bloody clothing. He then set everything on fire, watching it burn until he was sure all of it was ashes. Afterwards, he took the car to a car-wash and washed its trunk out thoroughly before he headed back to his motel for the night.

Being a gangsta may have been glamorized in today's society, but boy was it hard work.

***

Po sat on the bench leaning forward with his hands clasped. His head was tilted upwards and his eyes were taking in everyone that was inside of the holding cell with him. He wasn't tripping off any of the niggaz there, because he and his crew outnumbered them. Po and his niggaz had been there nearly a week; today the bus was coming to take them up to the County jail. He had been calling his older brother, Kennan's house since the day before, but he'd yet to get an answer. Po figured he'd try calling again today, in hopes that someone would answer.

There was laughter and talking amongst the men inside of the holding cell. Po's niggaz chopped it up amongst themselves about the time they were looking at for the guns and drugs they were caught with, while Po sat at the end of the bench lost in thoughts of his own. Out of all of his people, Po was the one looking at never seeing the sunlight again; being that he was already a two time loser. With this case, he was looking at twenty-five years to life under California's three strike law. If nothing short of a miracle happened, he knew that he was washed up, but he wasn't just going to lie down without getting some get-back. Fuck that. He wouldn't be able to sleep at night knowing that the bitch responsible for him being locked up for an eternity was still out in the free world.

Seeing one of the fools inside of the cell had just gotten off of the phone, Po jumped to his feet and strolled over to it, casually.

Picking up the telephone, Po placed a collect call to his brother again. He cracked a slight grin when he heard someone answer the telephone. It was a woman. His exchange with her was brief. Afterwards, she handed her husband the telephone.

"Bruh bruh, it's me, Po."

"'Sup, lil' nigga? Fuck you doin' locked up?" He took the time to take a pull from whatever he was smoking and blew out smoke into the air.

Po told Kennan exactly how he'd gotten locked up. He then went on to tell him in code what he wanted done about it.

"Yeah, my nigga, if this shit goes left, I'm not neva gone see a sunset again."

"Keep yo' head up, loved one. Yo' blood got chu faded."

"True that. Peace." Po disconnected the call and shuffled back over to the bench. Once he got to the space that he was sitting, he found a young nigga there that looked like he was with the shit. The fool had tattoos on his face that made little to no sense, and dreadlocks that hung over his eyes. His menacing eyes peered up at Po, but he wasn't pumping fear into his heart. Nah, that nigga Po was far from pussy. He was cut from a cloth that wasn't even made anymore.

Po's eyebrows arched and his nose scrunched up. He balled his hands into fists at his sides, making the old scars and missing knuckles there more prominent.

"Fuck up off of my spot, nigga!" he ordered with authority in his voice.

"Fuck you think you talking to?" Dreadlocks jumped to his feet, hair bouncing on his shoulders.

"You, pussy!" He spat the word 'Pussy' with emphasis, raining spittle in homeboy's face.

"Nigga, you got me fucked..." Dreadlocks went to fire on Po and all of his niggaz surrounded him. Their hard faces and twisted lips dared him to make a move so that they could use his dreadlocks to mop up his own blood.

Dreadlocks took a look around at all of the threatening faces encircling him and knew instantly that he didn't stand a chance.

"This not what chu won't, homie. Now, get the fuck…" Po kicked dreadlocks so hard in his ass; he fell to the cold, filthy floor. Him and his crew watched him scramble to his feet and retreat to the corner, holding his buttocks and looking over his shoulder to make sure that they weren't about to jump his ass.

"Punk-ass nigga!"

"Bitch-ass mothafucka!"

"Fuck-nigga!"

Were just some of the words uttered by Po and his niggaz. One of them asked could they pound dreadlocks out, but he told them to chill. Afterwards, on his orders, they disassembled and left him by his lonesome. Po pulled up his jeans and sat down on the bench, leaning forward and clasping his hands together. Deep in his thoughts, he stared at the ground and a wicked smile suddenly etched across his face. He started off giggling, then chuckling, and finally, full out laughing his ass off. The nigga laughed so hard that tears came running out of the corners of his eyes. He had his head tilted back and his hand on his stomach, cracking the fuck up. What was so funny you ask? Well, Po's brother, Kennan, was said to be one of the most feared men in Southern California. You couldn't help mentioning murder and his name in the same breath. He was known for gunplay. The mothafucka had a reputation that stretched longer than Crenshaw Blvd. Unleashing him was the equivalent of letting a lion loose in civilization. This was because there was sure to be chaos and pandemonium. Po was laughing because Ella didn't know the trouble that was headed her way, and she'd be surprised when old Kennan showed up on her doorstep.

"Hahahahahahahahahaha."

Po doubled over laughing, holding his stomach with both hands. His crew and the rest of the niggaz in the cell were standing around, staring at him like he'd lost his fucking mind.

"Hahahahahahahahahaha."

"Man, they locked us up with a real mothafuckin' loon," one of the detainees said in a hushed tone to one of the men standing near him, keeping his eyes on Po.

"Hahahahahahahahahaha."

"You ain't neva lied." The man replied, keeping his eyes on a laughing Po as well.

"Hahahahahahahahahaha."

***

The illumination of the street light shining through the cracked opened blinds, cast black diagonal bars on the couple that lay asleep in bed. There were two lumps in the bed. A large lump lying beside the smaller one was snoring noisily, but it was the crying of the baby inside of the other bedroom coming from the baby monitor that led the smaller lump beside it to stir. The smaller lump's movements started off slow, but began to speed up until a hand reached out from underneath the blanket it was bundled up in. The hand picked up the monitor and brought it to a pair of full lips and sleep brown eyes, which were narrowed into slits. All of which belonged to a homely looking younger woman in large lens glasses. She had a golden brown hue and had a black mole just above her top lip, like Cindy Crawford. She had thick eyebrows and individual braids that were tied off at the end by a golden thread.

The younger woman coughed with her fist to her mouth while listening closely to the baby. Once she was sure that it was indeed her child and she wasn't dreaming, she sat the monitor back down on the nightstand and threw the blanket off of her person. Sitting up in bed and sliding her feet into a pair of slippers, she rose to her feet. Treading across the room, she walked passed her husband, Kennan's, charcoal gray security guard uniform. It was hanging on the doorknob of the closet, right above his worn pattern leather boots, which were untied and polished to a shine. The younger woman grabbed her house coat from out of the closet and slipped her arms into it, one by one.

"I'm coming, Eden, I'm coming," she told her baby girl as she shuffled to the door. She glanced over her shoulder and found her husband still lying asleep, snoring. His breathing made the lump that was him increase and decrease in size. "Awww, my poor baby," she said of her husband of eight years. He had been pulling twelve hour shifts, six days a week to make sure his family was well taken care of.

Right then, the telephone began ringing, resonating throughout the house.

Briiiiing! Briiiiiing! Briiiiiiing! Briiiiiing

Kennan stirred awake. He threw off the covers and looked to the telephone, wiping the crust from the corners of his eyes. Picking up the telephone, he stretched and yawned a little. He then pressed the button that accepted the collect call from his younger brother.

"Yeah," Kennan spoke halfway asleep, his eyelids narrowed and his nose scrunched up. He snorted repeatedly. He then made an eerie sound with his throat as he dug in his ear. "What's up, man? I see yo' black ass is in trouble again." he looked over his shoulder at his wife. He found her pacing the floor with their baby, trying to get her to fall back to sleep. Seeing that she was occupied, he turned his attention back on the conversation at hand. He excused himself from the bedroom and entered the bathroom, shutting the door behind him. He turned on the faucet and shut the lid of the commode, sitting down on it.

"So, what's the situation?" he leaned forward, resting his elbows on his thighs and listening closely to the caller.

From there, they had a conversation that was so coded that you would have genuinely thought that they were talking about making an omelet and not about committing murder. At the closing of the conversation, the brothers wished each other well and hung up. Kennan took the cordless phone from off his ear and turned off the faucet. Leaving the rest room, he treaded across his daughter's bedroom and found his wife placing their baby girl inside of her crib.

"So, who was that?" Jewels asked, as they both stared over into the crib at their little bundle of joy.

"My younger brother."

"Hold on. I know you aren't talking about your younger brother, Po. The one that's always got his hands into some shit?" her brows furrowed. She knew everything there was to know about her husband's younger brother, including his criminal history. The only time her man heard from the knucklehead sibling was when he found himself in a jam. Otherwise, he was as quiet as a church house mouse on his part of town.

Jewels considered Po a con man and a manipulator, and she was sure that Kennan saw him as such, too. Still, that didn't stop him from running to the hoodlum's every beckon call when he was in trouble. She figured it was because they were the only existing relatives from their bloodline besides the child that she and Kennan were having together. Although that was absolutely true, she still didn't see the logic in her husband risking his wellbeing on account of his trouble making brother when he had a family to take care of.

"Yeah," He answered as he journeyed into the living and opened the closet door.

"What has he gotten himself into now?" she questioned with concern

"That, I cannot tell you, you know that," he stated as he triggered the light inside by pulling on the drawstring. He then reached up at the top shelf of the closet and took down a gun case. Sitting the case down on the arm of the couch, he opened it. Holding open the lid and staring down into it, he found himself observing his handgun and four magazines.

"And why is that?" she frowned and folded her arms across her breasts.

"It's best that you don't know anything about my dealings in the criminal world. In case I get jammed up, there isn't anything that you can tell 'em crackas about my involvement." He picked the gun up from out of the case and gripped it with both hands. Shutting one eyelid as his face winced, he aimed the gun across different stuff inside of the living room, imagining the items as his enemies and opening fire on them.

It had been a long time since Kennan had held a piece of steel in his hands. Although he still had the mentality, he was far removed from the street life. These days he was making his coins as a security guard and strip club bouncer to keep a roof over his loved ones heads and food on the table. He had to admit to himself though. The call to action had him excited. He couldn't wait until he could get back into the streets and into the thick of things.

"That's all fine and dandy, but what am I suppose to do if something happens to you? What am I suppose to tell our child?" she moved her head like ghetto girl's do when they're heated.

Kennan placed his gun back inside of the case, shut it and locked it. He placed his hands on the waist of his wife and kissed her lips, staring inside of her eyes lovingly for the moment. "Baby, I have life insurance policies that total up to five million dollars. Should anything happen to me, you and our child will be well taken care of. As far as what do you tell our child should something happen to me? I'm going to leave a recording just in case something goes left out there."

At that moment, staring into her husband's eyes, Jewels felt her eyes pool with water. Her bottom lip began to quiver as the thought of never seeing her man again broke her heart into one million pieces. She trembled all over, and she suddenly threw her arms around his neck and buried her face into his chest. She broke down sobbing loudly, and he caressed her back lovingly. For as much as she was a pain in the ass, none of that mattered because she loved him unconditionally. She treated him as if he came from a family of kings and queens, and he knew that there wasn't anything that she wouldn't do for him. He was sure that if he had asked her to die for him, she'd gladly do it without question.

When Jewels pulled her face back from Kennan's chest, she left a wet stain behind from her crying. Sniffling, she looked up at her husband and wiped her dripping eyes with her hands, saying, "I don't want to lose you. I don't want to be a widow and our child to be fatherless. It scares me, Kennan. It scares the hell out of me, and when I think about it paralyzed me with fear."

"I know, sweetheart, I know." He told her as he held her at arm's length. "But this is about family, and my brother is family. Besides our baby, he is the last living relative of our bloodline. I can't just let this shit ride. I gotta do something about it."

Jewels nodded and wiped her tearing eyes again, and said, "I understand."

"Good," he kissed her forehead. Afterwards, he took the video camera down from out of the closet. He set the camera down on the tripod and set it up. Next, he threw on a T-shirt and sweatpants. He sat down on the couch and began to film himself. Jewels stood off to the side continuously wiping her dripping eyes with her hands.

CHAPTER FOUR

Hahahahahaahahahaha! Mannnn, that Connecticut hoe really had yo' ass goin' with all that love shit! Feelin' yo' head with all of that nonsense. I told you, ain't nobody that chu can trust. Absolutely nobody!

"Already knew that." Kreon said in annoyance.

Obviously you didn't 'cause if you had, that lil' bitch wouldn't have been able to play you. You think it was a coincidence that she had the same nigga she fucked around on her baby daddy with ova there tonight? Don't be foolish! Homie was ova there layin' down that good wood, makin' lil' momma's toes curl! I guarantee she was suckin' and fuckin' 'em reallll good. I bet she called 'em ova 'cause you weren't knockin' it outta the park! See, if you woulda been fuckin' that bitch like a porn star then she wouldn't have been checkin' for that nigga again.

"Do you eva shut the fuck up, huh?"

Nigga, I'm tryna give yo' ol' green ass some game. D.Cot...D.Bot whateva the fuck he calls himself. The nigga'z from Connecticut, right? So, what the fuck is he doin' wayyyyy out here in Cali? That's right; he caught a flight way out here just so he could wax that ass. She probably let 'em back in the house once you made 'em walk the block naked. Yep, I bet that's exactly what she did.   He's probably mad and shit, and now she's smoothin' things ova with 'em by givin' 'em some slllllllllllllow neck. Shit, I know I'd love some slow neck, right about now. And homie's ova there gettin' it. Lil' momma's makin' that nigga'z toes curl up in them Timbs.

Kreon made an ugly face. His eyebrows slanted and he gritted his teeth. He balled his right hand into a fist and clenched it so tight that his knuckles bulged. Abruptly, he slammed his fist into the medicine cabinet's mirror and cracked it into a spider's cobweb. When he drew his fist back, glass debris trickled down into the sink. He drew his fist back again, again, again, again and again, until shards rained down into the sink. When he looked down, he saw a million images of himself in the shards. All of the images had different expressions on their faces. But the biggest shard had the image of the man behind the negative thoughts inside of his head. He looked exactly like Kreon, except, he had cornrows and wore a wave cap over it while his hefty frame filled out a long sleeve T-shirt.

You ugly, my nigga, you always have been. Why you think she doesn't want chu? You seen dude, right? He did look betta than you. Lil' momma has taste. Well, except when it comes to you,

By this time, tears were flowing down Kreon's face in buckets and he was sniffling. He bowed his head and sobbed with his shoulders shuddering. His teardrops splashed on the broken shards of glass that twinkled inside of the sink. The hand he'd used to break the mirror was covered in small cuts and highlighted by the bright red blood in them. The cuts twinkled from the glass residue sprinkled around

You're ugly, on the inside. Now, let's make the outside match.

Reluctantly, Kreon's wounded hand eased inside of the sink and picked up the shard that had the negative image of himself in it.

Aww, there we go, now let's do a lil' plastic surgery on that face of yours.

Kreon pressed the shard at the side of his face and slowly began to drag it. Quickly, the blood ran and started to trace the side of his face. He squeezed his eyelids shut and gritted teeth as he felt the pain engulfing the side of his face.

Thata boy, bring that sucka on around

Kreon brought the shard further around and caused more blood to run. He had squeezed the shard in his hand so it sliced into his palm and making it run with blood. The blood oozed down the curve of his hand and slid down his wrist.

Knock! Knock! Knock! Knock!

The rapping at the door caused Kreon to drop the shard. It clashed inside of the sink and broke in half. The young man blinked his eyelids like he was coming out of a dream and looked at his bleeding palm. There was a black gash inside of it, oozing blood. He balled his hand into a fist and tore off the sleeve of his shirt. He used the length of his sleeve to tie around his hand. He then snatched off some paper towels and patted the blood from the side of his head. Once he'd dissipated the blood, he balled up the paper towel and tossed it into the waste basket.

Knock! Knock! Knock! Knock!

"Hurry up in there; I gotta take a shit, man!" the man said from the opposite side of the door. "Jesus fuckin' Christ, I'm gonna fuckin' shit my pants!" he said to no one particular.

Knock! Knock! Knock! Knock!

Kreon unlocked the door and pulled it open. Standing before him, he found a trucker with a beat-up old baseball cap and a sleeveless jean jacket. He had a thick dirty blonde, bushy mustache and beard. He had one hand holding the bulge in his jeans while the other hand was balled into a fist. His fist lingered in the air because he was about to rap on the door again, until Kreon had pulled it open. The trucker didn't waste any time oozing inside of the men's room and slamming the door shut behind him. Kreon looked over his shoulder and shook his head at the man, before journeying over to the Nissan and jumping in behind the wheel. He threw his head back and shut his eyelids, as he took a deep breath. Suddenly, he made a hideous face and his bottom lip quivered, as negative thoughts invaded his head once again. He placed the

palms of his hands against his face and ran them downward.

*You almost won tonight, but I'm determined not to
allow you to beat me. I'm ashamed that I even let chu get
this close,* Kreon looked to his wrapped up hand and then
the wound on the side of his face that he'd made with the
shard of glass. If it wasn't for the trucker knocking on the
gas station's men's rest room door, he was sure he would
have carved his face up something awful.

Kreon wiped the tears that threatened to drip from the
brims of his eyes with the back of his hand. He took
another deep breath and glanced out of his vehicle's
window. At that moment, his cellular rang and vibrated.
When he looked down he noticed that he was getting a
call through Face Time. Seeing that it was Odette calling
him, he pondered on whether or not he should answer her.
Deciding to go ahead and answer the call, he pressed the
button that accepted the call and Odette's face filled up the
screen. Off top, he could tell that she'd been crying since
he'd left her house because both of her eyes were swollen
badly. It looked like she'd had an allergic reaction to
something she'd ate.

"Hey," she sniffled and wiped her nose with a Kleenex

For a minute, Kreon just stared down at the display of
his cellular. He was debating on whether or not he should
respond to what she'd said. He was still as hot as a fire
cracker at her, but he decided to go ahead and entertain a
conversation with her.

"'Sup, slim?"

"Please, don't hang up. I just want chu to hear me out,
okay?"

"Yep," he replied nonchalantly.

"Donald was out here on tour. He hit me up because
his conscience had been bugging him about Marquise. He
said that he believed that he was his, regardless of me

46

telling him that he wasn't. He said he wanted proof that Mar Mar wasn't his, so I decided to oblige him with an over the counter paternity test. He came right over with the test and did it. In fact, here it is," she held up the home paternity text box and sat it back down.

"He did it and gave it back to me. Afterwards, he asked could he have something to drink.I told him yes, but afterwards he' have to go. I was talking to my sister while he was having a glass of water and that's when you showed up. But I promise you that nothing happened between us. I don't want him or anyone else. I only want you, Kreon." She broke down sniffling and sobbing again, wiping her eyes and nose with fresh Kleenexes.

"I don't want chu to see him ever again."

"I promise. Once I give him back these test results and he knows the truth about Mar Mar, we're through. He and I don't have anything to talk about."

"No exes, period. I don't give a fuck what reason is behind it."

"I promise. Under any circumstances will I deal with my exes."

Kreon smiled inwardly, but he still wasn't letting her ass off the hook that easily.

"You gone have to do somethin' to make this back up to me, you gone have to do somethin' big. You Griff me?"

"Anything," she wiped her dripping eyes with her curled finger. "Just tell me what it is."

"Not ova this jack, you neva know who's listenin'. I want chu to meet me here, at this gas station on…" Kreon went on to give Odette the address of the Chevron gas station that he was posted up at.

"Alright. I'll be there."

"Smooth."

"I love you."

Again, Kreon was hesitant at first to respond, but eventually he responded back with, "I love you, too."

With that said, Kreon disconnected the call and laid his head back against the head rest. He shut his eyelids and swallowed the spit in his throat. He drifted off to sleep, but woke up when he heard the soft purring engine of a vehicle pulling up beside him. Peeling open his eyelids, he looked out of the driver's window and found Odette behind the wheel of her car. Marquise was sitting in the backseat in the booster seat with the safety belt strapped across him. He and Kreon smiled from ear to ear at one another. They then tapped their fists against their hearts and threw up two fingers for peace.

Odette hopped out of her Honda and made her way over to Kreon. She threw her hood on her head and zipped up her hoodie since it was chili outside. Looking into her face, Kreon could tell that the swelling of her eyes was coming down some. Her nose was red and he could still see the dried white tears on her face though. Stuffing her hands inside of the pockets of her hoodie, she stopped before her man and looked him in the face.

"Hey you," she said timidly and offered him a weak smile.

"Hey, back," he replied. Although he hated to see her in her current state, he wasn't about to console her. The way he saw it, if she wouldn't have broken their no exes' agreement then their falling out would have never happened in the first place.

Odette's brows furrowed seeing the dried blood on the side of Kreon's face and then the fabric tied around his hand.

"What happened to your hand and the side of your face?" she asked. She went to touch the side of his face, but he turned his head away from her.

"Nothin'."

"Well, that scar didn't just crawl there."

"Oh yeah? How you know that?"

"Always the smart ass, huh? What is it that chu want me to do to make things right between us?" she inquired, and pulled a few balled up Kleenexes from out of her pocket. She then used the tissues to blow and wipe her nose with.

Kreon cupped her face and stared deep into her soft brown eyes, asking, "You love me, right?"

"Of course I love you, Kreon, you know that."

"It doesn't matter what I know. The only thing that matters is what you can prove, sweetheart."

This caused her brows to furrow and she said, "What do you mean?"

Kreon took his hands off of her face and turned around. With his back to her, he bowed his head and massaged the bridge of his nose, taking a deep breath. He looked up, not seeing that she had a worried expression across her face.

"What do you mean, bae? Tell me." Odette said as she touched his arm.

He turned back around to her and said, "If you love me like you claim you do then help me kill Marquise's father."

For a minute Odette was silent. She just stood there staring into his eyes trying to see if he was sincere.

"Are you serious?" she asked.

"Slim, I've never been mo' serious about anything in my life." He swore.

"Jesus," she turned away from him and massaging her chin, thinking on it.

"Either it's yes or no," he said growing angry.

"Lemme think, Kreon. Damn, you're talking about me helping you murder my kid's father. That's a lot you putting on me."

"Much as you claim to hate the mothafucka it shouldn't be somethin' that you have to think on. But lemme guess, that was just bitta baby momma talk."

"Whatever," she turned back around, giving him the view of the side of her face.

"Fuck it. I'ma find this nigga and handle 'em myself, then." he moved to open the door of the Nissan. Just as he pulled the car's door open, Odette was calling out to him.

"Wait," she told him, looking between him and Marquise. The boy was nodding off to sleep in the car.

"What?" he spat heatedly and folded his arms across his chest. His eyebrows arched and nose scrunched up.

"I'll do it."

"You sure?" he cracked a one sided smile.

"Yes," She assured him.

"Good," He cupped her face and smiled. Afterwards, he pressed his lips against hers, kissing her deep and passionately.

Odette stared into Kreon's eyes, and at that moment, she thought about what she'd agreed to do. *Damn, I really love this nigga.*

"I've gotta go. It's late and I need to get Mar Mar in bed. We'll talk later, okay?" He nodded, and she held the side of his face as she kissed him on the lips.

Kreon bowed his head as Odette retreated back to her car. His shoulders rocked as his head bobbed and big teardrops fell from his eyes. His sobbing grew louder and louder as he pressed his hands to the sides of his head. Hearing her man in despair, Odette looked up from where she was beside her car. A line creased her forehead and she stashed her keys back inside of her hoodie. She made her way over to him and cupped his face, looking into his eyes. His entire face appeared to be wet and his eyes were pinkish.

"Are you having one of your episodes?" she inquired.

"Yeah, bae, a nigga sick. A nigga really sick."

"You'll be okay, bae."

"No, I won't," he took her hands from his face and turned to the Nissan, placing his hands on its rooftop. "I'm tired of people tellin' me that shit. Everything is not gonna be all right. I'm fuckin' crazy. A fuckin' whack job! I'm far from fuckin' normal, can't you see that? Look at what I have become. Look what people who claimed to love me did to me!" Kreon scowled and clenched his fists tightly, causing a vein to pulsate at his temple, "I fuckin' hate bein' Kreon!"

Kreon exploded like a barrel of TNT and punched the driver side window, repeatedly. The window began to crack from the force behind his punches. The only reason he didn't break his hands was because his adrenaline was pumping incredibly fast. He threw his head back and screamed at the top of his lungs, as tears came streaming down his cheeks. Suddenly, he dropped down to his knees and clutched his head. Wrinkles creased every corner of his face and he shuddered, dropping teardrops on the asphalt.

"What's...what's the matter, papi?" Odette questioned with concern.

"I keep seeing myself on the floor and I'm strugglin' to get up 'cause this life. My life has beaten the shit outta me, babe. I see me, I see me tryin' my hardest to get up and I'm on the sidelines hollered at myself. I'm sayin', 'Get up, Kreon, get up! Don't let this shit beat chu, man! You've been through too much! If you give up then we're done, we don't got nobody, but us! We all we got, baby! Get up; get up, no one loves us so we gotta love us! They gave up on us, so we gotta keep fightin', my nigga! We've gotta keep fightin'!" snot bubbled out of his nose and tears fell down his face, rapidly.

When he looked to Odette she was wipin' her wet face with the sleeve of her jacket. "I see me, babe. I'm crawlin' on the floor, trying to pull myself upon the ropes. And this sickness in my head, this fuckin' disease is steadily punchin' on me, hittin' on me! Trying its best to keep me down for the count, but I'm still trying to get up while its wailin' on me! I'm up and at 'em, baby. I'm on my feet and I'm throwin' them hands." he starts throwin' punches like a trained fighter, boxin' his invisible enemy.

"I'm throwin' them hands and he's throwin' them back. I'm giving it just as good as I'm takin' them, but then he starts makin' a comeback, and I'm gettin' sluggish, wobbly on my legs 'cause I'm tired. I'm fuckin' tired, I'm fuckin' tired of fightin' this never endin' battle with this shit!" spit flew off of his bottom lip and more tears came from his moist, pink eyes.

"Then I'll fight witchu, bae. I'll stand by your side fighting." she sniffled. "We'll take this mothafucka on together and we'll beat his ass. Nothing or no one is stronger than the love Kreon and O have for one another. You hear me? Nothing or no one."

"I'm drownin', O. I'm drowning," he threw his head up and screamed up at God. "Who's gonna love, Kreon, huh? Tell me ol' great Mighty Lord, who's gonne love me?" he sobbed and bowed his head again. Looking back up at Odette, he said, "I'm drownin', babe. I'm drownin'." he whimpered and cried, snot threatening to drip from his nostrils.

Odette hugged Kreon. "I hear you, Papi. You're drowning, and I'ma save you. I'ma love you like no one has ever loved anyone in this world before." she swore, tears slicking down her cheeks. They shared a loving embrace, both crying their eyes out.

Once Kreon had calmed down, Odette broke his embrace and looked him in square in the eyes. "Once you tie up this loose end, you and I are gonna see about getting you some help. That's the only way you're gonna get through this. You're gonna need meds and therapy, lots and lots of therapy. I'm gonna need it, too. 'Cause God knows I have issues of my own that I need to get through. You hear me, Kreon? We're gonna get through this together, as one. It's *Oreon*, Kreon and Odette together.That's us, Oreon."

"Right. Oreon, babe, that's us. You are me and I am you. Together we are us."

"That's right." she smiled happily and wiped the tears from her eyes. She then wiped his away, hugging and kissing him once again.

"I better get going so little man can get to bed."

"Okay."

Odette turned to walk away and Kreon held on to her hand as long as he could. Having finally released her hand, he watched as she walked around her car and slid in behind the wheel. She cranked up her Honda and looked to her man, smiling. She then kissed the palm of her hand and blew him a kiss. He caught it and pressed it against the left side of his chest, smiling back. With that sweet gesture given, Odette pulled out of the parking lot of the gas station. Once she was gone, Kreon jumped inside of the Nissan and drove away in the opposite direction.

****

Kreon cruised through the streets on his way home. His head was on a swivel as he took in his city. Thoughts of Odette corroded his mind. Although she'd hurt him, and caused him to grow insecure with her having an old flame inside of her home, he was willing to let the violation go, just as long as she went through with setting her baby's daddy up for him. The way he saw it, if she could go along with doing what he'd asked, then she was good enough to be called his woman. In fact, he'd be proud to have her on his arm with her showing loyalty and dedication like that.

Kreon made a left at the corner of Slauson and Vermont. As he drove down the street, he saw a woman hop out of her rental and make her way to its back tire. Figuring then that she had a blow-out, Kreon decided to pull over and help her out. When he got out of his whip and made his way towards her, she was kneeling down and examining her tire. Seeing his shadow approaching her on the asphalt, the woman looked to him and surprise enveloped her face. She slowly rose to her feet and saw the jovial expression drop from his face, as he recognized who she was.

"Nigeria." Kreon stated her government as his eyebrows sloped and he tightened his jaws.

"Hey, stranger, we finally meet." She approached him, but he held his hand up and let her know that she'd gotten close enough.

"It took me droppin' that ass for you to finally come out here to see me, huh?"

"I'm sorry ta say, yes. It took me losing ya fa me to see dat ya are da most important person in my life."

"Is that right?" he twisted his face up like *Bitch, I don't believe that shit* as he folded his arms across his chest.

"Yes, it's da honest truth," Nigeria admitted sadly. She wished she'd realized just how much she wanted and needed him in her life before she made a decision that dissolved their relationship. Little momma had caught two flights from her island, Bermuda, to the United States to try to salvage her relationship with Kreon. The last time that they'd talked, he told her that he was seeing someone else and gave her, her walking papers. Although he had told her that he didn't want anything to do with her anymore, she couldn't take his word for it. See, she was still gassed by the idea of being with him and settling down. Besides her next breath, there wasn't anything else in her life that she wanted more.

"You a lil' too late, Nigeria."

Her forehead furrowed and she said, "But...but I thought we had somethin' special."

"I thought we did too, but apparently not special enough for you to say fuck that trip."

"Oh my, Gawd, Kreon, are you really goin' ta crucify me ova dis trip? I said I was sorry," Nigeria cried, wiping her dripping eyes with her curled finger. "You don't think I feel bad enough? You already kicked my ass to the curb and gave your love to someone else."

"Right. And yet that didn't stop yo' tropical ass from flyin' out here and tryna get back with me."

"I know, I know, I shoulda stayed back home. But I don't know how ta leave you alone, baybe. I need ya in my life ya like...ya like water, oxygen or food...I need you, boo." She tried to touch his face, but he grabbed her wrist and turned his head. "Oh, it's like dat now?" her forehead wrinkled.

"That's how you made it, Nigeria. Like I told you when I first started choppin' it up witchu, I'm second to none. The moment you booked that punk ass plane ticket to Tampa is the day our shit ended. That same day I found that shit out, all my feelins for you died." He looked her in the face with his glassy eyes. "A nigga ain't got no love or nothin' for you. Our shit was already rocky, you neva had time for me. I mean, how long did you think I was gone keep holdin' on waitin' for you, huh? You wayyyy over there in Bermuda, across the fuckin' water, and I'm out here in the city. All we had was the jack and Skype to keep what we had goin'."

"But you hardly eva called me." Her voice cracked under her raw emotions.

"'Cause when I did, yo' ass was with yo' homegirl or you were too sleepy from work. Now, work, cool. I understand, niggaz be tired from punchin' that clock, gettin' to the money. But as far as your friend, you shoulda told her what was up and made time for me."

"Baybe, ya neva said nothin' though." Tears flooded down her cheeks and she sniffled.

"I shouldn't have to! You claim you love me; you wanna be with me, right? Well, show me that I'm important, make a nigga feel special! You didn't do that shit! Yo' ass got comfy thinkin' I was so far gone ova you that I wouldn't give anyone else the time of day! Well, you were wrong." She bowed her head and big teardrops fell from her eyes. What he had said was true. She really did believe that he was so into her that he didn't have eyes for anyone else, but she was sadly mistaken. "This is all yo' fault, you did it to yo' self!"

"Lemme fix it den, baybe, lemme show ya dat I am da woman dat ya want and need in yo' life, Kreon. Gemme just one mo' chance and I promise I will neva make ya regret it!"

"Have you gone deaf? I told you I'm with O. What about her?"

"Fuck ha! What about me? More importantly…what about us?" Nigeria took his hand and placed it against her left breast, where her heart was. "You see how fast its beatin'? It sped up da closer I drew here in da plane. My heart beats for ya, Kreon."

"Nah, nigga, yo' heart beats for Tampa." He tried to pull away but she held fast

"No, I'm serious." She assured him. "I can't stop thinkin' about our future together. Me movin' out here from home and us gettin' an apartment together, me workin' full time as a bartender to save up money ta go back ta fashion school over in Miami, ya coming home from a hard day's work and rubbin' one another's feet, eatin' TV dinners 'cause we too lazy ta cook, ya proposin' for da first time, ya kissin' my pregnant belly, ya standin' by my side as I push ya first child out into this world. Do ya rememba? Do ya rememba what we were goin' ta name our baybe?"

"Yeah," he said reluctantly, eyes welling up with tears and hatred at the same time, "Riya Cyan Williams."

"That's right. A beautiful baybe girl, with all da looks of ha motha and a fondness fa ha daddy. Our baybe was gonna be a daddy's girl, just like I was. And ya were gonna give ha all da love dat you neva got from ya fatha."

Kreon shut his eyelids for a moment and thought about the conversations on the telephone and Skype they had. A smile stretched across his face as fond and happy memories ripped through his mind. The smile grew broader and broader across his face, but then, his expression turned into one of spitefulness. This was because he thought of all the empty promises and/or the unreturned phone calls he'd gotten from Nigeria. Before he knew it, he was balling his fingers into his palms and making fists at his sides. His jaw twitched with animosity, but then suddenly, the tension left his face and his hands unclenched themselves.

"That was then, and this is now, Nigeria," he told her flat out. "That life we dreamed of together…it's gone. I share them with someone else now. Someone who loves and appreciates me, someone that won't have me second guessin' about them, you Griff me?" Kreon spoke from his heart.

Nigeria stared into Kreon's unforgiving eyes and solemn expression. From the look on his face she knew that all the love he'd had for her was truly gone from his heart. Knowing this hurt her deeply. It felt like someone had heated a knife on the burner of a stove until it glowed orange and stabbed her straight through the heart with it. Instantly, her bottom lip began to quiver and her eyes slowly accumulated water. Her face grew uglier and uglier by the second, until eventually, teardrops fell from the brims of her eyes.

Nigeria bowed her head and big teardrops trickled from her eyes. She wiped her eyes with her curled finger and looked back up at Kreon as she pulled out some Kleenex from her coat's pocket. Her eyes were pink and her face was soaked wet from crying. Kreon didn't show her any remorse as he watched her dry her eyes and blow her nose. Once she was done, Nigeria balled up the tissues and dropped them to the ground.

"Foolish of me…thinking I was gonna come here, and you were gonna come running back to me with opened arms."

"Yeah, very foolish," Kreon agreed. He was rubbing her face into the wrong decision that she'd made. She had hurt him and he was just trying to pay her back for it.

"Well, I gave love a shot, so if weren't meant to be then I guess we weren't meant to be." She shrugged.

"That's right."

"Can ya grab my tire out of da trunk and help me put da spare on, please?"

"Yeah, I got chu faded." He moved towards her trunk.

Kreon busied himself trying to get the spare tire from out of the trunk of Nigeria's vehicle. He was so engrossed into what he was doing that he didn't notice what Nigeria was doing behind his back. Sneakily, she opened her purse and pulled out a metal rod about ten inches long. She raised the rod above her head and brought it down with all her might. She struck him upside of the back of his skull and he fell over inside of the trunk, knocked out cold. Kreon lay there snoring with his eyelids shut. Nigeria scanned her surrounding for any witnesses. Once she saw that there wasn't any, she dropped the rod into her purse and finished placing Kreon inside of the trunk.

Afterwards, Nigeria kissed the tips of her fingers and blew Kreon a kiss. "I love you," she told him as he lay unconscious, and then she slammed the trunk shut and left him in darkness.

CHAPTER FIVE

Ella pulled up alongside the curb and killed the engine of her car. She picked up a pair of shades from where they were sitting on the front passenger seat. She slid them onto her face and grabbed up the black and pink leopard printed cap that was there also. She smacked the cap on her head. Next, she opened the sun visor and a small light came on, reflecting off the small square mirror that had been placed there. Holding the cap by its brim and back, she adjusted it to her liking as she stared at herself in the rearview mirror. Afterwards, she threw the hood on her head and tightened the drawstrings of her hoodie, enclosing the hood around her head. She gave herself one last look before shutting the visor and hopping out of the car. She was confident that no one would recognize her thanks to her disguise and the cover of darkness. Slamming the door shut, she tucked her hands inside the pockets of her hoodie and approached the curb. She then made her way down the sidewalk, walking past pedestrians as they were coming and going.

Ella came across a homeless woman pushing a shopping cart, a few teenagers playing around, a drunken Mexican man with a bottle of liquor inside a wrinkled brown paper bag, a stray dog and some fool talking loud as fuck on his cell phone. As soon as he past her, he looked over his shoulder at that big butt of hers, saying, Damn. Ella was oblivious to the loud man's ogling of her ass. You see, she was focused on something else. That something else was the young man posted up on the side of an out of order telephone booth. He was a slender fella of average height and a brown hue. He wore a blue snapback on his head backwards, jean jacket with fur around the collar and tight blue jeans with tears going up the legs. A blue bandana hung from his left back pocket.

Occasionally, a cool breeze would past and ruffle the hanging bandana, causing it to drift in the wind.

Boy, oh, boy, the drug dealers getting younger and younger these days. And this one looks more like this circa's rappers with the clothes he's wearing. If he's strapped I wonder where he's stashing his gun, 'cause it couldn't be in those tight ass jeans. I know those mothafucka'z got his nut sack in a Yoke, Ella thought, *it don't matter. I could care less about what he's dressed like, just as long as he has what I need to get my mind right.*

After the harsh tongue lashing she'd gotten from Kreon over her meddling in his life, Ella felt the lowest she'd felt in a long time. She cried and cried until she couldn't cry any more. When she went into the bathroom and looked into the medicine cabinet's mirror, her eyes were swollen and puffy. Her nose was red and her cheeks were stained white with dry tears. She was depressed, distraught and heartbroken. Ella felt a deep, deep emotional pain and she wanted it to stop.

Not only was Ella hurt over the actions of her son, but she was shaken up by the robbery that had taken place back at the gas station, that ordeal had rattled her nerves and had her jumpy as a mothafucka. On her way over to the block she was on now, she found herself looking over her shoulders constantly. She was expecting someone else to roll up on her and rob her ass again. If not, kidnap her or some shit. It was then that she realized that she was going to need something to calm her nerves, and fast.

All out of options, Ella thought about turning to a narcotic she'd vowed to never use again. Crack cocaine! Her addiction left her life in shambles and she was left to pick up the pieces.

She'd gotten it in her head to get herself a small taste of crack cocaine. You know, just a little bit to help her get over her heartache. Being that she was a recovering addict, this was a bad idea. Ella had been cleaned for ten years, so if she went off to get high. It was a good chance that she'd never come back from it. That's when she remembered a time when she'd gotten fucked up back in the day.

"Damn, you don't got no more weed?" Ella asked disappointedly.

"Nah," Sylvester shook his head no.

"Oh, well, I guess the party is over," she sucked her teeth and walked off. She'd gotten two feet before he grabbed her wrist, stopping her in her tracks.

"Hold up. The party is just gettin' started, baby." He smiled devilishly and held up a small saline bag of off white crack rocks. There were a total of six crack rocks inside of the bag.

Ella narrowed her eyelids and looked closer, forehead wrinkling, "Nigga, is that crack? I'm not smoking no mothafucking crack! What I look like? You musta slipped, fell and bust yo' head!" she grabbed her purse and went to rise from off the couch. He grabbed her arm again. She looked at him like he must be crazy, lying his hands on her. Slowly, he released her arm and held up his hand, showing her that he posed no threat.

"My bad, I didn't mean to grab you and shit...But look, don't knock it 'til you try it. Peep," he unzipped the saline bag and dumped its contents out onto the coffee table.

He then pulled out a glass stem from out of the small pocket that was above the big pocket of his jeans. The glass stem was scratched up and scorched black at its end from several usages. Ella plopped back down on the couch and sat her purse down beside her. She folded her arms across her bosom, watching Sylvester closely as he stuffed the stem with crack. He picked up the Bic lighter he'd been using earlier to light the joint with, holding its long blue flame to the end of his crack pipe.

As he sucked on the end of it, cheeks puffing up and smoke expelling in clouds. He sucked and sucked on the glass dick, pulling smoke into his lungs. Once the intoxicating smoke hit his system and he felt that high, he laid back on the couch, slumped. His eyes were hooded and his chin was touching his chest, nigga was high as a kite. "Gone," he began, licking his lips. "Gone give it a try, lil' momma, you only live once."

Something was telling Ella not to fuck with the drug, especially having seen its negative effects on her loved ones and people in her neighborhood. But how good it seemed to have made Sylvester feel changed her mind. Going against her better judgment, she plucked the items that Sylvester used to get high from his hands. Placing the pipe to her mouth and the flame of the lighter behind it, she sucked on the end of the stem. Smoke filled her lungs, and some of it even escaped from the stem, polluting the surrounding air. Initially, she didn't feel anything, so she took a couple more drags, and that's when it hit her like a sucker punch, unexpectedly. Before she knew it, she was laying back on the couch with hooded eyes, just like that nigga Sylvester.

Seeing Ella well under the influence, Sylvester decided to take full advantage of her. Smiling sneakily, he unbuckled her belt and then her jeans. As she continued to smoke the crack rocks, he slid off her jeans and opened her legs. He ate her pussy as she got high. Once she was laid out from her intoxication; he licked his top lip in anticipation. Next, he positioned himself and slid his thick, vein riddled penis into her awaiting vagina. A look of pleasure crossed his face as he gasped and felt her warm, wet pussy.

Ella stopped before the young nigga wearing the blue banadana hanging out of his back pocket. He spat off of the curb and looked to her. His brows furrowed as he locked her up and down. She didn't look shit like a crackhead to him, but he had been fooled in the past. Hell, he'd served doctors, lawyers, accountants, physicians, etc.

"'Sup, Auntie?" Donatello greeted Ella by a nickname he'd made up on the spot. He'd given her the name *Auntie* because she was an older woman around his mother's age.

"Shit. Listen, uh," she looked around to make sure that there wasn't anyone watching them. "You got four dimes?"

"Yeah, I got that." He said to her and pulled the crack rocks from out of his hoodie. He looked around one more time before making the quick exchange with Ella. As soon as Ella had gotten what she'd come for, she walked off down the sidewalk.

Damn, man, that old bitch gotta fat ass. I'd smash that shit out fa sho' fa sho'. Mmmmmhmmm, he said as he rubbed his hands together and pondered all of the sexual acts he'd perform on Ella.

***

After recording the footage that he wanted his daughter to see should something happened to him, Kennan shared an emotional goodbye with Jewels. He then kissed her and hopped behind the wheel of his vehicle. Cranking the automobile up, he turned it on to the oldies station and adjusted the rearview mirror. As he drove off he could see his wife through the reflection of the rearview mirror. She was growing smaller and smaller in the background as she waved to him and then blew his a kiss. Sticking his hand out of the window, he pretended to catch the kiss and then he pressed it against his heart. He didn't have to see Jewels' face to know that she had a smile to couple with the tears she'd shed before he left

Kennan hadn't even been gone five minutes yet and already he missed his family. It tripped him out how much in love he was with his wife and newborn baby. He'd always considered himself a bad ass, but once he'd gotten married and had his first bundle of joy; it put a chink in his armor. He found himself doing all of that corny shit that family guys do. Hell, if you would have told the people that knew him back home how he was now compared to how he used to be. Them mothafuckaz would never believe you, but then again, some people wouldn't believe that he was a cop at one point in time of his life either, if you told them. Yeah, old Kennan was a cop. A dirty cop, but the nigga was fair. He didn't take any shit and he didn't give any one shit that didn't have it coming.

The night was dark and quiet, except for the sounds of the crickets in the grass. The noise was broken up when a police cruiser pulled up. It idled at the curb of Trinity Park before its headlights and engine were executed by its driver. The driver side door flung open and out stepped Kennan, one black leather boot at a time. He slammed the door shut behind him and took a good scan of the area before he slid his nightstick into its holster. Whistling, he made his way to the trunk of his vehicle and lifted it. Inside he found a bound Patrick staring up at him. His eyebrows were sloped and his forehead was wrinkled. He looked like he wanted to beat the brakes off of Kennan but his restraints wouldn't permit it.

"You know I've cleaned up a lotta scum from off of these streets," Kennan began. "Rapist, murderers, drug dealers, pimps, child molesters; and you, sir, are by far one of the biggest pieces of shit I have ever had the misfortune of meeting. I saw what chu did to Caroline. Although she was too frightened to give a statement saying that it was you that put her in the hospital, I knew it was you. You fancy yourself a fuckin' monsta, huh?"

He looked to the tattoo on his forearm. It read exactly that, Monsta. He then leaned closer into the trunk, staring him in his eyes, madness dancing in his own eyes. "Well, meet the biggest monsta of them all, sweetheart...me."

Right then, the scowl was erased from off of Patrick's face and a ball of nervousness formed inside of his stomach. He felt his bowels shift and he struggled to keep from losing control of his asshole.

"Getcho punk ass outta the trunk," He grabbed him by the collar of his shirt and pulled him out of the trunk. Patrick hit the ground with a thud, wincing. A very pissed off Kennan went on to pull his ass across the asphalt and upon the curb. The son of a bitch struggled to get free, thrashing his legs around, but his attempts were useless. Kennan continued to pull him along, dragging him across the playground until he was standing before the jungle gym. Once he'd gotten there, he whipped out his hand-cuffs. He cuffed Patrick's wrists around one of the many bars of the jungle gym. With that done, he whipped out his nightstick and flipped it over in his hand.

"Fractured nose, hip, elbow and ribs, you did a real numba on that delicate flower of a wife of yours, son. The sight of her made me sick, but you know what made me sicker? Knowin' a sack of shit like you wouldn't be gettin' his just due." he pulled out a set of folded photos from his back pocket and tossed them at Patrick's feet. They were all up close photographs of Caroline's bruised and battered face and other parts of her body. Her left eye was swollen shut and her nose was twice its size from the beaten her husband had given her. "Take a good look, it's your handiwork."

Patrick looked down at the photos and didn't feel a mothafucking thing. As far as he was concerned, if his wife would have done what he had told her then she wouldn't be all knotted up and shit.

"Fuck that bitch!" Patrick snarled angrily. He then harped up phlegm and spat on Kennan's shiny boot. A nasty goo splattered against it and slowly slid off to the side of it.

Kennan's eyebrows arched and his nose wrinkled. With a grunt, he swung his nightstick against the side of Patrick's head and opened up a blackish red gash. The nigga looked dazed and confused from the impact of the black rod. Seeing this, Kennan sheathed his nightstand and retrieved some lighter fluid from his vehicle. He soaked Patrick's ass up with it. By the time Patrick was coming around from his dazed and confused state, Kennan was striking a big flame on his metallic Zippo lighter and tossing it on him. Before the burning lighter mingled with the flammable liquid on Patrick's clothing, the crooked cop was already strolling casually back to his car.

Froooosh!

He heard Patrick burst into flames. He also heard his horrified screams and the clinging of the handcuffs on the jungle gym as the man danced around where he was restrained. His burning and thrashing body had the night lit well. Without so much as a glance at his handiwork, Kennan jumped behind the wheel of his car and drove off.

Kennan turned the volume on his stereo up just as soon as he heard The Temptation's *My Girl* flowing from the speakers. Instantly, his mind was bombarded by thoughts of his lovely wife. He mashed the gas pedal and his vehicle ripped up the street. He busted a left and hopped on the freeway. He was coming from Marino Valley and headed out to Los Angeles, and when he got there, there was going to be hell to pay.

I've got sunshine on a cloudy day.
When it's cold outside I've got the month of May.
I guess you'd say
What can make me feel this way?
My girl (my girl, my girl)
Talkin' 'bout my girl (my girl).
****

Boom!

Kennan kicked open the door and splinters flew everywhere. The apartment was dark, but the light shining in through the door provided light. The ex-cop stood beside the door on the outside, taking two quick glances inside. When he didn't see anyone, he crept in cautiously, head on a swivel. He hit the light switch and walked over to the flat-screen, feeling the back of the television to see if it was warm. If it was, then he'd know that someone was still in the apartment or had just left. The TV was cool.

Seeing that, he peeked inside of the bedroom, gun at the ready, moving like he had a department issued gun and badge. He checked underneath the bed and the closet. The coast was clear. With that done, he entered the bathroom and rubbing his finger inside of the sink checking for wetness. It was dry. He took a deep breath; no one was inside of the unit. Gun at his side, he returned to the living room and looked around. Seeing a family portrait of Ella and a young Kreon, which was cracked down the middle sitting on the end table, he picked it up. Once he studied the face of the woman in the photo, he came to the conclusion that it was indeed the woman he was looking for, Ella. Taking the butt of his weapon, Kennan slammed it into the glass of the portrait, cracking it into a spider's cobweb. He banged the portrait against the edge of the end table and broken glass came raining from it. Carefully, he pulled the photo from out of the ruined placement and folded it up, stashing it inside of his coat. Next, he checked the answering machine, but there weren't any messages left.

Kennan gave the unit one good last look, before taking a deep breath and taking his leave.

***

Omar sat behind the tinted windows of his Excursion taking pulls from a withering blunt. He was slumped in the front passenger seat, observing Kennan kick in his sister's apartment door. Seeing this, he grabbed his tool from underneath the seat and chambered a live copper round into its head. Hurriedly, he smashed out his blunt in the ashtray and made to jump out. That's when Candy grabbed his arm, stopping him cold in his movements. His scowling face snapped in his chick's direction, looking from her hand to her face.

"Look," she nodded to the rearview mirror. He looked to the side view mirror and saw a Lincoln Town Car. This caused his forehead to wrinkle. "That Lincoln followed us all of the way here from off the freeway. It's just been sitting there the entire time…watching us. You think it's the feds?"

"I don't know…could be." He replied, still focused on the side view mirror. Bringing his eyes to the passenger side window, he saw Kennan climb behind the wheel of a black on black Cadillac and crank it up. The back lights of the vehicle came on and illuminated its license plate. "Gemme a pen," Omar told Candy.

He then removed a McDonald's napkin from out of the glove-box and smacked it shut. Candy handed him an ink pen just as the Cadillac pulled off. He looked back and forth between the napkin and the license plate, jotting down the digits scrolled on the placard. Having written down the numbers, he held up the napkin and read them over, wondering what kind of shit his sister had gotten into. Thinking about Kreon, he decided to hit him up. He called him but his cell phone rung and rung until it went to voice mail. He tried him again and still didn't get any answer. Giving up, he hit up his sister, Ella, who was Kreon's mother but her cell went straight to voice mail.

"Fuck! Ain't neither one of they asses answerin'." Omar sat his cellular on his lap and ran his hand down his face, as he took a deep breath. Not hearing so much as a peep from Candy, he looked over at her and found her attention focused on something in the rearview mirror, "Lil' momma, yo' eyes still on that Lincoln?"

Neither of them noticed that Kennan had just jogged across the front of their car, en route to his own whip. He jumped in, fired it up and pulled off without them ever noticing that he had.

"Yeah," Candy informed Omar, her attention glued to the vehicle idling behind them.

Omar slid low in the front passenger seat. He looked into the side view mirror again at the Lincoln Town Car. The vehicle had limousine tinted windows so he couldn't see inside of it. He had an idea that it was some detectives, but he'd also known rival gangs that did drive-bys and walkups from those model cars.

"I don't know if these fools are the enemies or the law." He said this as he popped the glove-box and retrieved his gun. Holding the handgun between his legs, he cocked the slide on it. Now he had one in the head and it was ready to go.

"I know. That's what sucks about it." She made a frustrated expression and shook her head.

Omar gave her instructions to drive off, and just like he thought, the Town Car followed behind them.

"It's betta safe than sorry." He said to himself as he rested his gun in his lap and whipped out his cellular. He speed dialed one of his little homies. A young hitta from around the way that didn't mind dropping a body and neither did the young wolves that he had under him. "Yo', Lil' Boom, what's poppin', Blood? Where you at?" he listened attentively as his little homie spoke to him. "Good, good, good. How many homies witchu, loved one? Bool. Look here, I need y'all lil' niggaz, ASAP. Nah, I'm not finna hang up, I'ma stay onna jack withchu 'til you get here." Omar went on to tell Lil' Boom where he was headed. He stayed on the phone with him, talking, and keeping an eye on the Lincoln Town Car in his rearview mirror.

Omar continued to give Lil' Boom his whereabouts while keeping an eye on the side view mirror. Taking his eyes from off the side view mirror, he looked up ahead at the stop light and saw that it had turned yellow. He gave Candy specific instructions. She floored the gas pedal and flew passed the yellow light, right before it turned red. Just as Candy cleared the intersection, a raggedy ass white van pulled up in front of the Lincoln Town Car. It's pulling out into the path of the Lincoln Town Car stopped it from flying through the intersection and giving chase to Omar.

The sliding door of the van came open and two niggaz wearing red bandanas to cover their head and the lower half of their face emerged. They wore black sunglasses over their eyes and their gloved hands clutched AK-47s, with long ass banana clips in them. They pulled the triggers of their deadly weapons and they rattled to life in their hands. The assault rifles shook like they were about to jump out of their hands as they spat rapid fire. The young bloods shattered the front tinted windshield of the Lincoln and put two hundred holes in the hood of it. When the choppas were done unleashing carnage, the Lincoln was full of holes and blood was splattered on what was left of the windshield

The shorter of the two gunners, who was Lil' Boom, jumped down to the ground and made his way over to the driver side of the Lincoln cautiously. He switched hands with the AK-47 and unlocked the driver's door, pulling it open. He eased his head inside and saw two dead men in suits. They were covered in black bleeding holes, eyes bulging and mouths twisted in a grotesque manner. Lil' Boom's forehead creased as curiosity had gotten the best of him. He reached inside of the driver's suit and pulled out what appeared to be a brown leather wallet. Flipping it open, he found the man's identification card. It read *F.B.I Joshua Burton.* Instantly, Lil' Boom's stomach twisted into knots and his heart sunk. He swallowed the lump of fear in his throat and turned around, walking over to Omar's vehicle which was parked and idling at the curb. Once he reached the front passenger window, Omar let the window down and looked out at him.

"Fuuuck!" Omar slammed his fist down against the dashboard. He knew he'd fucked up in having a couple federal agents hit. Their murders were going to bring one hell of a shit storm.

***

"Stupid, stupid, stupid," Omar smacked himself upside the head for ambushing the federal agents. Right now, he was behind the wheel of the same van that Lil' Boom and his crew had carried out the executions of the agents in. Loaded in the back of the van were the dead bodies of the agents. As of now, he was heading to the morgue to a buddy of his who he was sure he could get to burn the bodies to ashes.

While he was going about the task of getting the bodies disposed of, Lil' Boom and his homeboys were taking the Lincoln they'd Swiss cheesed to a junk yard to be destroyed. The junk yard wasn't too far away from where they'd slaughtered the federal agents, so he was sure they'd make it there without any problems. He gave Lil' Boom instructions to call as soon as they'd disposed of the vehicle.

Omar glanced at his watch and saw that he had an hour before his homeboy got off work. He knew that if he didn't make it on time that he'd be stuck with the dead bodies, and if it came to that, he was fucked. He didn't have any idea of what he was going to do with the corpses. Sure he could bury them somewhere, but if they were ever found that was going to lead to an investigation, which would eventually lead to arrests and niggaz possibly snitching. He couldn't have that under any circumstances.

"Alright, almost there," Omar made a left at the corner and crossed the threshold into the grounds of the mortuary. He parked at the rear of the building and hoped out of the van, slamming the door shut. He took another glance at his watch and knocked on the back door. The door was iron so the sound of it being knocked on resonated.

Omar glanced over his shoulders and impatiently tapped his foot as he waited for the door to be answered. Before he knew it, all of the locks were being undone and the iron door was being pulled open.

When the door came open, Omar was face to face with a tall white dude with a shaved head and a flabby body. He had a pinkish complexion, a bushy dirty blonde mustache and tattoos that covered his neck and sleeves. His headphones were around his neck. He had been listening to some heavy metal music when he heard someone rapping at the door. At the moment, he was in a short sleeve navy blue shirt, which he wore underneath an apron. Latex rubber gloves were on his meaty hands and black leather motorcycle boots were on his feet. His wallet chain hung from the loop of his jeans and connected to the end of his wallet which was stuffed inside of his back pocket.

"Omar?" Burrell's forehead crinkled seeing his old buddy standing before him. Sticking his head out of the iron door, he looked both ways to see if he'd arrived with anyone else. "What the hell are you doing here?"

"I needa favor."

"What kinda favor, man? This shit couldn't wait 'til I got off?"

"Afraid not. I need you to crank up that old crematorium and incinerate these bodies for me."

"Bodies?" Burrell's forehead crinkled further and he looked up to see the van. "You mean to tell me, you gotta couple of dead people in that van of yours?"

"That's right. Now, can you help me out?"

Burrell looked like he was about to say no, so Omar pulled a wad of money from out of his pocket and held it up before his eyes. Burrell stared at the dead presidents for a minute, before plucking them out of Omar's hand and stashing them into his pocket.

"Alright, let's make this quick." Burrell opened the door all of the way and put down the latch that would keep the iron door open. Afterwards, he followed Omar to the van and waited for him to open the sliding door. He was about to help Omar carry the bodies out until he seen something peeking out of the suit's jacket that belong to Agent Burton. Reaching inside of the van, Burrell pulled out what he saw peeking out of the dead man's suit's jacket. He opened what was a wallet up and saw the card, F.B.I beside the slain agent's face and other information.

"Omar, this man's a federal agent..." he stopped himself short and climbed inside of the van. He went through the suit's jacket of the other dead man and discovered that he was a federal agent, too.

"Shit, man, both of these guys are." He dropped the wallets on the slumped dead bodies and jumped down from out of the van.

"I'm sorry, man. I mean, you're my boy and all, but I'd be jeopardizing my freedom should this thing ever come back to haunt us."

Abruptly, Omar pulled out his gun and pointed it between Burrell's eyes, causing his face to turn red as he lifted his hands up into the air.

"You gone cremate these bodies or you gone be *jeopardizin'* yo' life. The choice is yours, homeboy." Omar mad dogged him. He hated to press the line on a friend, but he was desperate. He had to get rid of those bodies tonight and Burrell was the only one that could help him.

"So, it's like that now?" Burrell's forehead indented.

"That's just how it is, big dawg. Now, are you gone get these bodies out and dispose of 'em, or am I gone have to get rid of three of 'em, instead of one?"

"Alright, but after I take care of this, you and I are through. I want chu outta here and my life for good."

"You got it, boss. Now, get to carryin' these mothafuckaz out."

Burrell placed the headphones over his ears and went about the task of carrying the dead agents inside of the crematorium so he could burn them.

When Burrell disappeared through door with the first body to cremate it, Omar's cell phone rang and vibrated. He pulled it out and saw Candy's face and name on the display. He answered the call and brought the cellular to his ear.

"'Sup with it, lil' momma?" Omar spoke into the device.

***

Candy, Lil' Boom, and two of his homies watched as the Lincoln Town Car they'd sprayed up was crushed beyond recognition. Once the job was done, Candy looked to the man that was behind the controls of the machine that had handled the job and gave him a thumb up. He returned the gesture.

"What's our next move?" Lil' Boom inquired with his homeboys standing on either side of him.

"I gotta hit daddy up and see." Candy told him and pulled out her cellular. She dialed up 'Daddy' and pressed the device to her ear. As she listened to the ringing, she folded her arm across her bosom and shifted her weight to her other foot.

"Heyyy, daddy, it's done." She informed him and looked at her French tipped nails. She held them out before her face and turned her palm towards her, looking the nail job over again.

"You sure? Okay. Love you, bye, bye." She blew a big ass bubble out of the gum in her mouth.

"What the big homie say?" Lil' Boom asked curiously

Candy slid her cellular into the back pocket of her jeans and grabbed a hold of something at the small of her back. She brought her hand back around and pointed a gun at one of Lil' Boom's homeboys' forehead. The young nigga'z eyes stretched wide with fear and his jaw dropped

As soon as the bubble popped that Candy had blown up, so did her gun. The shot rang out throughout the night and old boy's head snapped back from the impact of the bullet. He fell to the ground awkwardly, and Lil' Boom's other homeboy took off running towards the exit of the junkyard. Seeing that the young thug was getting away from her, Candy continued to chew on her gum as she kneeled down to the ground.

She took a hold of her handgun with both hands and aimed it at the fleeing thug. Shutting one eyelid and tilting her head to the side, she pulled the trigger of her weapon, successively. The gun bucked in her hands as it cut down the fleeing gangbanga. He caught three in his back and collapsed while throwing his flailing arms into the air. His face hit the ground and he took his last breath. His eyes stared out into space and his mouth was wide open.

After laying down old boy, Candy rose to her feet and swung back around. She pressed her gun underneath Lil' Boom's chin and caused his head to tilt back. The young thug stared her in the eyes fearlessly, as he waited for the bullet to rip through the bottom of his chin and come out of the top of his head.

"Fuck you waitin' for, Blood, handle yo' business." Lil' Boom mad dogged her as he clenched his jaws and showed the bone structure in his face.

"You good, baby boy." Candy took the gun from underneath his chin and held it at her side. "Daddy said he don't trust them other niggaz to hold they tongue, but chu straight, so you get to keep yo' life."

"Right," Lil' Boom said as he stuffed his hands inside of his pockets.

"Uuuuuh!" the last nigga that Candy had gunned down was lying on his stomach moaning in agony. Once she saw him squirming around on the ground, she started in his direction to finish him off for good. Once she reached him, she checked her magazine and smacked it back into bottom of her gun.

The man that had crushed the Lincoln Town Car stuck his head out of the machine and placed his hand above his brows. From up high, and far off in the distance, he watched as Candy turned into a dot before his eyes. The next thing he saw was muzzle flashes. Candy had murdered off the last nigga she'd shot. Afterwards, he saw her walking back towards him and motioning him down with her gun. He was hesitant to come down for fear of being killed, but the way he saw it, he may as well come down because she could kill him anyway.

"Come on down, pops, I'm not gone hurt chu." Candy continuously motioned him over with her gun, until he was standing before her. "Listen, I can turn that three stacks into six if you help me tuck away those bodies I left behind me."

She spoke of doubling the money she'd promised to pay him, if he'd helped her get rid of the federal agents' Lincoln Town Car.

"I could definitely use that money, trying to help my granddaughter pay her tuition." The old man spoke. He was in a navy blue jump suit and the name tag on his breast pocket read, Pete.

"You gotta car we can use to move 'em? Nothing fancy, I just needa reliable ride that's gone get me from point A to point B."

The old man scratched his temple and looked to the ground, as he tried to figure out which one of his vehicles he'd be willing to part with. He snapped his fingers once an automobile of his came to mind.

"I gotta '67 Deville parked 'round back. It's gotta trunk as big as a dining room. You can fit the bodies inside of there."

"Okay."

"I'll bring it over." Pete ran off to retrieve the car he'd spoken about.

Candy, Lil' Boom and Pete dumped the bodies into the '67 Deville. Afterwards, she paid him the six grand and peeled off.

***

Candy pulled around back at the mortuary, where she found Omar waiting for her. Initially, Burrell refused to burn the bodies, but when Omar put his gun his face, he went with the flow. The big white dude incinerated the bodies and Omar broke him off a little something, something for his troubles. Omar, Lil' Boom and Candy took the van and the Deville to a car-wash where they scrubbed and washed them, thoroughly. Afterwards, they cleaned off the prints that they'd left in the vehicles and left them parked. They caught an Uber to their house and Omar got his other car to drop that nigga Lil' Boom off at home.

Tranay Adams

CHAPTER SIX

The doors of the 77th street division precinct opened as Donald and Khaos, two of the members of The Dope Money Klique, came walking out. Khaos was frowned up as he walked beside Donald, talking and moving his hands animatedly. Anyone watching him from a far would assume that he was angry, especially with the way he was moving his hands. Donald was listening attentively as he pulled the T-shirt over his head he'd brought him, since he was picked up off the streets by the police for walking butt naked. The cops winded up beating Donald's ass with their nightsticks. This was because he was very irate having been robbed and stripped down to his socks. The assault left Donald with a black eye and a busted lip.

"Yo', that whole shit with you disrespectin' The Klique went viral," Khaos complained. "Shit all ova social media, son! Niggaz sayin' you soft, you pussy, dat chu ain't livin' what chu rappin' 'bout! 'Cause if you were homie dat did dat to you would be food, right now! You know, the homies EZ and Fowl talkin' 'bout kickin' you outta Dope Money?"

Donald stopped dead in his tracks and scowled real hard, looking at Khaos as he made his way around his Mercedes Benz. "Nigga, what?"

Khaos opened the driver's door and said, "Yep."

"Well, what's yo' stance on it?"

"I say you stay, long as you redeem yo' self, of course," he jumped into the Benz and slammed the door shut behind him. He had just stuck the key inside of the ignition, when Donald slid into the front passenger seat and slammed the door.

"Redeem myself how?" his brows furrowed.

"By doin' some of the same gangsta shit dat chu rap about," Khaos cranked up his luxurious vehicle and the stereo came. *Gangsta Shit* by Dope Money Klique came blasting from the speakers. Donald was on the hook.

Nigga, who 'bout some gangsta, gangsta shit.
Dope Money 'bout some gangsta, gangsta shit.
My nigga Khaos, 'bout some gangsta, gangsta shit.
Nigga, who 'bout some gangsta, gangsta shit.
My nigga EZ 'bout some gangsta, gangsta shit.

Khaos drove off with the song pumping out of his car and into the ghetto streets he was driving through.

***

A few days later

Kreon's eyes fluttered as he slowly began to stir awake, hearing a power-drill. His head bobbled around as he looked up seeing through obscured vision. His eyelids narrowed as they strained to see the slim figure en route to him with something flat, long and brown. The figure stopped before him and said 'Hey, baybe' before striking him across the side of the head, knocking him out cold. He plummeted back down into darkness. An hour later, he pulled his head up, wincing in pain. He could feel the dry crimson blood on his face. His eyelids peeled open. Once they came into focus, he saw Nigeria sitting on the floor before him, Indian style. She had a bowl of something that looked like oatmeal in her hands and a bottle of water sitting beside her. He looked down and he was wearing a baby's bib. He frowned, thinking that this was strange. He looked up and she was stuffing oatmeal into his mouth. He didn't know what that crazy bitch was giving him so he spat it back out. Some of it hit her face and lip, pissing her off. Her skin turned red. Heated, she smacked him viciously across the face, snapping his head aside and splitting his lip.

"Bish, fuck wrong wit chu?" Nigeria spat.

"I'm tryna show ya some hospitality and look how ya ass act." She looked upon him like he was mad.

"You know what, if ya don't wanna eat, fine. I'm not makin' ya, ya aren't some baybe." She slung the bowl aside and began slipping off her clothes.

Once she had disrobed, she kneeled down to unbuckle his jeans and he kicked her dead in the face. She staggered backwards and slid across the surface, dragging her ass across the floor. She looked up at him with fire in her eyes. Gritting her teeth, she wiped her bloody lip with the back of her hand. She nodded her head and said, "Okay, baybe, ya wanna play? Alright, but like it or not ya gonna give me dat dick." She got to her feet and hauled her naked ass up the staircase, ass cheeks jiggling along the way. Twenty minutes later, she came back wearing a wielding mask and clutching a blow torch. She threw her head forward and snapped the mask shut. She fired up the blow torch and slowly approached him. The reddish orange flames from the torch illuminated her upper body.

Kreon looked alive with his eyes bulging, mouth hanging open as he struggled to get away. He jerked his arms several times trying to break his restraints and the chains made a clang sound. He thrashed around wildly as he tried to escape her wrath, but there wasn't any use. He would have to deal with whatever her crazy ass had planned. She brought the torch so close to his face that the fire singed his eyebrow, raping half of it off of his face. He snapped his head to the side, feeling the heat and trying not to be burned.

"Okay, okay, okay!" He panicked, looking scared as shit.

"Hahahahahahahahahahaha!"

The wielding mask muffled Nigeria's laughter as she doubled over. Afterwards, she threw her head back and snapped the face of the mask above her head. "Dat's what

I thought." She smirked, pulling off the wielding mask with one hand while holding the blow torch with the other.

She got down on her knees. Holding the blow torch at his face, she undid the buckle of his belt and pulled his jeans down around his ankles. She then yanked his boxer briefs down around his thighs. His dick was thick with veins, lying asleep. Feasting her eyes upon what she deemed a nice piece of meat, she licked her chops like a hungry dog. She knew he was terrified so she'd have to get him going if she wanted to bust one off. First she was going to bind his ankles though. She grabbed her spaghetti strap shirt and tied it tight around his ankles, making sure he wouldn't be able to move his legs. With that out of the way, she stuffed his mouth with her panties.

The natural smell of her pussy and the scent of her perfume invaded his nostrils. He looked down between his legs and watched her bring her lips to his flaccid penis. Once she had the entire thang stuffed between her cheeks, she motioned her head back and forth, while looking directly into his eyes. She knew from their explicit phone conversations how much he loved when a woman sucked his dick and looked him square in his eyes.

Nigeria made slurping and sloshing sounds as she sucked Kreon's dick, spilling her hot saliva down his meat and over his slightly hairy nut sack. His forehead wrinkled and he clenched his teeth, trying to fight off the erection that was surely coming. Nigeria smiled with a mouthful, knowing that the inevitable was to come. She had an undeniable head game; her shit was all of that: a bag of chips and a free soda.

Nigeria's head bobbed up and down his hardness. She made humming sounds as she worked his meat, feeling it beginning to grow inside of her mouth. Kreon's face was a mask of concentration as he tried to fight off his erection. His expression was of a man that had tasted something sour as he bit down on his bottom lip and a vein bulged at his temple.

Oh, shit! Ohh shitt! Ohhh Shiiiit! Don't give in, don't give in! This shit feels good, though! Fuckkk, man! You ol' freaky psychotic bitch, you! I hate cho mothafuckin' ass! This shit foul, it's wrong! I can't do this to my baby! Ugh!

The tension left Kreon's face and his body fell limp as his eyes rolled into the back of his head. He peeled his lips apart and moaned in ecstasy. Nigeria chuckled lightly and smiled as she blessed him with the best neck he'd ever received. The 98 degree temperature of her salivating mouth, chaperoned by the stud in her tongue, flew him in a plane across the sky and delivered him to a paradise called Utopia. His head turned from side to side and his mouth trembled; her plump juicy lips went up and down his meat. She held that thang at the base and whipped her head back and forth on it, sucking him off. She sucked that dick like it was an Icee melting away under the heat of an 87 degree sun. Nigeria got down on the dick sloppily and noisily, taking it all the way into the back of her throat, humming an inaudible song.

There was a wet suction noise when she pulled her mouth off of his dick, bring a length of saliva with her. She wiped her lips with the back of her hand and jerked him off. She then smacked it against her cheek, hard, and then softly. Looking into his eyes lustfully, she opened her mouth at the tip of his One Eyed Snake. She stuck out her tongue and allowed a hot river of saliva to roll off of it and coat his dick. Its appearance made it look like a glaze donut. She sucked the saliva back up and spat on it, like she hated it. Her face scrunched up and she did it again.

Nigeria stared dead in Kreon's eyes as she tickled the head of his dick with her tongue, jerking his meat up and down. Once she thought that he was hard, she grabbed him by the face and turned him towards her. She slowly lowered the thick lips of her pussy near the swollen head of his fuck-organ. Her hot juices flowed freely from her hollowed opening, pelting his grown man. It looked like she was peeing on him but she was just stupid wet, and hornier than a teenage boy. She was only about five inches away from meeting his girth, but he could feel the heat exhausting from her gushy hole. Her thick lips swallowed his massive head whole and she inched down onto his meat, until she had half of him up in her.

"Ohhh." She smiled and giggled. "I can already feel you in ma stomach."

She positioned herself on top of him and wrapped her arms around his neck, slamming her chunky ass down to his stubble mound. She rode that dick like a buck wild horse at a rodeo show, moaning and groaning. She squeezed her eyelids shut and slightly peeled her lips part. Her tongue peeked out of the corner of her mouth and slid around to the other side. "Mmmmm," the sound fled her lips as she went all of the way down on him and brought her moist cave up, letting the head of his hardness peek at it. She went back down again slowly, all of the way until her ass was resting on his nut sack. She moved to the sound of the beat playing in her head. At that moment, it was only her and that dick in the basement.

Finding her G-spot, Nigeria started talking shit. "Ohhhhh, Goddamn, nigga, sheeiiiiiit, sssssssss, ya gettin' ta da bottom of dis pussy," Her voice lowered and her eyes fluttered. "Fuuuuckk," she held the letter *F,* speeding up; moving faster and faster. "I can feel ya, deep, deep inside of me." She whispered into his ear as she rode him slowly, moving like she was in a hula-hoop. "Mmmm, bring it home ta momma, Big Daddy, bring dat dick home ta momma and make dis fat pussy cum! Make dis mothafucka cum! Show me what dat dick do!" She whispered in his ear, her hot breath tingling it.

Kreon hated Nigeria's ass with a passion. He didn't know that it was possible for a man to be raped until now.

Growing angry, his lips started twitching like a mad dog, as he stared straight ahead with her panties stuffed into his mouth. He fought back the only way he knew how; with his wrists and ankles bound...he used his mind. Kreon began to think of disgusting shit that would make him loose an erection; slowly, but surely, his erect began to die until it had grown limper than a cooked noodle. The mask of pleasure was rinsed from Nigeria's face once she felt his hard steel melt to butter. She looked down at him with disappointment. Her eyebrows arched and her nose scrunched up.

"Get 'em back hard or else." She brought the blow torch to his face, its fire licking the air.

"Fuck you bitch, you think you just gone take some dick?" he sneered, looking like he was about to spit in her face. "You gotta pay to play! I make hoes break bread or play dead!" he harped up phlegm and spit in her face. Her head jumped as the glob splattered against her face and dripped from the corner of her brow. "Go ahead and burn me, bitch, I don't give a fuck!"

Nigeria snarled and rained punching on his exposed face. He turned from left to right, dropping his head to avoid the punches but they kept on coming. She didn't stop until she was exhausted and his face was bleeding. Fist speckled with blood, she rose up and headed up the staircase, talking more shit than a little nigga with a Napoleon complex. She returned shortly, still naked, but this time toting his.38 revolver. She stood off to the side of Kreon and pointed the revolver down at his meat.

"I'ma blow dat mothafucka off if ya don't act right, ya hear me?" she barked, spittle jumping from her lips. "We'll see if ya little gurl fren wants ya with dat handi-cap!"

Kreon groaned in pain as he slowly came around. Turning his head to the left, he saw a blurred version of who he knew was Nigeria threatening to blow his wang off while pointing a pistol below his waist. That cleared the fog lingering over his brain quickly.

"Ah shit! What the fuck?" He hollered out. "Bitch, what the fuck is wrong with you? Your ass is fuckin' crazy, you're outta your mind...goin' through all this trouble ova some dick!"

"Not just any dick, the best dick ever!" she licked her lips and felt her southern lips moisten at the thought of his cock massaging her pink walls. She groaned like Homer Simpson, when thinking of sweets, *uhhhh*. She quickly snapped out of her trance. "Fuck all of that shit! Either you're gonna act right, or I'ma blow dat bitch clean da fuck off!" Not really having a choice in the matter, Kreon turned back over bringing a sinister smile to her lips. "Yeah, dat's what I thought." She lowered her gun beside her naked thigh and approached him. She blessed him with some of that world famous head of hers, but his manhood wouldn't standup like snitch-ass niggaz that pointed out their homeboy in court. Having grown frustrated, she shot him an evil eye and twisted her lips. She grabbed his limp member and pressed the revolver to its head. Her eyebrows raised and she looked at him like *You better get him hard 'fore I blow his head off.*

"Alright, alright," he squeezed his eyelids shut and tried to will himself a hard dick, but his wang wouldn't submit. He was softer than coke out of the grinder. *Shit!* He thought to himself when he couldn't rock up. He knew he wasn't far from being castrated, with this fucking nympho psychopath holding that banga to his joint. "I can't, I can't."

She exhaled and looked up at the ceiling, mouthing something he couldn't quite understand. She rolled her eyes and got to her feet. She came back with a glass of water and kneeled to him. Sitting the .38 on the floor, she shoved a blue pill into his mouth.

"Fuck is this shit?" Kreon frowned when his taste buds came into contact with the bitter taste of the pill.

"Take a wild guess." Nigeria gave him a sip of water. She sat her nude body on the floor, holding the gun and occasionally glancing at her watch. A few minutes later, she looked up and his meat was standing strong, like a G refusing to turn state evidence. She hurriedly crawled over to him, sucking him off so that he'd enter her with ease. She gasped when she felt him sliding up in between her walls. Her interior felt like the softest, warmest, wettest silk he'd ever had the pleasure of caressing. But it didn't matter, because he hated the air she breathed. He closed his eyelids, imagining himself somewhere beautiful and serene. He ceased to exist down there in that basement, the only thing there was Nigeria's pleasured noises.

"Uhh, yesss, yessss, God—Jesus—Ohhhh," Nigeria grinded on his thick penis and shuttered, meeting that first orgasm. She licked and sucked on his earlobe, as she continued to wind her hips on top of him, prolonging her orgasm. Once she was through, her face and body were shiny from perspiration. She lay there against him, with the side of her sweaty face against his, as she panted out of breath. "Whew, that was good, baybe, dat was da shit! Mauh!" she kissed him on the cheek. "Lemme get dat up out chu one mo' time, okay?" she didn't wait for him to answer. She answered herself. "Okay." With his dick still in her, she grinded again and started back up with the noises. A couple of minutes later, her juices were soaking his balls and thighs, darkening the cement floor that they were on.

With a smile plastered on her face, Nigeria un-straddled a zoned out Kreon and got to her bare feet. "Good looking out, baby daddy," she giggled and rubbed her stomach thinking of the pre-cum she felt ooze inside of her womb. Next, she ruffled his head. After wiping herself off, she slipped her panties and clothes back on.

She then tucked the .38 into the small of her back. She picked up the wielding mask and the blow torch. Stopping at the door, she tucked the wielding mask under her arm and turned around to Kreon.

"I love you, baybe." Nigeria kissed her palm and blew him a kiss. She then chuckled, turned off the light and headed back up the steps.

Besides the street light shining through the basement on him, Kreon was sitting in darkness.

For the next few days Kreon was forcefully fed Viagra and used as Nigeria's fuck-dummy. She got off on him at least four times a day. At the end of every day, she'd clean him up and feed him her nasty ass oatmeal. She fixed him with a diaper for him to shit and piss in while she when she'd go to sleep at night.

A fly whizzed back and forth across Kreon's face, eventually landing on his nose. The bug crawled across his face towards his bottom eyelid, causing his eyelid to flutter. Once it seemed like it was going into his wondering eyeball, he shook his head and the fly flew away from him. Kreon's eyes followed the fly and his eyes landed on Nigeria's dark figure, which was standing on the staircase and holding something the shape of a revolver in her hand. The sight of her caused Kreon to panic. He thrashed around trying to get free of his handcuffs, but he couldn't get loose. Realizing that he wasn't going anywhere, he went slack in the metal bracelets and breathed heavily.

"You know, Kreon, I finally realized dat I'll never have yo' heart." Nigeria's voice cracked under her raw emotions. Kreon could tell that she'd been sobbing before she entered the basement. "Sadly, I'm too late ta salvage our relationship, and now ya heart belongs ta another. I can't live with knowin' someone else out there has my soul mate's love. I just can't." holding her pistol at her side in one hand, she used the other hand to slide down the guard railing, as she made her way down the staircase, slowly. The closer she drew to Kreon, the harder his heart thudded, and he began to sweat.

Nigeria flipped on the light switch and made her way over in Kreon's direction. For the first time since she'd entered the basement, he finally got to see her face. Her eyes were pink and her cheeks were wet from crying her eyes out. She stopped before him, and the light kissed off the .38 in her hand. When he looked to it he knew that it would seal his fate.

Fuck! This bitch 'bouta knock me off, this is it!

Kreon looked beyond Nigeria and smiled inside, seeing Odette slowly descending the staircase. She moved stealthy with a shovel in her hand and held her finger to her lips, signaling for him to keep silent about her presence.

"I'm sorry, baybe," Nigeria wiped her dripping eyes with her curled finger. "But if I can't have you, then no one can. I love you and I'll see ya soon." She pointed her .38 down at Kreon. She intended to kill him and then herself. At that moment, Odette was standing behind her and cocking her shovel back, as far as she could. She was just about to swing the shovel with all of her might, when Nigeria suddenly whipped around and kicked her in the chest. The impact of the kick sent Odette sliding across the basement floor, losing the shovel in the process.

"Bish, ya think ya slick, huh?" Nigeria scowled and glanced back at Kreon. "So, dis da hoe ya chose ova me? I gotta tell ya, she does not compare," she chuckled and threw her revolver aside. "I don't needa gun, I can beat cha at cha own game." She picked up a shovel that was at the corner of the basement. Gripping the tool with both hands, she stepped to the center of the basement floor and addressed Odette. "We fight ta da death, bish!"

"Bring that shit then, bitch!" Odette picked her shovel back up and got to her feet.

"Come on, O, you got this! Take her ass out!" Kreon called out to his lady.

"Ya just think ya gone swoop into ma life and take ma muddafuckin' man? Ya got me fucked up!" Nigeria nose twitched and she clenched her jaws, as she and Odette circled one another.

"Well, if you woulda been on yo' shit, I couldn't have taken him in the first place! You can't take a nigga that don't wanna be taken!" Odette spat off to the side and continued to circle Nigeria, looking for a flaw in her defense.

"Aahhhhhhh!" Nigeria's eyes exploded with rage and she screamed like an African warrior. She ran at Odette and brought the shovel above her head, swinging it downward with all the might she could muster. Seeing the shovel coming at her, Odette swung hers upwards and the tools collided.

Claannnnggggggg! The sound of the shovels coming into contact rang throughout the basement and sparks flew.

Cling! Clank! Ching! Zing!

Blood, sweat and sparks flew at the ladies engaged in combat. Their faces and bodies were hot and dripping with perspiration. Their shadows danced on the wall as they fought long and hard. They grunted and hollered, swinging the shovels and trying to decapitate one another.

"Get her, O, get her! Fuck her ass up!" Kreon called out from where he was shackled.

Odette swung at Nigeria's head and she ducked. She swung at her legs and she hopped over it.

When Nigeria came back down on her feet, she punched Odette square in the face. The punch sent blood flying and Odette stumbling backwards. She almost fell but she quickly righted herself by using the handle of the shovel. Stopping, she touched her top lip and felt the blood that came from her nose. She then licked it and spat it out. When she looked up, she saw a battered and bruised Nigeria. She was glaring at her and laughing.

"Aaaahhhhh!" Odette went charging at Nigeria swinging her shovel. Nigeria jumped back three times to avoid the onslaught of the shovel, but the fourth time the tool sliced through the front of her clothing. Odette faked swinging the shovel at her side, and when she went to blocked it, Odette cracked her in the jaw and kicked her in the chest. She went slamming up against the basement wall. Nigeria blinked her eyelids like she was coming out of a dream, she then shook off her daze and looked up. She found Odette about to stab her in the stomach with the shovel. Swiftly, Nigeria moved out of the way and the shovel deflected off the wall.

Cling! Ching! Bing! King!

Sweat and sparks flew as the ladies fought on. Their shadows continued to dance on the wall and Kreon continued to cheer his woman on in the brawl.

Nigeria aimed the shovel for Odette's throat and swung it like a sword. Odette avoided the deadly threat. Once Nigeria swung the shovel at her head, she ducked it and came back up. Odette swung the shovel at Nigeria's kneecap, breaking it and sending blood flying. Once her foe screamed out and reached for her kneecap, she swung the shovel upwards with all her might.

Clang!

The impact from the shovel opened up a gash and sent blood splattering on the wall. Nigeria had a dazed look on her face as her head flew at a funny angle. Her body was about to smack down on the floor, when Odette swung the shovel again. The metal collided with Nigeria's skull and sent her head flying in the opposite direction. Sweat and blood went everywhere and Nigeria's body smacked down on the surface. She lay where she was looking at Kreon, blood oozing out of her nostrils and forehead.

"I…I love you," Nigeria claimed. She outstretched her hand, trying to reach out to Kreon.

Kreon shook his head shamefully and looked away. He shut his eyelids and bowed his head. Seeing this, Nigeria became teary eyed and her bottom lip quivered. It was from Kreon's actions that she knew whatever love he had for her had truly died some time ago. Suddenly, her arm and head dropped. Her eyes stared out at nothing and her mouth remained opened.

Odette stood over Nigeria's slain body, huffing and puffing out of breath. Her chest jumped up and down while her eyes slowly watered. Although she was victorious, taking someone's life fucked with her conscience. She was a genuinely kind hearted person, so murdering someone made her feel conflicted.

"Suck that shit up, slim. Don't chu cry ova her. You did what chu hadda do to save me and yo' self. You hear me? What chu did was necessary." Kreon told Odette from where he sat on the floor handcuffed. He was staring right into her face and wearing a stern expression.

Odette nodded and began wiping her face with the inside of the lower half of her shirt. She nodded her head and said, "You're right, you're so right."

Odette, with her eyelids shut, sniffled and took a deep breath. Having calmed herself, she approached Kreon and hacked away at the chain that bound him by the shackle. Kreon turned his head and squeezed his eyelids shut, hearing the clanging of the shovel as it repeatedly clashed with the chain. Eventually, the chain broke and clashed to the floor.

Kreon got upon his feet and lovingly embraced Odette. He kissed her on the forehead and tightened his hold, feeling her body shudder and hearing her crying. The couple stood in the basement wrapped in one another's arms for a minute before they made their way up the staircase.

"How did you manage to find me?" Kreon inquired curiously, as he held her hand and made his way up the staircase.

"I put in a missing persons report to the police days ago, but they couldn't find you. That's when I remembered that our cell phones are linked through the GPS app. That's how I found you."

"Thanks."

"Don't mention it. You would have done the same for me."

"No doubt."

CHAPTER SEVEN

Hearing knocks at his door, Drennen stopped cleaning his .45 automatic handgun and set it aside along with the copper bullets, magazines, and items used to clean it. Pulling up the right leg of his slacks, he un-holstered the .32 handgun that was there and chambered a live round into it. Cautiously, he crept up to the door and placed his shoulder up against the side of it. He pulled the curtain back slightly and eased his head out. Right there at his door, he found that nigga Omar holding onto a black leather briefcase. Identifying his guest, his shoulders slumped and his breathing steadied. Afterwards, he unchained and unlocked the door, pulling it open. He dapped up Omar and allowed him in over the threshold and into his apartment, shutting the door behind him.

"What up, Omar?" Drennen dapped him up after locking the door behind him.

"Ain't shit. You mind if I have a seat?" Omar swayed his hand towards the kitchen table.

"Go ahead; I'm just cleanin' out this banga out. Slide some of that shit off to the side. Matta fact, hold on," he made his way over to the kitchen table and pushed some of the items that he was using to clean his gun off to the side. Once he was done, the OG sat down at the table and sat his briefcase down upon it.

"Nice place you got here, I love what you've done with it." Omar complimented him on the décor of his home. The gangsta hadn't been home very long but he already copped his own pad and had it furnished and decorated.

"Thanks. A nigga try, but I haven't been home in a minute, so I really don't know what's in or out, when it comes to decorating and shit. I just picked out the shit that I liked, you feel me?"

"Well, my nigga give yourself a pat on the back, you did okay here." He turned his focus away from the décor of the room and looked to Drennen. "Anyway, I came here to holla at chu on the business tip." Hearing this, Drennen holstered his .32 and draped his pants le over it.

"What's the deal?" Drennen's eyes went from Omar's face to the briefcase that he was opening.

"Now, I know you just came off of that thang that I had you take care of, and I hate to be right back at chu so soon, but my sister is in a situation that I need handled, ASAP."

"Don't even worry about it. That's sis, so that's family off top, so don't worry about getting back at me so soon. Niggaz fuck with the bloodline then they gotta pay with interest."

"That's love, here," Omar pulled a file of documents out of the briefcase that he'd gotten from Roland and passed it off to Drennen. The file contained a lot of information on Kennan that would aid Drennen in finding him. Drennen's forehead crinkled as he sifted through the documents inside of the file and found the only photograph among the paperwork. Once he saw the face on the photograph, he knew that he didn't have to read over the rest of the paperwork. He knew the nigga on the photo very well. Seeing the look of familiarity cross his homeboy's face, Omar assumed that he knew old boy on the photograph.

"You recognize this fool?" Omar's forehead ran with lines.

The gangsta tossed the photograph upon the table top along with the documents. He then took a deep breath before speaking, "Yeah, I know exactly who old head is, surprise you don't." he said, nodding his head.

With that said, Omar picked up the photograph and studied the nigga that was on it. "Nah, I can't say I know homie like that. The mothafucka does look vaguely familiar though."

"That's that ex-cop turned hit-man for hire, Kennan. I ain't holdin' homie's dick or nothin', but he's a reputable out here."

"Yo' my man," Kennan called out to homeboy in the doo-rag as he advanced in his direction. When old boy saw his fear filled his eyes and his mouth formed an O. Swinging around, he took off running in the opposite direction, his thin gold chain floating in the air and his T-shirt ruffling. The wind was blowing against him as he hauled ass towards the backyard of the house. "Don't chu run from me, don't chu run." Kennan whipped out his nightstick and took off running after the nigga in the doo-rag. He witnessed him leap upon the gate of the backyard. As he went to crawl over it, Kennan threw his nightstick with all of his might. The sleek black weapon spun around so fast that it looked like a black helicopter propeller. It curved at an angle and struck old boy in the back causing him to holler out in excruciation. The impact of the attack took doo-rag's his mind off of his escape and he grabbed at his back, falling backwards. He hit the surface hard and winced, turning from side to side.

"Unh huh, didn't I tell yo' ol' bitch ass notta run, huh?" Kennan stumped his stomach and kicked him in the side, cracking his ribs. The nigga howled in pain. "Now, I told yo' ass 'bout pushing that poison out here to these kids. I gave you a break and even gave you a safe haven to hustle, where the law wouldn't fuck witchu but chu wasn't tryna listen, were you? Now, it's time I set an example for you and the rest of the drug dealas out here." He sheathed his nightstick and reached for doo-rag's waistline, drawing his .9mm Beretta. He pointed the banga at both of his kneecaps, popping him in them one by one.

"Aarrrrh!" Doo-rag's face balled up in agony, try-ing to clutch both of his aching kneecaps at once.

After firing the Beretta and tucking it on his waistline, Kennan grabbed old boy by the back of his collar which tore a little, and dragged him down the driveway, leaving crimson smears behind. He tied the bitch-ass nigga to the back of his whip and drove it throughout the ghetto for all of the drug dealers to see. He knew that this would set an example for the rest of them to know not to sell narcotics in the school zone. Once he was sure he'd gathered an audience, he stopped his car in the middle of the residential street and hopped out. Making his way to the back of the vehicle he came across homeboy in the doo-ray. He was bloody and smoking, the pinkness beneath his dark skin shown. The speeding around the ghetto had stripped a lot of the flesh from off of his form and had left him looking like something out of a horror movie. His pupils were rolled up to the back of his head and his lips occasionally twitched. That was the only way that you could tell that the poor bastard was still alive.

Kennan made it his business to use his victim's body as a stepping stone, making his way around to the rear of the trunk and popping it open. He lifted the trunk, holding it open with one hand; he took in his surroundings and saw that he had not only the drug dealers, but everyone else in the neighborhood's full attention. People whispered among one another while others exchanged glances and ordered their children into their homes. They could only imagine what Kennan was about to do and they didn't want their kids there to witness it for fear of them having nightmares. The regular Joes and their wives in the neighborhood knew, loved and respected Kennan, they didn't fear him. In fact, a couple of their kids had gotten hooked on heroine and they complained to him about all of the drug dealing that had been going on in the hood and by the schools. This is one of the reasons why homeboy was out there today busting a head open. He wanted hustlers to get the message that he was about to send loud and clear.

Kennan removed the megaphone from out of his trunk and planted his boot on the chest of doo-rag. After activating the device, he looked around to make sure that he had everyone that was there attention. Clearing his throat with his fist to his mouth, he placed the end of the megaphone to his lips and spoke, "You see this piece of shit at my feet here?" the people cringed seeing his victim, looking like a charred rib. "Let 'em serve as an example to all of you poison peddling mothafuckaz out here. The next time I see a child walking around high out of their minds, moving around like a goddamn zombie or any of you fucks slinging that shit in a school zone, you gone end up just like my friend here," he lowered the megaphone to his side and pulled the gun that he had taken from doo-rag off his waistline and pointed it at his skull, pulling the trigger. Homeboy's head burst like a rotten tomato, splattering all over the street. The shot that rang out startled and horrified nearly everyone in attendance. Once the job was done, Kennan tossed the murder weapon and the megaphone into the trunk, slamming it shut. Afterwards, he untied doo-rag from the back of his vehicle, jumped in behind the wheel and cranked that bitch up, pulling off

"Well, reputable or no reputable," Omar began as he placed his hand on Drennen. "I want this mothafucka silenced...forever. You feelin' me? Now, I know how you ain't no joke, and from what chu say, this mothafucka ain't no joke either. But if it comes down to it, I'm willin' to bet the house on yo' skills when it comes down to this hitta shit. I'm willin' to lay all of mine on the table when it comes to you versus this nigga Kennan. Ain't a nigga on this planet that can convince me that my right-hand man can't crush any other nigga when it comes to the business of murda." He smiled as he stroked that nigga Drennen's ego.

"If you bettin' all yo' marbles on me, then you gone come out a winna every time, homeboy. That's for damn sure." Drennen said, wearing a dead serious expression across his face.

"That's what I like to hear," Omar's smile stretched further across his face and he patted his homeboy on his shoulder, brotherly like. "Here's a lil' initiative," he reached into his deep pocket and pulled out two big ass wads of money secured by rubber bands. He then smacked them down on top of each other on the table top. As soon as he moved his hand back, the top wads of money fell off to the side of the other wad. Drennen's eyes shot to the money on the table top. That's what he loved about fucking with Omar. That nigga paid like he weighed and he wasn't stingy with his wealth. "That right there is ten grand, big dawg. You knock this mothafucka off for me and I'ma send anotha five yo' way."

"Dead or alive?" Drennen asked.

"Dead or alive." he nodded.

The homeboys dapped one another up and Omar made his departure.

As soon as Drennen was alone, he took a quick shower and started getting dressed. Afterwards, he began readying all of his weapons. Oh yeah, it was on now!

***

Omar hopped into the passenger seat of his car where Candy was waiting for him in the driver seat. He gave her the signal to drive off, and she obliged him. With his eyes focused out of the passenger side window, watching the streets pass him by, he couldn't help thinking, *Where in the fuck is my sister?*

***

Ella sat on the edge of her bed in her bra and panties. She was hunched over with her eyes concentrated on the glass penis in between her fat lips, as she held the big flame of a Bic lighter to the end of it that crack rocks resided in. It was dark inside of her motel room and the blue illumination from the television's screen flashed on her upper half. The air conditioner was broken and it was pretty hot inside. This was why her entire body was shiny from her perspiration. Small trickles of sweat ran down her forehead, as she sucked on the end of her stem and pulled the smoke into her lungs. After taking a long deep pull, she threw her head back and blew out a little smoke before indulging in her habit again.

Kreon not contacting his mother had really gotten to her. She started to try to call him, but her pride wouldn't allow it. She was as stubborn as a bull, so she knew where he had gotten it from. She wanted so badly for her him to call and check up on her. It would definitely make her feel good knowing that he was worried and concerned about her. But she wouldn't hold her breath. Knowing Kreon, he was probably going on with his day like he didn't give a shit. That hurt her thinking that this was true. Although she made some mistakes while raising him, she really did love him. He was her first born, her baby boy, her reason to live, her excuse to die.

"Fuck Kreon, fuck 'em. And fuck Omar too, mothafucka hasn't even thought about calling me," Ella brought the crack pipe back to her lips and the flame of her lighter in behind it. The flame licked at the end of the glass dick and she sucked the smoke from out of it. Her eyelids fluttered as she brought her head back and blew out a cloud of smoke into the air.

Unbeknownst to Ella, she had been so preoccupied with getting high that she hadn't paid her cell phone bill. In fact, her cellular had been off for the past few days so neither her brother nor her son could contact her. At that moment, her cell phone, which had half of a battery on it, was lying on the nightstand.

***

After Odette had broken Kreon out of the homemade prison that Nigeria had confined him, he didn't waste any time in making her keep her promise. He had her call up Carlos so they could get the ball rolling on their plan. He listened intently as she chopped it up with him on the phone, he promised himself that if she shed any tears behind the setup that she was doing for him, then he was gone stop fucking with her ass. Surprisingly, well, at least surprisingly to him, Odette talked to her baby daddy as natural as she always had. When she hung up with him, she told Kreon that they'd agreed to meet up at a park not too far from where they were at, at 9 o'clock. Before they knew it, that time came rolling around and it was time for the meeting to begin.

The lighting inside of Trinity Park was dim and the night was cold, with the occasional breeze. The wind would whisk through and cause the collar of his coat to flap against his chin, slapping up against it repeatedly. Carlos sat on the park bench with his hands in the pockets of his trench coat. While one hand was just filling the void inside of his coat the other was holding firmly to a Glock. His eyes, which were just below the brim of his Atlanta Falcons cap, moved around suspiciously. This was because he was watching everything around him. For all he knew the fool that he had taken a shot at was going to leap out of the shadows and pop a cap in his ass. Now, don't get it fucked up. He trusted his baby momma. Mainly because he knew her like he knew the back of his hand. Odette was a very sweet girl that wouldn't harm a fly; not to mention she was gullible as hell. The poor girl wanted to believe that there was good in most people. You know, the kind of individual that looked at a glass as half full instead of half empty? See, he knew that with all the right words, no matter what kind of fucked up shit he done to her, he could be back in her good graces in no time at all.

This was the only reason that he believed that she wouldn't try to set him up. Well, that and the reason that they had a son together. Shit, you would have to be a pretty fucked up person to have the father of your only child whacked.

Where da fuck is she? Carlos pulled back his sleeve and looked at his watch. He looked at the time and saw that his baby's momma was ten minutes late. Lifting his head back up, he tapped his foot impatiently and waited for a couple of more minutes. *Fuck it,* the giant rose from off the bench and made to leave. Homeboy froze in his tracks when he saw a short, dark figure moving in his direction. His brows furrowed wondering who it was advancing towards him and he reached for his gun. He was about to drawn down on whoever it was but he caught the person's walk, immediately identifying who it was that was approaching him. With that in mind, he took a breath and his shoulders slumped, relaxing a little bit.

"Odette, what's up?" Carlos's forehead creased seeing his son's mother with teary eyes and a red nose. Her eyes were partially swollen, which indicated to him that she had been crying for quite some time.

Odette shut her eyelids briefly and looked down, taking a deep breath. She looked back up at him and said, "They snatched Marquise up...they snatched up our baby."

"What? Who?" Carlos leaned closer and his forehead creased further.

Suddenly, Odette's eyebrows sloped and wrinkles surrounded her nose. Clenching her jaws, she smacked fire out of his ass, snapping his head to the right. When he turned back around to her, there was a red hand imprint on his cheek and the area was stinging. He rubbed the side of his face.

"Who the fuck you think, stupid, huh? The motha-fucka you shot at!" she spazzed out on his ass, punching and kicking him. Hunched over, he balled up and covered his head with his arm. "You shot at him and he took Marquise..." her punches came slower and landed softer against him, until finally she stopped. Her arms dropped at her sides and she bowed her head. Big teardrops fell from her eyes as she shuddered, entire form rocking.

Slowly, Carlos took his arms from his face and stood upright, watching the mother of his son cry. Although he'd taken her through a lot of shit in their marriage and didn't feel too much about it. As of now, he felt a twinge of guilt creep up into his heart. This was because he knew that everything had fallen upon his shoulders. If it wasn't for him busting at that nigga Kreon then that mothafucka wouldn't have snatched up his son. Now, he had to get him back. In fact, he was going to do everything in his power to make sure his little man made it back home in one piece.

Carlos embraced Odette and swept his hand up and down her back, rocking her from side to side. "Don't worry about nothin', we gone get 'em back. On my mothafuckin' momma we gone get Mar Mar back home."

"You promise?" she sniffled and wiped her dripping eyes with her curled finger.

"Look at me," he tilted her chin upwards so that she'd be looking up at him. Once she was looking him directly in the eyes, he continued, "I promise."

Carlos went to kiss Odette and she turned her head, not wanting his lips to touch her. He dropped his head feeling the sting of her not wanting his affection.

Odette composed herself as best as she could before addressing him. "He said that he'll only give Marquise back if you ..." at that moment, a cellular rang and killed any words that attempted to roll off of her tongue. She reached inside of her purse and pulled out a small cell phone, looking at the screen. Carlos looked at it too, forehead crinkling with wonder.

"Whose cell phone is that?" Carlos asked curiously.

"It's Kreon's phone. I mean, the one he gave me to give to you."

"Fuck he want me to have his cell for?"

"I don't know. That nigga got my son, so I did whatever he told me to do. Hold up," She told him and answered the call. After a brief exchange with the caller, she extended the cell phone to her son's father. His forehead creased, pointing his finger to the cell phone and then to himself. "Yes. He wants to speak to you."

Carlos took a deep breath and his shoulders slumped, motioning Odette to give him the cell phone.

"Gemme the jack," he said, taking the device from her and placing it to his ear. "Fucks up?"

"'Sup, pussy? I guess by now you got word that I got cho lil' nigga, right?" Kreon spoke, voice coming through a voice alternator.

"Yeah, I got word, mothafucka."

"Well, if you want 'em back, here's what chu gotta do… It ain't gone be that easy, homeboy. That's just the icing on the cake; you gotta do something else for me, slim."

Carlos blew hot air and rolled his eyes, listening to what Kreon had to say. He looked at Odette who was staring at him curiously, wondering what was being said over the phone.

Suddenly, Carlos's face balled up hearing what Kreon wanted him to do in order to get his son back.

"What the fuck? Hell naw, I ain't doin' that shit! Fuck you think I am?"

"What I think you are? I don't know. But I know for a mothafuckin' fact you gone be the man that's gone receive his little boy back in pieces, through the mail, if he doesn't do exactly what the fuck I said."

"Alright, alright, alright," Carlos said, throwing up his hand in surrender. "I'll do it...we gotta deal?"

"Yeah, we gotta deal, bitch, just make sure you record the act so I can confirm it. You got me, homeboy?"

"Yeah, I got chu."

"Alright, give our bitch a kiss for me." Kreon disconnected the call.

Carlos took the cell phone from his ear and stashed it inside of his coat, looking up at his baby's mother in defeat.

"What's going on? What did he say?" she asked anxiously.

He licked his lips and said, "He wants me to kill Royce and film it. That's the only way he's gonna give up Marquise."

"Well...well, what're you going to do?" she inquired, interlocking her fingers, hoping that he was going to go through with it.

Carlos took a breath and looked up at her with teary eyes. "I'ma do what I gotta do to make sure our son gets back home in one piece."

With that said, Odette collided with him and wrapped her arms around him, kissing him on the cheek gratefully. He brought his deluxe arms around her and squeezed her tight, tears sliding down his cheeks. He silently cried in her arms knowing that he was about to do something that was going to break his heart and haunt his memories for as long as he lived.

***

After her meeting with Carlos, Odette made her way back to her Honda and hopped in behind the wheel. As soon as she shut the door behind her, Kreon slid up in the backseat. He had Donald's Glock in one hand and his cellular in the other.

"That nigga went for it?" Kreon asked, looking up at her. She looked up at him through the rearview mirror and met his eyes. They were cruel and unforgiving. She knew right then that there wasn't any way that she could salvage her baby daddy's life. His life was gone if it was resting in Kreon's hands.

"Yeah. He's on board. Matter of fact, he's gonna do him tonight." She said sadly.

Hearing the emotion in his lady's voice caused Kreon to frown up. He hated hearing his woman so emotional behind another nigga, it enraged him.

"Yo', I know yo' ass bet not be lettin' no teardrops fall behind this sucka ducka ass nigga."

"No."

"Lemme see ya face then." He commanded.

She turned around and he saw that she hadn't been crying, but she was sad. He could deal with that because it was her son's father, but tears? Nah, he wasn't having his lady dropping tears behind any nigga that wasn't him. And if she thought that she could go on being his woman after she'd shed tears for another man then she had him fucked up.

"Good. The only males you should be shedding tears for is me or Marquise," he looked over his shoulder and seen Carlos's car stopping at the stop sign. "Yo', catch up with cho B.D, try to stay like two cars behind that nigga." He ordered her, and she cranked up her whip and hurriedly pulled off. She busted a U-turn and pursued Carlos, keeping two cars behind him like she was told.

Odette looked into the rearview mirror and saw the light of Kreon's cell phone shining in his face as he texted someone. "Who are you talking to?"

"My unc." He answered without looking up. "Nigga said my mom's been missin' for a while now. He said he tried callin' her but her phone is off."

"You have any idea where she is?" Odette asked as she made a left turn

"Nah, we gone take care of this business with cho B.D, then we lookin' for my momma tomorrow. We gone find her, and she betta be good too, or else it's gone be hell to pay. My old lady hasn't always done right by me, but she has been there for a nigga sometimes. Besides, that's still my moms, you know?"

"Yeah. I feel the same behind my mother." Odette looked up into the rearview mirror and saw Kreon's attention focused out of the passenger side window. When he shut his eyelids and silently mouthed something, she knew that he was praying to God to watch over his mother. It was from this that she knew that people would always love their parents, whether they did well by them or not, simply because they were all that they had.

***

An hour later

Carlos pulled up across the street from Royce's house and five houses down from it. He killed the engine and lay back in the seat, resting his head against the headrest. He shut his eyelids and took a deep breath. This was his way of preparing himself for the murder that he was about to commit. It wasn't going to be easy for him to lie down at all. And how could it be? The man was told to murder his cousin in cold blood in order for his son to be set free from kidnappers. He knew that if he didn't carry out the mission that was handed down to him that his offspring would pay with his life.

"Fuuuuck, man! Fuck, fuck, fuuuck!" Carlos punched and pounded the steering wheel with his fists, accidentally blowing the vehicle's horn. Settling back down, his nostrils flared and his chest heaved. He reached into his back pocket and pulled out his wallet. Opening it, he searched it until he found a picture of little Marquise. The boy was smiling and showing off his missing front tooth. He was so cute in the photo. The little dude was the perfect mixture of him and Odette's features.

"I can do this, I can do this. I have to if I wanna save my lil' man." He kissed the photo and then held it to his heart, shutting his eyelids.

Taking a deep breath, he placed the photo back inside of the wallet and slid it into his back pocket. Afterwards, he opened the door of his Maybach and slid out. Slamming the door shut, he took a look around and made his way towards Royce's crib. When he found himself at the front door, he knocked on it and waited for someone to open it. It wasn't long before he heard the locks coming undone and the door being pulled open. Before he knew it, he was standing before his cousin, Royce.

Royce was rocking a burgundy P fitted cap backwards and no shirt, so all of his tattooed form was on display. His hands were in a pair of latex gloves at the moment.

"'Sup, reli?" Royce slapped hands with Carlos and embraced him. He then stepped aside to allow him inside over the threshold. Once he'd entered, he closed and locked the door behind him. "So, what's this, a social call?"

"Nah. I came through 'cause I found out where dude laying his head at." Carlos said, looking at Royce. He was standing over the stove whipping up crack in a see-through Pyrex pot. Seeing that his cousin was focused on the task at hand, Carlos pulled out his cell phone and activated the video camera on it. Once he saw that it was filming, he propped it up against the window pane.

"Oh, yeah? Where that fool at?"

"Off of seventy-fifth and Hoova...peach apartment complex." He informed him. "I got the number of the unit and every thang, cousin."

"Bool. This gone be an easy one, just lemme finish whipping up this work and we gone handle that." Royce told him.

"Cool." Carlos replied, walking inside of the kitchen, still talking to Royce. He was at his back and reaching for the butcher's knife, which was in the wooden block on the counter. He slowly drew it as he chopped it up with his relative. The light from the ceiling kissed off the blade and caused it to gleam. "I'm sorry about this, Royce." He said apologetically, with tears misting in his eyes.

Royce's forehead wrinkled and he stopped whipping up the drugs. His back was still to him when he said, "Sorry about what?"

Carlos sniffled as tears slid down his cheeks. His eyes were glassy and red webbed. With a trembling hand, he looked up at the ceiling and mouthed *'Please, forgive me, father'*.

"Sorry about what I'ma 'bouta do." A serious expression crossed his face.

Royce's eyebrows rose and his heart dropped to the pit of his stomach. He went to grab his gun from off the stove top, where he'd left it and Carlos sliced his hand.

"Aahhhh!" Royce snatched his hand back and whipped around, swinging on his cousin. His fist connected with his jaw, but it barely budged him. So, he kicked him in his balls, slammed his elbow down onto his shoulder blade and then into his temple. The attack dropped the giant on his hands and knees, but he held tight to the butcher's knife.

Royce turned around and snatched a dish rag, wrapping it around his wounded hand and tying it tight with his teeth. His blood quickly absorbed it but he didn't pay it any mind.

"You came here to kill me, nigga. Yo' own flesh and blood?" Royce screamed on him, with spit jumping off his lips. He then hauled off and kicked him in his side, causing him to howl in pain and fall back down to the floor. He tried to get back up, and he kicked him again. "Who sent chu, nigga? How much they give you to off me?" he kicked him in his side once again. "Huh? Tell me! Tell me!"

Royce kicked his cousin until he was out of breath and his forehead was shining from sweat. He wiped his forehead with the back of his hand and reached down to pick up his gun. His palm had just brushed against the handle, when Carlos hurriedly got back upon his feet. He rushed Royce and grabbed him by his neck, slamming him up against the refrigerator. His eyebrows slanted and his nose crinkled as he held back the butcher's knife.

"I love you. Please, forgive me." Carlos sniffled and teardrops fell from the brims of his eyes. He slammed the butcher's knife into Royce's stomach and his eyes bulged, mouth stretching wide open. He gurgled blood and attempted to claw at Carlos's face, but he moved his face from side to side to avoid his attack.

Carlos yanked the knife out of his cousin's stomach and blood splattered on the floor. The Dominican then slammed Royce back up against the refrigerator, so hard that the magnetic colorful letters of the alphabet fell to the linoleum. Looking away from Royce's pain streaked face; Carlos cried and continued to stab him repeatedly.

"I'm sorry, man. I'm sorry." He apologized repeatedly and squeezed his eyelids shut, turning his head. He couldn't stand to see the horror etched on Royce's face, as he kept stabbing him, making his blood rain on the floor.

All that could be heard throughout the kitchen was Royce's pained voice and sharp metal puncturing his flesh, over and over again. When Carlos released his grip from around his relative's neck, he collapsed to the floor on his behind, legs stretched out in front of him. Hoarsely breathing, and bleeding profusely from his stomach, Royce stared up at Carlos accusingly.

"Don't look at me, don't look at me, man!" Tears flooded Carlos's cheeks as he gripped the butcher's knife with both hands and brought it high above his head. He turned his head away from his victim and squeezed his eyelids shut. He didn't want to be haunted by his cousin's face after he murdered him.

"P...please..." Royce begged weakly, tears pooling in his eyes.

"I'm sorry, bro," Carlos took his bloody hand from off the kilt of the knife and crossed himself in the sign of the crucifix. He then gripped the knife with both hands again, clutching it so tight that his knuckles bulged. With a grunt, he slammed the knife down through the top of Royce's skull with all of his might, burying half of it at the top his head. Blood oozed up out of the wound that he created and came running down either side of his face. Royce's eyes rolled into the back of his head and his mouth hung open. His head fell back against the refrigerator and he sat slumped, palms facing upwards.

Carlos dropped the murder weapon and it clanged to the floor. Sobbing aloud, he got down on the floor and pulled his cousin over into him; letting his upper half lie against him. He looked down at Royce's lifeless body, his hot teardrops pelting his face. His entire form shook as he cried, holding his deceased relative in his arms.

"I'm sorry, Royce, man. I'm sorry... I...I had to, bro. I didn't have a choice." Carlos rocked back and forth, still crying as he held his loved one.

Having shed his tears and taken a deep breath, the giant got to his feet and walked over to the kitchen sink. He turned on the dial and water came bursting from the faucet. He rinsed off as much blood as he could and lathered his hands up with dishwashing liquid, rinsing a second time.

After he was finished, he turned off the faucet and wiped his hands dry on a couple of paper towels. He stared at Royce's corpse as he picked up his cellular and cut off the video. Balling up the paper towels he'd used to dry his hands, he tossed it into the trash can and headed to the front door, using the sleeve of his shirt to open it and leave out.

***

Carlos, with his hands shoved inside of his pockets, hurriedly made it back to his Maybach taking cautious looks over his shoulders. Once he made it back to his luxury vehicle, he opened the driver's door and slid inside on the leather. He then reached inside of his jacket and pulled out the butcher's knife wrapped in the news paper. He opened up the glove-box and stuffed the weapon inside of it along with car's registration, manual, and a bunch of napkins. Smacking the glove-box shut, he went to draw his arm back and was cracked at the back of the head. Knocked out cold, his face went slamming face first into the horn and sounding it off, without pause.

Kreon, who had been hiding inside of the backseat of the car, pulled Carlos back from off the horn of the vehicle. He then pressed his Glock to his temple, his finger rested on the trigger as he thought about pulling it back. Odette's saddened expression when he told her he wanted her to help him kill Carlos, as well as Marquise's jolly face, crossed his mind several times. As bad as he wanted to bring that bastard's life to an end, he knew that it would break Marquise's heart and have Odette over-whelmed with guilt. Having realized this, he decided to let homeboy live and put his gun away. He then took Carlos's cellular off of him and took the butcher's knife that was wrapped in news paper from out of the glove-box. Afterwards, he opened the back door and hopped out.

Kreon took cautious looks over his shoulders as he headed back to Odette's car. After he figured that the coast was clear, he climbed into the backseat and slammed the door shut. He then gave his lady the word to drive off and she did like she was told. Two blocks down, he saw two police cars heading into the direction that he was leaving. Their red and blue lights shined in through the windshield into his face and he narrowed his eyelids. He then slid down in the backseat and told Odette to act natural as she drove. She cleared her throat and continued to drive, acting as casually as she could. Once the police had passed them up, Kreon sat back up in the seat and looked through the back window. The police were definitely heading to the murder scene where Royce's dead body was left.

"Babe, you okay?" Odette asked concerned.

"I'm straight, slim." he answered when he turned back around.

There was silence for a minute as they were both tending to their thoughts.

"I have to know, so I'm going to ask. I hope you don't get upset, but if you do then it is what it is."

"What is it?"

"Did you...did you, you know?" she looked into his eyes through the rearview mirror as she waited for his response. Her heart thudded and she swallowed the lump of nervousness in her throat.

"Nah, I let that nigga breathe. I shouldn't have, but I did...for you...for y'all."

Odette shut her eyelids briefly and sighed with relief. She was thankful that her man hadn't killed her ex-husband.

"Oh, thank you. Thank you so much." Her voice cracked with emotions and she sniffled. "These tears aren't for him, I promise you. But chu gotta understand, bae. He is Marquise's father. I don't want baby boy growing up without him."

"I understand, and that's why I spared 'em." He placed his hand on her shoulder and she grasped his wrist, kissing him tenderly on it. She then laid her head against his hand for a minute and rubbed on it lovingly, kissing it again.

"I love you, Kreon."

"I love you, too, Mocha Brown." He called her by one of the nicknames he'd given her.

CHAPTER EIGHT

Kennan had been combing the streets for the last few days trying to find Ella, but he couldn't manage to locate her. He found himself getting two hours asleep a day over his obsessing over her. He called every precinct and morgue in L.A County, but they didn't have any one by the name of Ella Williams in their custody. It was from this that he knew that she had to be in the streets. And since she was, he wasn't going home until he found her and puffed her wig out for opening her mouth. If that bitch thought she was gone live after possibly getting his younger brother a life sentence, then she had him fucked up. He wasn't even about to let that shit slide. To do so would be a slap to the face of every G there ever was.

Kennan pushed the door of the diner open and the bell above it chimed as he crossed the threshold. He took a quick look around and headed for one of the stools at the counter. He removed his hat and his overcoat, lying them down on the stool beside him. He called the waitress over and ordered up a cup of black coffee. Looking to his right, he saw an older Caucasian man in a short sleeve button down. He had a balding scalp and long graying hair that he wore in a ponytail. At the moment, he was sitting at the counter and cutting a slice of lemon meringue pie with a fork, while checking his email through his cell phone. Lying beside the balding man's elbow was a folded news paper he'd been reading earlier that night.

Kennan glanced at the paper and then pointed to it, saying, "Say, do you mind if I..." the older man nodded yes and the ex-cop picked up the paper and unfolded it. Straightening the wrinkles out of the news paper, he took the time to look it over.

At that precise moment, the bell hanging over the door chimed again. A five foot seven African American cat walked inside. He had a fresh fade that swirled with waves and a goatee that lined the lower half of his face perfectly.

The snazzy suit that he wore fitted him to the T. His suit, accompanied with his luxury watch, made him look sophisticated, like he was one of them mothafuckaz working on Wall Street. The cat unbuttoned the button that held his suit's jacket around him and approached the counter. Kennan looked up from his news paper and saw the cat in the snazzy suit in the lengthy mirror behind the counter. He called the waitress over with a wave of his hand; she came right over to take his order.

"What can I get for you, suga?" the waitress asked as she chewed gum. She had an ink pen and a small tablet ready to jot down whatever he wanted.

"Gemme a sec', love." the cat stated, sitting down and flipping through the menu. He made up his mind rather quickly and shut the menu, tossing it back on the counter, "Gemme a cup of apple cinnamon tea."

"Will that be all?" she asked, closing the small tablet. Homie didn't want much so she didn't bother to write his request down.

"Yep," He plucked a toothpick from out of the small container on the counter and stuck it between his lips.

"Coming right up," She smiled and sauntered off.

Once the waitress was gone, the cat sat down on the stool opposite of Kennan.

"Well, well, well, if it isn't the infamous Kennan Bledsoe," Drennen smiled devilishly and rubbed his hands together.

"You know me, homie?" Kennan asked, narrowing his eyelids.

"Do I?" he looked at him like he was crazy. The way he came off was like *of course I know you, nigga. Who doesn't ?* "You're a legend out in these streets, my man. I'm real, real familiar with your work."

"A legend? Hmmph, someone's been blowing smoke up your ass, chief." Kennan took the time to take a sip of his coffee. "I ain't a legend, far from it. You got the wrong Kennan Bledsoe."

"Nah, I'm sure I've got the right one," Drennen, still wearing a smile across his face, took a sip of tea that the waitress had just sat before him.

"Is that so? Well, what makes you so sure I'm *the right one*?"

Drennen sat his glass of tea down on the counter top and licked his lips. He looked up in the mirror behind the counter and made direct eye contact with the seasoned killa.

"I like to do my homework on my prey."

At that moment, Kennan's face twisted into a scowl and his nostrils flared, staring at his enemy in his reflection. He unfolded the newspaper on the counter top and revealed his gun, which he'd been hiding. He went to grasp the gun, but he stopped his hand when Drennen called his hand.

"Unh unh," Drennen shook his head disapprovingly of the Kennan's actions. He was still smiling when he wagged his right hand, moving his gun from side to side.

When Kennan looked to him, he found that he had his .45 automatic handgun peeking out of his suit's jacket, where no one could possibly see it.

"I wouldn't do that if I was you, bruh. I got chu dead to rights, but if you feelin' froggy...by all means...make that leap." He kept his eyes on him as he took another sip of tea. As homie was indulging in his cup of tea, he observed his rival closing the newspaper back over his weapon.

"Wise man," He cleared his throat and sat the cup down on a saucer. Afterwards, he stashed his gun on his waistline and pulled out a pack of Newport 100s. Holding up the packet of smokes for the waitress to see it, he wagged them to see if it was okay for him to smoke inside of the establishment. She nodded her head and he thanked her. Once he received the go ahead from her, he tossed her a ten dollar bill on the counter top for her tip. Next, he took the time to light up a cigarette and threw his head back, blowing smoke up into the air. His eyes shot to their corners and he cracked a smirk, seeing that Kennan was watching him closely.

"Relax; we're both in the same game. You know, if I wanted to put the love on you then it would have already been done, right? Hell, I coulda got chu without steppin' foot in here. I gotta AR-15 with an infrared laser, scope, and silencer attachment in the trunk of my car. I coulda picked you off from that apartment complex across the street," he looked to the gray apartment building in the mirror that was across the street and nodded to it.

When Kennan looked he saw the tenement that homie was talking about. It was from this that he knew he wasn't bullshitting about being able to knock him off from that distance. He was a vet in the murder game and he would have picked that exact location to have carried out the hit on the man sitting beside him.

The kill would have been quick, clean, and he would have been gone on his way to collect while the police were en route to the murder scene.

Kennan composed himself and took another sip of his coffee. "What're you following me for?"

"Drennen...you can call me Drennen. I'm sure it will ring a bell."

"I'm afraid not."

"Do yo' homework...ask around...niggaz know about me."

"Anyhow, my original question."

"Right. Why am I followin' you? I was expectin' somethin' harder. That's an easy one." Drennen took the time to take a pull from his cancer stick. "Your steppin' on toes…goin' after the people of a man that is like a brother to me…his sister to be exact.

Now, I was sent here to cut cho lights out, but then I realized who you were. I must say that I am a very, very big fan of your work. I respect your gangsta. Allow me to tip my imaginary hat," he tipped his imaginary hat down at Kennan. "That's the only reason why you aren't slumped forward with a bullet at the base of your skull. I came to give you fare warning, leave Ella Williams alone before you find yourself in a situation that you really don't want any parts of." He looked at Kennan through the reflection in the mirror. The gangsta's eyes were glassy and serious. The mothafucka looked like the Devil to the ex-cop's just then, but he wasn't scaring him. Kennan had once gone up against some of the roughest toughest street niggaz that American ghettos had ever had the misfortune of spawning. He didn't know what it was to lose and he sure as hell wasn't about to find out now. Fuck that! This nigga Drennen had another thing coming.

"That sister of his ratted out my kid brother…with this charge he's facing a lifetime behind bars. Now, you tell me, what kind of big brother would I be if I let this shit slide?"

"What're you sayin'?" a line creased his forehead.

"I think I've already said it."

"I know the Williams' like I know the back of my fuckin' hand, and ain't no bitch in these people's blood. So for you to even suggest that they told on a soul is an insult within itself. In fact, it's so mothafuckin' disrespect-ful, that I got it in mind to blow yo' top off inside of this diner in front of all of these people."

Kennan took a sip of his coffee before replying, "You could do just that. I mean, you do have the drop on me. You got me by the balls."

"Unh huh."

"But that would be a dumb ass move with all of these witnesses in this place, and you, you don't strike me as a dumb ass...not in the slightest bit."

This made Drennen give him that infamous smile of his again. "Kennan, you keep strokin' my ego like this, and pretty soon I'm going to think you wanna cock yo' legs open and gemme some pussy."

He put his gun away, stood up, and buttoned his suit's jacket.

"I gotta hand it to you, you're right. I just got my black ass outta prison and I don't plan on going back anytime soon. Hell, a nigga loves his freedom," he glanced at his Rolex and dropped his hand at his side.

"Here's some advice, stay away from Ella Williams. It's very, very important that she stays healthy 'cause should she take a turn for the worse, I'm gonna go see that wife and that beautiful lil' baby girls of yours at..." before he could give him the address, Kennan spun around on his stool and hopped to his feet.

He grabbed Drennen by the collar of his suit and pulled him closer, staring him dead in his eyes.

"You threatening my family, huh?" Rage bled from Kennan's eyes as he squared his jaws. The scene he caused had everybody and their momma inside of the diner staring at them.

"You hit the nail on the head." Drennen mad dogged him.

"You motha..."

"Nigga, get cho mothafuckin' hands off me!" Drennen shoved him back violently, causing him to stagger backwards and nearly fall. Kennan straightened out his suit and gave him a few parting words. "Bust a move like that again, and you'll be mournin' your entire fuckin' family." Scowling, he looked him up and down like he wasn't shit. He then pushed open the door of the diner and headed out over the threshold. When he left out of the establishment, all that could be heard was the ringing bell hanging over the door.

***

Kennan made his way to his vehicle, keys jingling in his hand. Stopping at the driver's door, he stuck his key into the key-hole and turned it, popping the driver's door open. He went to pull the door open and saw a red dot moving from within the shadows, shining on the driver's door window. The red dot went across the window's glass and disappeared. At that moment, Kennan's eyes bulged and his mouth dropped wide open. This was because he realized that the red dot had been lined up with the back of his skull. Acknowledging this, he dove out of the way just as the first shot went off, shattering the driver side window and making broken glass rain on the ground.

When Kennan dove to the ground, he tucked and rolled. Coming back up, he drew his Glock and took cover beside his whip. His nostrils flared and his chest jumped up and down, breathing huskily. His heart was racing like a mothafucka. A nigga had just tried to take his head off and he didn't know who it was...or did he? Shutting his eyelids briefly, he took the time to gather his wits and swallowed the spit in his throat. Peeling his eyelids back open, his listened closely to the oncoming police car sirens, The Boys in Blue were hurriedly approaching. For the first time in his life he was glad to hear that the law was coming. This was because he had a sniper on his ass and he didn't know how he could avoid being killed before they arrived.

Hunching over, he made his way to the opposite end of the vehicle, gun held low. Cautiously, he slowly raised his head over the hood of the car and that's when the front passenger window exploded, sending broken glass flying. Kennan whipped his head away at the last minute, narrowly missing the bullet that was meant to blow a hole in his skull. From there, the sniper blew out two of the tires of the vehicle as well as the windows that he could see. From where he was perched, Kennan scanned the ground and discovered a large piece of glass. The shard was the size of a handheld mirror. He picked up the glass and slowly lifted it in the direction where he saw the red dot come from. Peering into the shard, he saw the shadows stirring from the muzzled sniper rifle moving around. Before he knew it the glass exploded in his hand, sending pieces of it flying, looking like crushed diamonds.

With knowledge of where the shots were coming from, Kennan jumped to his feet and turned around. He lifted his Glock swiftly and opened fire in the direction where the sniper was shooting from. As the men banged it out, he backed away from the scene of the shootout so that he could make his escape. Backing up, he neared the doorway of a liquor store, whose door was slammed shut, locking him outside with lingering death. Kennan turned around and ran to the corner of the store, a bullet missing him by an inch. The shot caused debris to fly, and him to duck and wince.

Right then, Drennen came running from out of the shadows with his AR-15. He looked both ways before hauling ass across the street and jumping behind the wheel of his vehicle, tossing his assault rifle into the front passenger seat. He cranked that big bastard up and busted a U-turn in the middle of the street, speeding across the liquor store's parking lot. Adjusting his rearview mirror, he saw that nigga Kennan still posted up beside the liquor store. The ex-cop was looking in his direction. Suddenly, Kennan threw up the middle finger and took off running across the street, ducking off inside of an alley.

"Next time, son, next time," Drennen cracked an evil smile and focused his attention back on the street ahead.

A couple of nights later

Drennen was slumped low in his seat as he followed behind Kennan. Unbeknownst to the ex crooked law enforcer, the gangsta had been following him all that day. The file that Omar had laid on him contained a shit load of useful information. In addition to Kennan's address, were the addresses of his family members, as well as places that he and his wife frequently visited. This was how Drennen knew he could find Kennan's ass at the diner they bumped heads at. Luck happened to be on his side when he walked inside of the establishment and found his target there that night.

Drennen followed Kennan to his house out in Marino Valley. He trailed him as he dropped off his daughter at daycare, his wife at work and to the post office. After that, the nigga went to his house where he stayed for a few hours, and then left, toting a case that Drennen believed housed a couple of guns. Drennen passed several opportunities up to murder him because he was hoping that he'd led him to a place he was possibly holding Ella hostage. Omar had been up his ass about knocking Kennan off and finding his sister. Drennen was all for the tasks, especially once Omar threw in an extra five stacks as an incentive to get the job done. With that in mind, Drennen set out with the sole purpose of finding Ella, dead or alive.

Drennen had one hand gripping the steering wheel while the other was holding tight to his gun. His eyes were focused on the windshield on the back of Kennan's vehicle. Ahead of it, he saw a man chasing after a woman with a firewood poker. The woman that was being chased cleared the street and managed to avoid being struck by the oncoming automobile. The man with the firewood poker wasn't as fortunate, he winded up getting hit by the car. The man traveled the full length of Kennan's vehicle and he crashed to the ground, firewood poker landing beside him. Before he knew it, Kennan was hopping out of his vehicle and checking on the man he'd hit. A few moments later, he was drawing his gun and busting at the woman that was getting chased by the man he'd accidently hit. His bullets hadn't hit her because she already ducked low and ran from out of his firing range. When Kennan jumped back inside of his car and went after the fleeing woman, Drennen went right after him. He didn't know if he was right, but something told him that the woman that was getting chased was Ella.

"Fuck you goin', nigga?" Drennen, having seen Kennan peeling off at his right, flew down the block. He made it to the corner of the block where a stop sign was waiting for him at the corner. He didn't even bother to stop at that mothafucka, he bent the corner with an *urrrrrk* and kept on going, pursuing Kennan's ass.

***

Odette drove through the streets with Kreon riding shotgun. As he gripped his gun, he kept a close eye on his surroundings, hoping he'd come across his mother. He and Odette had been to several cities in L.A County trying to find Ella, but their efforts didn't bear fruit. Kreon was determined to find his mother, but he was beginning to lose hope and think that maybe she was dead. He hoped and prayed to God that she was okay, but if she wasn't, he had prepared himself to deal with her passing. This wouldn't be the first time he'd lost someone close to him. The death of his grandfather still stung like a son of a bitch, and that was thirteen years ago.

Fuck, momma, where are you? Kreon thought to himself as he bowed his head and massaged the bridge of his nose. He licked his lips and down on his bottom one, taking a deep breath. Looking back up, he saw Odette dozing off behind the wheel. Reaching over, he shook her awake and she looked alive, looking sleepy as hell.

"Wha...what's wrong, baby?" Odette asked, wincing. She took one hand off the steering wheel and wiped her eyes.

"Mocha, you fallin' asleep, pull over so I can drive. Matter of fact, I'ma shoot chu back to the crib and I'ma get back out here."

"Oh, no the fuck you not, I'm staying right out here witchu." She protested, looking very alive after hearing he was thinking about dropping her off. He was a roller and she was his rider. They both came hand in hand. One couldn't exist without the other.

"Nah, you good, I'ma just..." he began again but she cut him off.

"Yo' I'm not even tryna hear you right now, you talking crazy. You my man and I'm your woman, and we gone find your mother together. Just like me and Marquise is your family, she's our family as well." Hearing this caused Kreon to smile broadly and bite down on his bottom lip. He interlocked his fingers with hers and brought her hand to his lips, kissing it affectionately.

"What chu smiling and stuff about, papi?"

"I got me a real one." He held her hand and continued to scan the streets for his mother.

"I thought chu knew, boo." She hurriedly gave him a kiss and focused her attention back through the windshield. Glancing over at Kreon and seeing the sadden look on his face, she felt for him. "Don't worry, bae, we're going to find your momma." She held his hand up to her lips and kissed it tenderly.

"I know, babe, I know," he responded as he stared out of the passenger window.

***

Kennan had spent the last few days driving around aimlessly looking for Ella. He'd been to several cities, Inglewood, Lynwood, Lawndale, Gardena, Redondo Beach, and now he was in Watts, looking for her ass. He was determined to find her and put her to sleep forever. Once he'd laid her out, then he was going to see about getting his younger brother a lawyer. He had one in mind that he was sure could help him out, but homie was going to want a pretty big bag to take the case. Kennan had a couple of racks in the bank. That wasn't including the loot he had saved up to buy Jewels' dream house and their baby girl's college fund. He was pretty sure putting the paper up for Po to fight his case was going to take a nice chunk out of what he'd saved up, and his wife was going to pitch a mothafucking fit, but his brother was family, and there wasn't any amount he was above spending to guarantee his freedom.

Kennan rolled down his window, and let the air inside of his vehicle, which ruffled his clothing. He then cranked the volume on his radio because another oldies song came on. The ex-crooked law enforcer gripped the steering wheel and gangsta leaned in his ride, cruising through a residential block. He crooned along with the lyrics being sung by Al Green as he felt the cool air on his face.

"I'm not gone bat an eye until I find yo' ass, notta mothafuckin' eye, hoe. I promise you that." Kennan said to no in particular. He was just speaking aloud, but he meant everything that was being said.

***

Ella sat at the foot of her bed holding a crack pipe to her lips and a flame at the bottom of it. The drugs inside of it crackled and popped manifesting smoke, which she drew into her lungs. She sucked and sucked on the end of the stem, causing her eyelids to flutter like a butterfly's wings.

After blowing smoke up at the ceiling, she brought her head back down and took another pull from the stem. Her brows furrowed when she realized that she hadn't drawn any of the intoxicating smoke inside of her lungs.

Ella looked to the crack pipe and saw that it was empty. Sitting the pipe and the lighter down upon the nightstand, she patted her bra down and didn't feel anything. That's when she realized that she didn't have any money to pay for another night at the motel or buy drugs with.

"Fuck." Ella rose to her feet and sat down on the bed. Frustrated, she ran her hands down her face and took a deep breath. She tried to think of something she could sell to get herself some more crack, but nothing came to mind. She could have always ran home and got one of the televisions sets, but her fear of bumping into Kreon made her think otherwise. She wanted him to worry sick about her and miss her presence. The only way she was going to draw those emotions from out of him was staying gone.

Ella got up from off the bed and walked over to the mirror residing over the dresser. She pulled her hair back into a ponytail and cupped her breasts. Puckering up her lips, she leaned forward and gave her reflection a kiss. Seeing how she looked in the mirror, she couldn't help thinking about how she was forty seven years old and still had it. She could still bag a nigga like she could in her twenties, now it was time to put that confidence of hers to the test.

***

Thirty-five minutes later

"Uh! Uh! Uh! Uh! Uh!" Ella rolled her eyes in annoyance as she faked pleasure. Donatello was fucking her from the back doggy style, with each thrust she lurched forward. Ella had gone to go holler at the young nigga wearing a little bit of nothing to entice him into purchasing her goodies. Her proposition was simple: Give me some crack and I'll give you some ass. Needless to say, Donatello's thirsty ass was sold without a sells pitch. All he could think about was running up in the woman that was old enough to be his grandmother.

The young nigga took her around the corner to his granny's house since she wouldn't be home on the account that she was at a Spades game at her friend's house. As soon as he had gotten Ella behind closed doors, he was stripping down and trying to slide up in her raw.

She had to slow his roll because she wasn't going for that. The way she saw it, if he was so eager to raw dick a bitch he didn't know from a can of paint, then there wasn't any telling how many other bitches he done slung dick to without strapping up. Even after he offered to throw her an 8-ball for the experience, she still declined. He had this lustful look in his eyes and she thought that he may try to just take the pussy. Fearing so, she carefully slid the box cutter she'd brought along within arm's reach, just in case he was got on some rape shit.

After several failed attempts at trying to get Ella to let him smash without a condom, Donatello finally gave up and slid on a rubber. Now, although safe sex wasn't nearly as good as bare backing, he was wearing a thin latex condom so he could still feel a little something, something.

Donatello stood behind Ella with her bodacious ass cheeks spread apart. His fingers were buried into her meaty buttocks as he watched his dick pump in and out of her hot, gooey womb. Sweat trickled from his brow and splashed upon the slit of her slightly hairy ass crack. The veins bulged in his forehead and neck. He gritted and licked his lips, feeling his nut sack swell and the mushroom tip of his penis throb.

Wap! Wap! Wap!

His pelvis collided with her rear as he deposited and withdrew his hardness. "Yeah, bitch, you like that, huh? You like how a young nigga get off in them mothafuckin' guts, huh? Huh?" "Ooooh, yes, daddy, fuck me, fuck me harder, harder, faster, faster, oh, yessss!" She called out with her eyes rolled to their whites. He had her head pulled back by her hair and the bottom of her chin was exposed. She jolted back and forth as he pummeled her from behind, the sound of wet flesh smacking against each other bounced off the walls, inside of the living room.

Smack! Whack! Whack! Smack!

Donatello smacked Ella across her dampened ass cheeks viciously and caused her to wince in pain. His smacking her buttocks left red hand imprints behind like his palms had been painted or some shit. Releasing her hair, Donatello held his hands behind his back and ordered her to throw her ass back into him. He watched excitedly and licked his lips, seeing her booty mash up against his pelvis and then bounce back into form repeatedly

"Faster, hoe, throw that ass back!" *Smack!* He smacked her ass again and she threw herself into him faster. This caused the slapping sound that their flesh made when meeting to grow louder and louder. Before he knew it he was about to explode, so he grabbed her aggressively by her hips to stop her while she was in motion.

"Stay right there, ma, don't move!" Donatello ordered.

He pulled off his condom and stoked his meat back and forth. His creamy white jizz oozed out of the head of his penis and splattered in droplets on Ella's buttocks, sliding between the crack of her ass. Wiping the sweat from off of his forehead, he took a deep breath and looked down at that bodacious ass of hers. He smiled and boasted his shiny gold grill which twinkled. He licked his top lip and smacked his conquest on her supple behind, sending a ripple through her meaty buttocks. Afterwards, he hopped out of bed and walked towards the bathroom, holding the nut filled rubber pinched between his fingers. He shut the door halfway and opened the lid of the commode, dropping the used condom inside of the toilet. He threw his head back and shut his eyelids, whizzing inside of the bowl and relieving his bladder. He farted and his nose scrunched up, that's when he looked down and flushed the toilet.

"I gotta take a shit," Still holding his dick in his hand, Donatello kicked the bathroom door shut and plopped down on the commode. As soon as Ella seen this, she sifted through the pockets of his jeans until she came up with a wad of his wrinkled drug money. It was mostly singles but she didn't give a fuck. It was more than what she had which was nothing. Having hit what she believed was the jackpot; she recovered the sandwich bag of off white crack rocks that were stashed beneath the cushion of the couch that they were fucking on. Holding up the sandwich bag, she smiled up at it in delight. She then wiped the semen from off her ass with the blue bandana that Donatello had left behind and tossed it aside.

Hastily, she pulled up her sweat pants and stashed the bag inside the front of her sweats. Next, she reached over the bed and picked up her trick's .9mm from off the floor. She heard Donatello breaking wind as he went about the task of taking a shit, the sound resonating from out of the bathroom.

Ella pushed open the window and flung the handgun out, sending it hurling across the way into the yard of the neighboring house. Hearing the toilet being flushed startled her and she dashed across the bedroom, hearing the door squealing as it was open. Donatello's eyes stretched wide open and his mouthed formed an O, not believing his eyes. The middle aged woman looked like a blur flying across his line of vision. His eyes darted to the couch and he noticed that a cushion was missing as his gun had been taken. Furious, he took off running behind Ella who had just threw open the door, flying out of the house and hurrying down the steps.

Donatello grabbed a firewood poker from out of the living room and went chasing Ella out of the house. He was about fifteen feet away from her in the middle of the residential street. She ran for her life and occasionally glanced over her shoulder, eyes fill with fright and mouth hanging open. Her face was shiny from sweat and she was breathing huskily, breasts rising and falling with each breath she took.

"I'ma kill you, I'ma kill you, you fuckin' bitch!" Donatello called out as he ran behind her, gripping the firewood poker with both of her hands. He clutched it so tight that veins bulged in his hands. When he finally caught up to her he was going to crack open her fucking head.

The occasional car passing through the block would slow down to see what was going on between the two of them, but they would keep on going. Donatello lifted the firewood poker above his head seeing that he was closing the distance between him and Ella. He was crossing into the intersection when blinding lights came from his right. By the time he whipped around, he was being over-whelmed by the brightness of an approaching vehicle's headlights. His eyelids stretched wide open and his mouth formed an O.

Ba-dunk!

Donatello went over the hood of the approaching car and scathed its rooftop. He bounced off the trunk of the car and landed on his side wincing, firewood poker clanging to the ground. The vehicle's driver's door opened and an older African American man hopped out, running to the rear of his automobile. Concern was plastered across his face as he took a closer look at Donatello. He was still breathing. Feeling someone at his back, he turned around, and the woman that was approaching at his rear froze in her tracks. She looked afraid, and didn't know what to do.

"Argh, fuck, my back! I broke my mothafuckin' back!" Donatello squeezed his eyelids shut and gritted his teeth, turning his head from side to side. He tightened his jaws repeatedly causing the veins at his temple and forehead to throb. He was in great pain and he couldn't move. He was pretty sure that he was paralyzed from the neck down.

Kennan, the man that had hit Donatello, heard him complaining of his pain, but he didn't even bother to address him. The woman that seemed to be frozen stiff had his undivided attention. Kennan's brows furrowed as he stared at the woman. He wasn't for sure if she was Ella, but she sure as hell resembled her. He had to be sure that it was her before he got at her though. He didn't want an innocent life on his conscience.

Taking this into consideration, Kennan pulled out the folded up photograph that he'd taken from Kreon and Ella's apartment. Quickly, he unfolded the photograph and looked at it. He looked back and forth between the photo and the woman. That's when it dawned on him that the lady standing before him and the one on the photo was indeed one in the same.

"Ella? Ella Williams?" Kennan called out to her to see if she would answer.

Hesitantly, Ella responded to him, "Y…yes. Do I know you?"

Instantly, Kennan dropped the photograph and swiftly drew his gun from the small of his back. Seeing him going for what she believed was a weapon, Ella's eyelids stretched wide open and her heart pummeled inside of her chest. Realizing that she was in immediate danger, she took off running in the opposite direction.

"Funky bitch!" Kennan roared angrily and opened fire on her as she retreated with her life. "Fuck!" He cursed when he realized that Ella had gotten out of his firing range. Hurriedly, he ran over to his vehicle and jumped in behind the wheel. He threw that bitch in *reverse* and floored the pedal. The automobile went flying backwards until its driver whipped it back around in the intersection of the conjoining residential streets. He then threw his car into *drive* and floored the gas pedal, flying down the block trying to catch up with Ella. Seeing her coming up ahead, he got a grip on his gun and looked out of the driver side window. Coming up on his target rather quickly, he pointed his gun out of the window and shot at her. Ella hollered out in terror but she wasn't hit. She ducked down low, holding her arms over her head and running for her life. Seeing that she was getting away, Kennan backed his whip up and took off after her.

"You can run, bitch, but chu can't hide! That's for damn sure 'cause I'ma get that ass! You hear me, huh? I said, I'ma get that ass!" Kennan said aloud as if she could hear him from the distance she was. Gripping the steering wheel with one hand, he used the other to reload his gun. If he didn't do anything else that night he was going to kill Ella's ass.

***

Odette and Kreon was looking all around as they cruised through the residential block. Something ahead stole Kreon's attention. He saw someone hauling ass in his direction with a car following beside them. The driver was hanging outside of the window blazing shot after shot at fleeing person, trying to lay them down forever. Kreon didn't know what it was, but something told him that they should follow the car that was chasing after whomever it was running.

"Babe, follow that car," Kreon told Odette as he checked the magazine inside of his gun.

"What, are you nuts?" Odette frowned up at him.

"You know I am. Now follow that car." He smacked the magazine back into the bottom of his gun and chambered a live round inside of its head. He then impatiently tapped his weapon against his thigh as Odette went flying down the street after the car that was pursuing the person that was on foot.

CHAPTER NINE

Urrrrrrk! Boom!

Kennan pulled his car upon the sidewalk and knocked over a trash can, spilling its contents. He was just in time to see Ella hauling ass passed him. Grabbing his gun, he threw open his door in a hurry and jumped out on the sidewalk. Seeing Ella running as fast as she could towards a shabby looking house, he took off running after her. Heart pounding, adrenaline pumping, Ella darted into the yard of the shabbily looking house and up the steps. She frantically looked over her shoulder and pounded on the door.

The impacts from her pounding caused paint chips to fall from the old peeling door. As soon as the door of the shooting gallery was pulled open, she barged her way inside. The door slammed into the nigga that opened it and he bumped his head up against the wall. Scowling, he looked her way and called her a *crazy junkie bitch*. When he went to slam the door shut, Kennan came charging up the steps, gun pointed.

Old boy that had opened the door, went to lift his Tec-9 to open fire, but the ex-cop sent one through his forehead. The bullet left a nickel sized hole in his forehead, but it blew a large chunk out of the back of his skull. Blood and brain fragments splattered against the wall and homeboy collapsed where he stood. Kennan ran into the house over the threshold and jumped over the dead body. His adrenaline was jacked and murdering Ella was his sole focus, so he didn't smell the overwhelming odors of feces, urine and vomit consuming the place.

Running down the graffiti sprawled walls of the corridor, he took shots at Ella, who was ducked down running for her life. The thunderous claps of the ex-cop's gun resonated throughout the entire house. While some dope fiends scattered and fled for their pathetic lives, others sat or stood right where they were in their dope head leans.

Bloc! Bloc! Bloc!

The crowds of junkies screamed and hollered, as they ran wild in fear of catching a hot one that would end their life. Kennan's shooting cleared a path to the living room of the enormous house.

Kneeling to the floor, he gripped his gun with both hands and pointed it at Ella's calf as she ran. He squeezed one eyelid shut and bit down on his bottom lip, pulling the trigger. The gun jerked and released an empty shell casing. Fire spat from out of its barrel and Ella howled in pain as she fell dramatically to the floor. She landed hard on the floor amongst trash and drug paraphernalia. Wincing, she crawled on the floor as fast as she could. Stopping momentarily, she looked over her shoulder to see junkies zipping back and forth across her line of vision. Beyond the junkies was Kennan casually strolling towards her. His menacing eyes were focused on her and his gun was down at his side.

Ella's heart thudded so loudly that she could hear it in her ears and her stomach twisted into knots. She continued to crawl on the floor, this time harder, so hard that her finger nails broke off and stained the floor with traces of her blood.

"Help me! Someone help meeee! Oh my God, someone please help, please!" She called out with tears in her eyes. She glanced over her shoulder again and saw Kennan almost on top of her, pointing his gun at her as he hastily approached. She threw her head back, tears encircling her face, she screamed as loudly as she could, "Heeeelllllllllp!"

"This is for my brotha, bitch!" Kennan curled his finger around the trigger of his weapon. He went to pull it.

Poc! Poc! Poc!

Kennan's shoulders danced as he took fire and he bumped up against the wall. Wincing, he looked up and found Drennen with his .45 automatic handgun pointed at him, both hands wrapped around it. He had a dangerous look in his eyes and his jaws were locked as his nostrils flared angrily. He put a fourth bullet into Kennan, but not before he sent two his way, catching him flush on the chest. He gritted his teeth and went down. As soon as he met the floor, Kennan backed up off the wall, where the bullets had propelled him, and moved to finish off Ella.

Ella threw up her arms to shield her face and turned her head, waiting for the shots that would end her life. A wicked smile spread across Kennan's lips and revealed his teeth. Once again, he went to pull the trigger of his lethal weapon.

"Say goodnight, bitch!" Kennan said.

"Goodnight, bitch!" a voice rang from across the living room.

Kennan gasped and his eyebrows lifted. His head snapped up and his eyes bulged when he saw Kreon with his gun on him. He had a murderous scowl on his face and he'd bitten down hard on his bottom lip. Kreon squeezed the trigger of weapon, back to back. The gun roared furiously in the young man's hands as he slowly advanced on Kennan. Once he'd let off of the trigger, Kennan fell up against the wall and slid down to the floor, still holding his banga in his hand. A smear of blood was on the wall above him and he was staring off to the side at nothing, his lips slightly apart.

Kreon, keeping his gun on Kennan, cautiously moved in on him. He kicked his gun from out of his reach and it spun around in circles as it slid across the floor. He then kicked him twice to make sure the nigga was dead. Seeing that he was, he lowered his gun to his side and walked over to his mom.

"Ma, you okay?" Kreon kneeled down to Ella.

"I'll...I'll be, okay, son. I think it's just a flesh wound."

"Lemme see," He examined the wound in his mothers' calf, frowning up seeing how bad it was. Looking to the sleeve of his shirt, he tore it off his arm and used it to tie around her leg to stop her bleeding. Afterwards, he pulled his mother to her feet. She hobbled on one leg as he pulled her arm around his shoulders.

"Daddy?"

Hearing Odette's voice, Kreon and his mother looked up to see Odette looking down at Drennen. She walked over to him and kneeled down. Grasping his hand, she studied the holes in his body.

"Daddy?" Kreon and his mother exchanged glances.

"Daddy, what happened? What're you doing way out here?" Odette's brows furrowed.

Drennen winced as he talked, "Hey...hey, baby girl. It's been a while since I laid eyes on that beautiful chocolate face." He caressed the side of her face with the back of his hand, affectionately. He was truly in awe of the gorgeous young woman that his daughter had grown into. He hadn't seen her since that day he ran into her and her sister at McDonalds. "I missed you, Missy. I love and I missed you so much."

"I've missed you too, daddy. It's good to see you." She sniffled and wiped her dripping eyes with her curled finger.

Drennen touched his chest and his fingers came away bloody. Letting his hand fall at his side, he went on to address his youngest daughter.

"What am I doin' here you asked? Well, I was here protectin' Ella over there. Kreon's uncle put me on her once he found out that homeboy lyin' over there dead was out to kill her." He shut his eyelids briefly and took a breath, taking the time to gather himself before he continued on with what he had to say. "I came out here not long after I ran into you and yo' sister outside of that Mickey D's on Flatbush back in CT. But listen, Missy, this is not the time for us to talk about this. We can do this some otha time. Right now, y'all needa be gettin' the hell up from outta here 'fore Jake turns out."

"Ok, we'll catch up later." Odette sniffled and wiped her face with the back of her hand.

"Gemme...gemme yo' gun, Kreon," Drennen motioned the young man over.

"For what?" Kreon frowned.

"When them people do an autopsy on ya boy ova there, they gone discover two types of bullets in 'em and I only have one gun on me. That means, they gone come lookin' for whoever else was here. You understand me?"

Nah, OG," Kreon shook his head. "I can't let chu hold the weight for me. Let's try to get chu on up outta here." He looked to Odette. "Baby, take momma while I get cho pops up to his feet."

"Nah, nah, nah," the gangsta shook his head. "By the time you manage to get me up outta here. Them people woulda been done come runnin' through that door, just gemme yo' hamma and bounce."

"OG, just lemme..."

"This is not up for discussion, nigga! This an OG call, now kick in yo' strap! Right now, goddamn it!"

Kreon took a deep breath and hesitantly gave his banga to Drennen. Holding his own gun as well as his street son's, Drennen gripped them both and looked between them.

By this time, the police cars' sirens were blaring loudly and on the block. It wouldn't be long before the badges came spilling through the doors of the shooting gallery.

Looking to his daughter and seeing her tears fall down her cheeks in buckets, caused Drennen's eyes to well up with water. This would be his third strike, so he knew he'd never have a relationship with her beyond the barbwire, tall fences he was going to be spending the rest of his life behind. It saddened him greatly, but he knew that his sacrifice was necessary if she and Kreon were ever going to have a shot.

"I love you, Odette. I swear before Christ I neva stopped lovin' you, baby girl. I hope you find it in yo' heart to one day forgive me screwin' up as much as I have with you and yo' sister."

"Oh, I do, daddy. I do." She hugged him lovingly and sobbed aloud over his shoulder, body shuddering. Still holding his guns, he rubbed his hand up and down her back, soothingly. Hearing the police cars' sirens at the door of the shooting gallery, he broke his embrace from her. "Okay, baby girl, y'all got to go. Them boys are here now. Gone! Get outta here!"

Odette wiped her eyes and kissed her father on the cheek. Standing up, she took off running through the kitchen and headed for the back door.

Looking to Drennen, Kreon mouthed to him 'thank you' and he cracked a smirk and gave him a nod.

With the goodbyes given, Kreon assisted his mother through the back door. As the cops entered the shooting gallery with their weapons drawn, the sound of a car peeling off in the alley carried into the living room. Drennen smiled with relief knowing that Kreon and Odette had gotten away.

Lying on his back, he stared up at the ceiling as the cops surrounded him with their guns pointed at him.

"Drop your guns, drop your guns now!"A red face cop ordered with a vein bulging at his temple. Spit flew from off his lips as he hollered out with authority. With the command given, Drennen dropped his weapons to the floor and eased his hands into the air, surrendering.

I do this all for you, baby girl. All for you, Drennen thought to himself. He hoped by forfeiting his life that he'd somehow make up for not being in his daughters life like he should have.

***

Kreon brought his car to a screeching halt just outside of the emergency room's electronic doors. Hopping out of the car and leaving the door open, he ran around to the other side. Together, he and Odette took his mother under either arm and helped her towards the entrance of the emergency room.

"Aaahhhh, sssssss, shiiiiit," Ella squeezed her eyelids shut and threw her head back, exposing underneath her chin and the vein on her neck. She hobbled on one leg towards her destination, keeping her weight off of her wounded calf.

"It's okay, Ms. Williams, we're almost there." Odette said to her.

"Now, remember, ma. There definitely gonna run some test on you, so crack is gonna show up in your system. Stick to our story, you were on your way home from gettin' high and you got caught up in a drive-by, it's as simple as that. You got it?"

"Yeah, I got it, son. I got it…grrrrrr." She brought her head back down and tears were seeping from her eyes. "I'm sorry, I'm sorry about everything, Kreon. I know I was a horrible, mother."

"You weren't a horrible mother, ma. You just made some very bad mistakes, that's all. People make mistakes. The best we can do is ask for forgiveness and try to make things right."

"I apologize, Kreon, from the bottom of my heart. I hope you forgive me someday."

"We gone be straight, ma. Once you get outta here, we're gonna get chu into rehab and then we gone go to family therapy. God knows we need it. That's the only way we gone hash things out, is if we get help. 'Cause we can't do this on our own, that's for damn sure."

"Okay. I'll do it, whatever it takes."

Kreon grasped her bloody hand and looked at her. "Whatever it takes, ma."

Ella kissed her son on the cheek and on his forehead. "I love you."

"I love you too, old lady." He looked from his mother and his eyes scanned the emergency room. There were people sitting around waiting to be seen and some had shocked looks on their faces. There were blood stains on Kreon, Ella, and Odette. They'd also left a small trail of blood on their way inside of the emergency room over the threshold. "Yo' I needa doctor, my momma is bleeding, and she's been shot! I need a doctor! I said, 'I needa mothafuckin' doctor!'"

***

Later that night

Carlos came in through his motel room's door rubbing the back of his head. It had been quite some time since he'd been clocked in the back of his head, but the lump that had grown there was giving him grief. It was the side of a baseball and sore as a mothafucka. Carlos didn't know who had struck him upside the skull, but he had a pretty good idea that it was Kreon's ass.

When he awoke, the butcher's knife he'd wrapped up in newspaper was gone and so was his cell phone. The crazy part about it was, all of his money and jewelry were still on him. All fingers were pointing to Kreon because if it had just been some knucklehead that robbed him, they would have stripped him for everything of value.

Carlos had just shut the door to his room and locked it when the distinguished sound of a film projector came on at his back. At that moment, a bright illumination filled the center of the room. Eyebrows slanted and nose scrunched, Carlos pulled out his gun and turned around, pointing the deadly end of his banga at someone sitting on the bed. That someone was Kreon. He was sitting on the edge of the bed with the light coming from the projector flickering on his face. His eyes were focused directly on the image as he took casual pulls from a Black & Mild and expelled smoke. From the way he was carrying on, anyone looking at him would have thought that Carlos wasn't even inside of the room. It was like the six foot five, Dominican man was a ghost, as far as Kreon was concerned.

"You got some set of balls on you, nigga!" Carlos said, nostrils flaring

"Correction. I have the *biggest* set of balls on me."

"I'll make sure it gets chiseled on your tombstone," he leveled the gun at Kreon's head.

Kreon took a pull from his Black & Mild and blew out a cloud of smoke. "You not gone pop me, big boy. You ain't stupid. You don't want this here footage to get sent to them people. Or do you?"

"What?" Carlos's face twisted up. It wasn't until Kreon nodded to the projected image on the wall that he turned around and realized what he was talking about.

Playing out on the wall was Carlos stabbing Royce to death.

"Don't look at me, don't look at me, man!" Tears flooded Carlos' cheeks as he gripped the butcher's knife with both hands and brought it high above his head. He turned his head away from his victim and squeezed his eyelids shut, so that he wouldn't be haunted by his face after he murdered him.

"P...please..." Royce begged weakly, tears pooling in his eyes.

"I'm sorry, bro," Carlos took his bloody hand from off the kilt of the knife and crossed himself in the sign of the crucifix. He then gripped the knife with both hands

again, clutching it so tight that his knuckles bulged. With a grunt, he slammed the knife down through the top of Royce's skull with all of his might, burying half of it at the top his head. Blood oozed up out of the wound that he created and came running down either side of his face. Royce's eyes rolled into the back of his head and his mouth hung open. His head fell back against the refrigerator and he laid slumped, palms facing upwards. He was dead.

Carlos whipped back around to Kreon, who he still had his gun pointed at. "But how did you?"

"I have my ways, homeboy, now take that fuckin' gun outta my face." Kreon spoke calmly.

Carlos lowered his gun at his side and massaged the bridge of his nose.

"Now, if you like your freedom, you gone do a couple of things for me that'll ensure you keep it." Kreon took the time to mash his Black out inside of the ashtray. Smoke billowed from out of his nose as he went on to speak. "Me and O want to be together and we gonna be together. In fact, we gone get married. What chu gone do is, stay the fuck up outta what we got goin' on and you gone be a father to Marquise. As a matter of fact, nigga, you gone be the model mothafuckin' father to my lil' homie, 'cause if not, that footage and the murder weapon is gone find its self in the hands of some homicide detective down at the 77th street precinct. Is that understood?"

"Yeah, I got it." Carlos responded with defeat in his tone.

"I've made a few copies of this footage, so if somethin' happens to me. I don't know, sayyyyy, I should trip and fall, catch a cold or stub my fuckin' pinky toe on the bed railin', a copy of it gets sent to some people you don't want gettin' their hands on it. Got it?"

"Yes, I understand."

"Good." Kreon rose from the bed and walked over to Carlos. Looking him straight in the eyes, he said, "Now, shoot yo'self in the foot."

"What?" Carlos's brows furrowed.

"I said, shoot cho self in the goddamn foot."

"F…for what?"

Smack!

"'Cause I told you to! Now, do it!"

Carlos snarled at Kreon and shot daggers at him. As bad as he wanted to put hands on him, he wasn't anyone's fool. Taking a deep breath to calm himself as best as he could, Carlos leveled his banga at his foot and looked away. He squeezed his eyelids shut and squared his jaws, a vein pulsated at his neck. His arm shook uncontrollably and he sweated bullets, as he tried to gather the courage to pull the trigger.

Blowl!

"Aahhhh, fuck, man! My foot, my mothafuckin' foot!" Carlos dropped his gun and fell to the floor. He rocked back and forth as he clutched his sneaker. He growled and gritted as the blood from the hole in his foot, slicked his hands wet. "Aaahhhh, fuck, dawg! This shit hurts, it hurts!"

Kreon grinned and continued through the door, shutting the door on his way out of the room.

***

A few weeks later

Po had been locked up and was now awaiting trial. After several calls to his brother, Kennan's house, he wife finally picked up. As soon as he mentioned his brother's name she broke down sobbing. When he heard her go to pieces at the mere mention of his sibling's name, he knew then that he was dead, and it weighed heavily on his shoulders. He knew that if he hadn't put in the call to have Kreon's mother knocked off then his brother would still be alive and well. The thought of it killed him inside and he contemplated suicide. The only thing that stopped him from going through with it was the hope of beating his case and getting back on the streets to exact revenge.

Jewels managed to pull herself together long enough to let Po know what happened to Kennan. Right after, she tore into him something fierce blaming him for his death. Before she could say anything incriminating, he disconnected the call and went to sulk in his cell. It was there he thought about all of the niggaz in the streets that owed him money, the loot he had stashed, and the shit he could sell off to get himself a good lawyer to mount himself a decent defense. Using a rubber pencil, he made a list of all the cats that owed him as well as the amount of gwap he had saved and his assets. If no one bullshitted him on the money they owed and he was able to sell everything, then he was looking at *at* least fifteen stacks, give or take. He figured that fifteen G's was more than enough for him to get himself a decent lawyer.

He made a mental note to call all the fools in debt to him over the next few days so he could see about collecting his just due. He was going to be sure to call his homeboy, Loco, to make his rounds to pick up all the money owed to him. Loco was tall, buff as fuck, had a gangsta you had to respect and the willingness to pull a trigger if need be. With him on the job collecting what he was owed, Po was sure he'd be able to gather up the chunk of change he'd need in order to get a lawyer.

Po stood before the small metal reflector that was his mirror, brushing his teeth. He worked the brush back and forth across his grill, creating foam that made him look like a dog with rabies. Once he was done with his teeth; he put some more tooth paste on his brush and scrubbed his tongue. He then spat residue out into the toilet bowl and rinsed his mouth out with water. Afterwards, he splashed water on his face and his fresh shaven head. Bringing his head back up, he looked himself over in the mirror and was satisfied with his appearance. Having taken a deep breath, he dabbed his face dry with a towel and sat it to the side.

After Po had finished with his hygiene and had gotten dressed for the day, he withdrew his shank from its hiding place in his mattress. He stashed it on his person and decided to head out of his cell. He'd just reached the entrance of his cell's door when someone in a prison made ski mask appeared before him. The first thing he noticed at the corner of his eye was something sharp and silver gleaming in the masked man's hand. Instantly, a shank came to mind and he went to brandish his blade. He was a little too slow on the draw though. Before he knew it, the masked man was jabbing his shank at his face, seeing himself in his victim's pupils.

"Aahhh! Arrggh!" Po hollered out in agony as his eyes were poked out by the masked man. His wounded eyes oozed a colorful gunk and blood steamed down his cheeks. He covered his ruined eyes with his tattooed hands, and his attacker pulled out a second shank. The masked man grunted as he attacked Po, hatefully. His twin shanks came fast and furiously, putting holes all over Po's chest and back, soaking his ass up. The only things that could be heard coming from the cell was the killa's grunts, his prey's hollering, and sharpened steel repeatedly puncturing warm flesh.

"Fuck you think you going?" the masked man kept hacking away at a defenseless Po's back as he blindly made his way towards the cell's door, feeling on the wall along the way.

The masked man ducked under Po's arm and came back up before him. He stabbed him in his chest, all of the way down to the kilt of his sharpened weapon. Po made the ugliest pain streaked face that the killa had ever seen, and he hollered out like a wounded animal. The masked man then allowed him to stagger out of the cell. He stood in the background breathing heavily and toying with the last shank in his hand. He observed his victim bump up against the guardrail of the tier.

Suddenly, the masked man charged out on the tier and slammed the last blade into the back of Po's skull. The impact of the steel made the bleeding man's eyes to stretch wide open and his mouth twisted in grotesque manner. The pain was so intense that Po couldn't even form words. He struggled to reach the shank that was poking out of the back of his head, but he couldn't grasp it.

"Give Kennan my regards," Drennen, who was the masked killa, wrapped his arms around Po's legs and lifted him up off his feet. With a grunt, he tossed his ass over the guardrail. He didn't even bother to look over the guardrail once he'd tossed the man over. He retreated back to his cell where he flushed the prison made ski mask and removed the blood speckled jumpsuit. He passed it off to his cellmate, who he'd given strict orders to get rid of, before washing the blood off his face and neck. Afterwards, he slipped on a brand new jumpsuit and retrieved the book he was reading earlier. He lay back across his bunk and slipped on his eyeglasses, pretending to read his book.

Drennen laid on his mattress reading his book as the alarm for lock down blared loudly. He licked his thumb and turned the page as if he just didn't catch a body.

***

Kreon and Odette stood outside of the bathroom door watching Marquise as he gargled and rinsed out his mouth. Once the boy was finished, he wiped his mouth on a towel hanging on a rack and jumped into his mother's arms.

Good night, Kreon," Marquise kissed Kreon on the cheek as his mother held him in his arms.

"Goodnight, lil' dude," Kreon did their exclusive handshake with him. They finished it off by tapping their fist to their chest.

"I'ma read him a bed time story, then I'll be back in there to attend to our guests." Odette told Kreon.

"Okay, gemme some lip," he puckered up and she kissed him. Once she turned to walk away, he playfully smacked her on her behind and she walked off, throwing that big old thang from side to side. He cracked a smile as he eyed her booty in her sweatpants.

Kreon headed back inside of the living room where his uncle, Omar, and his little homeboy, Lil' Boom, were. While his uncle was taking the occasional sip from his glass of Hennessy, Lil' Boom was rolling up a blunt expertly.

"'Sup, Blood, old head hit chu back yet?" Lil' Boom inquired as he licked the blunt closed.

He was referring to Drennen. He was suppose to holla Kreon once he wacked Po's bitch-ass.

"Nah, not yet." Kreon answered.

"For real?" Omar asked as he sat up and placed his glass on the coffee table.

"For real. I'm startin' to think he botched the hit, though.

"Nah," Omar shook his head, disagreeing,"Any mission I sent Drennen on he smashed. My nigga don't know how to fail. Believe me, if Po ain't layin' up dead then he will be...soon."

"Yo' rememba that rappa nigga you robbed and blasted on the net? Well, I meant to ask you what chu did with that nigga'z jewels?"

"I still got 'em, left them shits in the car; inside the glove compartment."

"Them shits phony or somethin'?" his forehead creased.

"I can't even tell you, man. I neva bothered to get them bitches appraised. The way these rap niggaz be stuntin' and frontin', I wouldn't be surprised if them jewels are fugazzi."

"If you ain't sweatin' 'em, you should let a young nigga sport 'em, Blood. You know my B-day comin' up and shit." He sucked on the end of the blunt as he sparked it up with his red Bic lighter. The young nigga sucked on the end of his bleezy and blew out smoke into the air.

"You want them shits?" Kreon cracked a one sided smile.

"Hell yeah, I'm tryna floss, and if them mothafuckaz real, ain't no tellin' how much I can get off 'em."

"Well, happy birthday, they all yours."

"You sho'?" he raised his eyebrows.

"Yeah, I don't won't that shit. Lemme hit that bleezy, and I'll go get them for you." He outstretched his hand to take the withering blunt from his little homeboy.

"Since when did you start smokin' weed, nephew?" Omar's forehead crinkled.

"Since tonight, you only live once." Kreon responded as he took the blunt.

Lil' Boom blew out smoke from his nostrils and mouth and said, "That's right, Y.O.L.O, Blood."

Kreon took a couple of pulls from off the blunt and released smoke into the air.

****

He came out of the house and took one last pull from the blunt, before flicking away what was left of it. After he blew out a cloud of smoke, he was about to make his way down the steps, but seeing a car creeping down the block with its headlights off stopped him. He narrowed his eyelids and peered closely trying to see who it was inside of the vehicle, but all he could make out were two shapes, which were in the front seats of the automobile. Once the car stopped at the center of the block, which was also in the front of Odette's house, he reached up under his shirt for his gun. When he did this, the car sped off down the block and made a right at the corner, disappearing from out of his sight.

"Bitch-ass niggaz," He said to no one in particular and took his hand from underneath his shirt. Afterwards, he continued on down the steps and made his way out of the yard. He looked up and down the street for the fools that had drove passed the house, but them niggaz weren't any where in sight. He chuckled and said, "Just like I thought, bitch-ass niggaz." He shook his head as he thought about how mothafuckaz always claimed to be so tough, until they ran into a nigga whose gangsta was larger than theirs. With that in mind, he proceeded towards the car. He got about five feet away before the unthinkable happened.

Ka-boom!

The explosion lifted him high off his feet and sent him crashing down upon the black top. Blood ran from out of his head and soiled the asphalt. The fire flash had left black soot over his clothes and face. He lay where he was with the fingers of his right hand twitching.

***

"Is dat him?" Khaos asked Donald as he slowed his car past Odette's house. They saw someone standing out on the porch smoking what they assumed was a cigarette.

"Yeah, that's him, yo'. I'd never forget that motha-fucka'z face." Donald scowled as he leaned forward in his seat and looked out through the driver's window. He held a detonator in his hand that looked like it was capable of operating a toy helicopter. "Fuck is he doin'?" he inquired, noticing that Kreon was going for his waistline. "I think he's about to start blastin', son. Pull off."

Khaos did exactly as he was told. When he got to the end of the block he made a right and drove down the street. He then stopped at the corner of the block he'd made the right turn. He left himself just enough room to be able to see the yard that they'd saw Kreon standing in. They were sure at their distance that they'd never be seen by him. Not only was it too dark for him to make them out, they were idling pretty far away.

"Can you see 'em from here?" Khaos asked as he leaned forward trying to see over Donald who was also looking out of the passenger window.

"Yeah, I see 'em, he's goin' towards the car."Donald told him as he pinched the small joystick on the detonator and stared out of the window at Kreon, observing him as he approached his vehicle.

"There he go," Khaos stated the obvious, seeing Kreon advancing in the direction of his car.

Right then, the automobile grew silent as the men focused on their target. Donald's heart thudded and a bead of sweat slid down his temple. He was scowling as he waited for the perfect time to activate the kill-switch. Once Kreon had gotten within spitting distance of the Nissan, Donald operated the kill-switch and that's when it happened.

Ka-boom!

They watched as the explosion sent Kreon high up into the air and he went smacking down on the pavement. Khaos and Donald sat where they were watching for a time. Donald looking satisfied and Khaos looking surprised he'd gone through with it. The flames of the fire shone in their pupils.

"That's what I'm takin' about, dawg. That's how you murda a mothafucka. You feel me?" Khaos patted Donald on the shoulder.

Donald cracked a smile. He was feeling himself after finding the courage to blow that nigga, Kreon, up.
****

"Oh my God, no! Kreeeooooon!" Odette screamed aloud from the porch, where she stood with the front door wide open. Tears welled up in her eyes and slid down her cheeks. The fire from the wreckage shown in her pupils as teardrops continued to fall from the brims of her eyes. She ran down the steps and darted out of the yard into the street. The golden orange flames shined on her as she approached and cast her shadow at the back of her. Fresh tears danced in her eyes and made them look like they had crust diamonds in them. Her bottom lip slowly began to tremble as she advanced in his direction. She got down on her knees and pushed him over onto his back; her brows furrowed once she saw it was Lil' Boom and not Kreon lying at her feet.

"Dope Money mothafuckaz!" A voice called out from down the residential block.

Odette stood up and looked down the street, holding her hand above her brows and narrowing her eyelids. She saw Donald down the street in the front passenger seat of a car with some nigga behind the wheel. The driver threw up the middle finger from out of the driver's window and peeled off.

"O?" Someone called out to Odette and her head snapped over her shoulders. At the end of her line of vision were Kreon and Omar. They were coming out of the house.

"Kreon! Oh, my God, I thought that was you," Odette broke out running towards her man. He started running out of the yards towards her, too.

The lovers collided and wrapped themselves up in each other's arms. They kissed hard and passionately. When they broke their lip lock, they stared into one another's eyes lovingly.

"I was so scared, bae. I thought I'd lost you." She caressed the side of his face affectionately.

"Never," he looked beyond her on the ground and found Lil' Boom's body. His eyes were bulging and his mouth was stretched wide open. He wore The Face of Death. "Damn, they got my lil' nigga." Sadness etched across Kreon's face and he crossed himself in the sign of the crucifix.

"Fuck, Lil'Boom, Blood," Omar gripped the sides of his head, seeing his little homeboy laid out dead in the streets. Instantly, his eyes misted with tears and he shook his head, hating to see what had been done to his comrade.

Kreon looked to his uncle feeling sorry for him. He went to touch Omar's shoulder to comfort him, but he shrugged him off, heading for Lil' Boom. Reaching the youngsta, he sat down on the ground and pulled him into his arms. He held him in his arms as tears fell from his eyes and splattered on his cheeks. Using his finger tips, he brushed his hand downwards and shut his eyelids. He then shut his mouth. Afterwards, he rocked him back and forth, crying and mouthing a silent prayer for him. The sounds of fire trucks and police car sirens filled the air.

CHAPTER TEN
A few days later

It appeared as if the entire neighborhood came out for Lil' Boom's funeral. There were several Bloods present, but there were also a few Crips and Eses sprinkled throughout the mourners. Although there were a few sets in attendance that didn't get along, niggaz left the static they had with one another back in the streets. They'd come out to pay their respects to the little homie, so bygones were going to be left to be bygones.

"I want that mothafucka bad, nephew. I want that mothafucka real bad." Omar said as he walked beside Kreon, Candy and Odette. He snatched the red handkerchief from out of the breast pocket of his suit and wiped dabbed his tearing eyes dry.

"We gone get 'em, unc, don't even trip." Kreon told him, gripping his shoulder in assurance. He then caught up with Odette. He interlocked his fingers with hers and kissed her. As they walked beside each other, he began talking to her.

"Babe, get that fuck-nigga Donald onna jack and see if you can get 'em to agree to a fair one with unc."

"Okay. I'm not making any promises, but I'll see what I can do." Odette dipped her hand inside of her purse and pulled out her cell phone.

She then walked over to Omar's Excursion, accompanied by Candy. Looking ahead, Omar and Kreon watched as Odette leaned up against the SUV and dialed up Donald. Seeing her lips moving they knew that she was talking to old boy.

"You think yo' girl gone be able to talk this dude into linin' it up?" Omar inquired, keeping his eyes on Odette as he talked with his nephew.

"I don't know," Kreon shrugged, "If she can't, fuck it. We'll find his bitch-ass and put the love on 'em. This nigga on our turf, I'll be damned if he makes it back home after touchin' one of ours. You Griff me?" he extended his fist.

"Fa sho'." Omar dapped him up.

Omar and Kreon became silent once they saw Odette take her cellular from her ear. She looked up at Kreon and smiled, nodding her head.

"Got 'em," Kreon said to his uncle.

"Good. 'Cause I'ma beat the brakes off that ass once I get a hold of 'em."

Once Omar and Kreon reached the Excursion, they climbed inside of the beast and pulled off.

"So how'd it go?" Kreon asked his lady as he caressed her hand.

"He was hesitant at first, but I heard his boys in the background egging him on. He didn't want to look soft in front of them so he agreed."

"Good. Thank you, baby, gemme a kiss."

Odette turned to him and he kissed her lips.

"There's something I got to tell you." Odette told him, looking nervous. She didn't know how he was going to take the news she was about to lie on him, but she had to tell him regardless.

"What's that, slim?" he asked, sweeping her hair from out of her face.

"I, uh, I, ummm," Odette struggled to find the courage to tell Kreon what was on the tip of her tongue, as she fidgeted with her fingers. "I'm...I'm pregnant." She looked him in his eyes, waiting to hear his response and hoping it was something she wanted to hear.

"Pregnant? Wow." Kreon's eyelids stretched wide open, she'd just dropped a bomb on him. "When...when did you find out?"

"A few days ago...when Lil' Boom and Omar were at the house." She told him. "You remember, the night of the explosion."

"Yeah, I remember." Kreon looked down at the floor, trying to digest what he'd been told.

Odette took this as him not wanting her to have his baby. The thought of it hurt her, but she wasn't going to give birth to a fatherless child. She knew how it was growing up without hers and she didn't want to subject her kid to the experience.

"Listen," she began, wiping her dripping eyes with her curled finger. "I won't have it if you don't..."

Odette's words were cut short, as Kreon pulled her close, kissing her romantically. He then pulled back and looked her in her eyes, caressing the side of her face with his hand.

"I want chu to have my baby, and I want chu to be my wife, too."

"You sure?" she said, continuing to wipe her eyes.

"Yes, here." He whipped out his handkerchief and passed it to her, watching her dry her eyes.

With that having been said, Kreon reached inside of his pocket and pulled out a burgundy velvet box. Instantly, Odette's eyes bulged and she started crying again, placing her hands to her lips.

"Oh my God, babe, is this really happening?" she smiled and continued to cry, fresh hot tears bursting from her eyes. The tears slid down her face and slicked her cheeks wet.

"Yeah, slim," he responded and opened the box, revealing the platinum and diamond engagement ring propped up inside of it. "Odette Drennen, will you do me the honor of marryin' me and makin' me the happiest man that has ever lived?"

"Yes, Kreon, yes!" She said excitedly, jumping up and down in her seat. She fanned her face with her hands trying to stop from crying more, but it didn't do any good. The tears kept running like they were coming from out of a faucet.

Omar adjusted the rearview mirror and smiled, watching his nephew remove the engagement ring from its box and slide it on his fiancée's finger. Right after, Odette grabbed him by his face and kissed him over and over again. She then threw her arms around him and hugged him lovingly.

Odette let the window down and hung halfway out. Looking around at the pedestrians and the cars in traffic, she waved her engagement ring back and forth across the air. The sun rays kissed off the diamonds in her ring and she smiled, saying, "Aye, y'all I'm about to get married, my man popped the question. Took a bitch off the market!"

"You go girl!" one woman said standing at the bus stop.

"Congratulations, boo!" another woman said from behind the wheel of her late model Toyota Camry.

"Honk the horn, Omar, so I can let the world know." Odette looked over her shoulder. As Omar drove through the streets, little momma continued to wave her ring around and brag that she was married. She received cheers, applause and congratulations from everyone she came across.

"You crazy, girl," Kreon chuckled and told Odette as she pulled herself back inside of the Excursion.

"Crazy about chu," Odette smiled at him.

"Awww, look at the lovely young couple, babe." Candy finally said something from the front passenger seat. She watched Odette and Kreon's interaction through the small rectangle shaped mirror in the sun visor. Her eyes misted with tears and she placed her hand on Omar's thigh, rubbing it.

"Come here." Odette let the window back up and turned to Kreon. She threw her arms around him again, kissing long, deep and passionately.

***

That night

Kreon and Omar stood in front of the Excursion waiting on Donald's arrival. They were posted up at the back of a construction site of an unfinished apartment complex, keeping a close eye on everything surrounding them. They didn't trust a goddamn thing because for all they knew, they could have been sitting like ducks in the middle of an ambush.

"Fuck this nigga at, nephew?" Omar asked before taking a pull from his withering Newport.

"I don't know, unc, but if this fool don't turn out in the next few minutes, we Swayze." Kreon said, looking ahead to see if any vehicle was approaching.

"You got cho banga on you?" Omar asked for what seemed like the millionth time.

"Yeah, unc, and it's off safety just like you told me to keep it." Kreon sounded annoyed. "Why you keep askin' me about my burna."

"I just wanna make sure you cocked, locked and ready for action should this shit go left."

"We good unc, I'm on my shit. The question is, are you on yours?"

"Nigga, I was on my shit when you were just an itch in yo' daddy's nut sack."

"Yeah, whoever the fuck he is."

"What's that 'pose to mean?" Omar's forehead wrinkled.

"Nothin'. Here this nigga comes now." Kreon narrowed his eyelids as he stared ahead at an approaching BMW X5 truck. The SUV stopped before Kreon and his uncle and caused them to narrow their eyelids into slits, holding their hands above their eyebrows.

The X5s headlights continued to shine on Kreon and his uncle, even after the engine of the SUV had been killed. As soon as the doors of the truck popped open, and niggaz started hopping out, their hands moved towards the bangas on their waistlines.

"Easy now, easy," Strategy said. He was a tall light-skinned dude wearing a doo-rag with the flap. He wore a black leather jacket with fur around its collar. His platinum and gold DMK chain hung loosely around his neck. "We came here to get dem results, and for my homie to catch the fair one."

"Here you go," Kreon passed the paternity test results to Donald. He snatched the paperwork out of his hand and read it over. His hushed words could be heard by everyone near him as he read the document as quietly as he could. Once he was done, he looked up at Kreon and balled the results up into a ball. "You happy now? Lil' man ain't yours."

"Yeah, whateva, nigga. What's up with that fair one though?" Donald asked.

"Oh, I'll be needin' that," Omar stepped up before Donald, pulling off his jacket.

Donald's forehead crinkled as he looked Omar up and down. He could see all the graying hairs coming out of his cornrows and goatee. It was because of this and him being overweight that he believed that he could take it.

"This what chu want, pops? An ass whoopin'? Cool, long as I go back home havin' whooped somebody's ass." Donald removed his baseball cap, jewelry and jacket. He then pulled his sagging jeans upon his ass and buckled his belt tighter around his waistline. He then threw up his bare fists before his eyes and slid his legs into a fighting stance.

Having seen this, Omar threw up his shit and got into a fighting stance. He shadowed boxed a little bit, just like Donald was doing at the moment. Taking notice of what was about to go down, Kreon and Dope Money Klique stepped back, allowing the two warring parties to have their space so that they could brawl.

Omar and Donald moved around one another, searching for the right time to launch an attack. Donald was the first one to take action. He faked left and threw a right, which landed flush on Omar's mouth. The impact from the punch threw the older man's head back, and set off a round of cheers and applause from the Dope Money Klique.

"Get his ass, unc! Fuck 'em up!" Kreon called out to Omar, fists and jaws clenched. He was anxious to see how this event would play out.

Bwap! Wap! Wam! Brack!

Omar's head jutted backwards repeatedly, having been assaulted by Donald's lightning fast fists. When he brought his head back down he was bleeding from his nose and his bottom lip was busted.

"That's right, D. Dot, fuck 'em up, fuck 'em up!" Khaos called out from the sidelines.

"Unh huh, old head, you done fucked up and opened a fresh can of whoop-ass!" Donald gritted his teeth and jabbed Omar in the face several more times. Omar spat blood on the ground and kept moving, fists up, eyes studying the younger man before him.

"It's beena while, youngin', I'ma lil' rusty, but once these old bones start shifting and settlin' and I'm back in step, it's gone be hell to pay." Omar assured him.

He'd been fighting for most of his life. If he wasn't defending the honor of his gang in a street brawl then he was banging it out against enemies in county jail. But ever since he'd taking up hustling as a trade, he kicked his feet up and let his soldiers put in work. It had been fifteen years since he'd gave a nigga a fair one, but his muscles memory had begun to set in, and he was recalling how to handle himself in a fight.

"I hear you talkin', gramps, but chu gone have to show me, fuck tellin' me." Donald said, before striking out once again.

Bwap! Wap! Wop!

Back to back hard punches sent mists of sweat flying from Omar's head. He took a step back and shook off his daze. Now he felt rejuvenated and ready. It was as if those last few punches to his head had fixed him, like a couple of slaps to the back of an old television set would get rid of the static on its screen.

"Yeahhhhh, that's what I'm talkin' about." Omar's lips stretched across his face and curled at their ends, showcasing a smile.

At that moment, time seemed to slow down and everything turned black and gray. This left Donald in color and made him pronounced. Omar saw him in 3D, high definition quality. He could also hear his own heavily breathing and the sound of his heart beating. As of now, he could see Donald's movements before he even made them. And right now, he was throwing an overhand right.

"There we go," Omar smiled, realizing that his muscles had recalled how to fight. He ducked Donald fist and came back up, clenching his fist at his side. He clenched it so hard that his knuckles bulged in his hand. With a grunt, he slammed his fist into Donald's gut causing his eyes to bulge and knocking the wind out of him. His mouth hung open and he gasped, but he didn't get a chance to recover, because Omar was on that ass like stink on shit.

Bwap! Wap! Wop! Wam!

He heated up Donald's ribcage with vicious punches and cracked him in the jaw. The last blow loosened his tooth and sent blood flying everywhere. Right after, Omar followed up with a three punch combination that lifted Donald off of his feet, leaving one of his Timberland boots on the ground. He went high up into the air and landed on the hood of the car he came there in, leaving a huge dent in it. He lay on his back moaning in pain with his eyes rolled to their whites. He turned his head from left to right as blood ran from out of the corner of his mouth, dripping off to the side of him.

Omar stood where he was, sweaty, staring at his defeated opponent. His hairy chest expanded and shrunk each time he took a breath. He was hot and sticky with perspiration. A bead of sweat ran down the side of his face and alongside his jaw line. He clenched his teeth and his nostrils flared, as he waited to see if Donald was going to get back up to fight.

"Get up, D. Dot, man, get up!" EZ Money Bagz called out to him.

"Son, you makin' the squad look bad out here!" Strategy said.

"Get up, yo, get cho ass up!" Khaos shook Donald hard and fast, but his ass still wouldn't get up from where he was lying.

"Blood, that nigga through, gone get 'em outta here," Omar told them Dope Money Klique niggaz as a grinning Kreon untied the red bandanas from his hands.

"Video, turn that goddamn camera off," Khaos called out to homeboy they'd brought along to film the brawl. As soon as old boy turned off the device and lowered it at his side, Khaos came from under his hoodie with a long ass revolver. He pointed his pistol at Kreon and Omar, just as the other members of his crew were pointing their guns at them.

As the men were pointing their guns at Kreon and Omar, he and his uncle were pointing their guns at them as well.

"Blood, I shoulda known you Connecticut niggaz was gone be some sore losers," Omar said, taking in all of the hard faces that were pointing their bangas at him. "You niggaz can't stand to hold an L." he shook his head disappointedly.

"Fuck you!" Khaos shouted at him.

Omar looked him over and said, "Nahhhh, you not my type."

"Reallllllll fuckin' funny," Strategy said.

"You should come and see my standup."

All the men with the guns pointed at each other, glared into one another's eyes. Their hearts pounded inside of their chests and beads of sweat slowly slid down the sides of some of their faces. At any moment, the first gunshot would rip through the air, and set off a string of others and end with several lives lost. The hostile men were about to bang it out when a feminine voice cut through the air.

"Is there room for one more at this party, boys?" Candy spoke from the sidelines. Her voice drew the guns and stares of Khaos and his niggaz. They found the young lady expanding a large pink bubble out of her Bubble Yum as she peeled herself from the shadows. She moved towards Kreon and Omar with her .32 pointed at Khaos. If he budged then she was going to send one right through his forehead, and from that distance, she was sure that she wouldn't miss. Candy went to stand beside Omar and Kreon, continuously blowing bubbles with her gum.

"Where the fuck did you come from?" Khaos asked.

"Suga, you didn't know, I'm heaven sent?" Candy replied.

"Bitch, if you don't knock it off," Khaos mad dogged her.

"No, *bitch*, you knock it off," Omar's eyebrows arched and his nostrils flared.

"Homie, I gotta admit, you got some set of balls on you. I mean, you talkin' like you ain't got about seven different on you." Khaos cracked an easy smile and tapped homeboy standing beside him.

"Yeah, and you talk like yo' daddy made bulletproof vests for a livin'." Kreon interjected himself in the conversation.

"Fuck you!" Khaos spat at him.

"Fuck you!" Kreon spat back.

"Hold on. Now, everybody just keep calm," Omar said, looking around at everyone. "Now, we can end this one of two ways. One we can empty out these clips and be a couple shot up dead mothafuckaz, or two, we can lower our guns, let bygones be bygones and get the fuck from up outta here. I'm for the second call to action, how about chu, gentlemen?"

Khaos and the Dope Money Klique exchanged glances. It was from their exchanged looks that they communicated that they would much rather get out of there than exchange gunfire.

"Alright," Khaos began as he nodded. "We gone let this shit go. It ain't worth nobody dyin' tonight. Besides, we don't have any casualties on our side." He lowered his gun at his side first, and then he motioned for his homeboys to do the same.

They followed his orders and tucked their guns on their waistline. "Alright, squad, let's gather D. Dot and move out."

Khaos and Omar mad dogged one another. Omar was as hot as a firecracker for what that rapping ass nigga said about his crew not having any casualties. He knew that the punk mothafucka was referring to the death of Lil' Boom. The young homie was only one he'd lost on their side.

Once Dope Money Klique had gotten a barely conscious Donald into the back of one of their vehicles, Khaos allowed his menacing eyes to linger on Omar before he turned around and headed to get inside of the car he'd came to the location in. Pulling out his gun, he opened the driver's door and gave Omar one last evil look.

Afterwards, he slid inside of his car and slammed the door shut behind him. He cranked up whip up and turned around, heading out of the location. He made a right turn and so did the other automobiles that were following him.

Once the Dope Money Klique was gone, Candy approached Omar and handed him a detonator. He threw his arm around her shoulders, looking back and forth between the device in his hand and the cars as they drove away.

"For Lil' Boom," Omar said.

"For Lil' Boom," Candy stated.

"For the homie, Lil' Boom," Kreon said lastly.

With that said, Omar pressed the button on the detonator and a loud explosion erupted that rocked the streets. They heard burning wreckage flying and crashing onto the ground and fireballs rushed up into the air.

"Rest in peace, Blood," Omar looked up into the sky and crossed himself in the sign of the crucifix. Kreon and Candy crossed themselves in the holy sign as well.

****

Omar and Candy took Kreon back to his house where he jumped behind the wheel of a rental. He drove back to his house to find a bunch of badges spilling through the gates of his apartment building. He coasted past his complex seeing one of the cops pound on the door of his unit.

Knock! Knock! Knock! Knock!

A cop with a flattop haircut rapped on Kreon's apartment door. He'd been at it for a minute, but he hadn't gotten a response. Having grown tired of knocking, he stepped aside and gave his men the go ahead to bust the door down. The men didn't waste any time with slamming a battering ram into the door, which had a dozen stickers on it and was labeled the *Big Bad Motherfucker*. As soon as the battering ram was slammed against the door, it came crashing down upon the floor off its hinges. The cops that had knocked the door down stepped aside and allowed the others to flood the apartment, guns at the ready.

"What the fuck is goin' on?" Kreon wondered with a wrinkled forehead. He then pulled away from the scene before anyone could identify him.

***

"Are you Odette Drennen?" the detective asked as he stood outside of Odette's door.

"Yes," Odette replied, looking between the two detectives standing outside of her door.

"Ms. Drennen, you are under arrest," the detective began placing the handcuffs on Odette.

As the detective was snapping the cold metal bracelets around Odette's wrists, his partner was reading her *her* Miranda Rights.

"You have the right to remain silent..." the detective's partner went on and on until he finished. Afterwards, the detectives to Odette by either arm and ushered her outside.

"Wait a minute, what am I under arrest for?" Odette's head snapped from left to right as she took in the law enforces faces

"The murder of Nigeria Forgit."

***

Sitting parked on the opposite side of the street, Kreon watched through the rearview mirror as Odette was ushered to a Crown Victoria by two detectives. From the look on the detective's face he could tell that he couldn't get Odette back to the station so he could probe her for any information that he wanted.

Once the detective had Odette secured inside of the back of his car, he cranked up his Crown Victoria and drove off. As he passed Kreon's rental, the young man slid down in his seat trying not to be seen. Slumped where he was, he watched the back of the Crown Victoria until it made a left and disappeared out of his sight.

"What the fuck happened?" Kreon's forehead wrinkled, wondering what the fuck was going on. He didn't have a clue but he had to get down to the bottom of it…fast.

Kreon put his car in gear. He was about to pull off when he felt his cellular vibrate and ring. Pulling it out, he saw *Unc* on the display. Wondering what he wanted, he decided to answer his call and see what was up.

"'Sup, unc?" Kreon asked, watching his surroundings. He listened intently to what he was being told.

"Man, man, man, have you seen the news?"

"Nah, what's up?" Kreon's forehead wrinkled further and his stomach twisted into knots. Whatever his uncle saw on the news had something to do with him and his boo. He had a gut feeling about it.

"You and yo' girl is on damn near every fuckin' channel, nephew." Omar told him. Kreon could hear the different voices of the anchors as his uncle flipped through the channels with the remote control, so he knew he wasn't over exaggerating.

"For real? For what though?"

Kreon's heart was thudding now.

"They sayin' ya'll are suspects in the murda of Nigeria Forgit."

Fuuuuuck, Kreon thought to himself. Instantly, he recalled the night that Odette had knocked off Nigeria and rescued him from his impending doom.

Kreon went over everything that occurred the night of Nigeria's murder. He rewound his memory over and over again trying to see any evidence they'd left behind. That's when it dawned on him that Odette finger prints from the shovel had been left, and most likely, his DNA was still inside of Nigeria from when she'd forced herself on him.

The way he saw it they could try to take the shit to trial and fight it, but then what would be their reasoning when it came to not reporting what had occurred that

170

night? Not only that, he knew that the justice system was totally fucked up, and that they'd be inching to bury a couple of 'niggers' if given the chance. There was no way that he was going to try to get them an attorney and try to fight the case. Fuck all of that! He'd have a better chance running.

Fuck would a nigga go though? It would have to be some place far…somewhere where the United States is out of jurisdiction, but where though?

Kreon casted his eyes down at the floor as he thought on it, massaging his chin, *I got it. Cuba. We gone take our asses to Cuba.*

"Nephew? Nephew? You there?" Omar asked.

"Yeah, I'm here." Kreon replied.

"Fuck yo' head at, nigga?"

"Just thinkin' is all. Check it out though, you know that Fed you be dealin' with? Well, you think he could help me out?"

"Depends on what? My guy plugged in with some of everybody. What chu got in mind though?"

"Hold on, unc," Kreon connected his Blu-Tooth and sat his cell phone on the front passenger seat. He then pulled off, making a right a left at the end of the block and then a left on Manchester, driving down the block. "Yeah, I gotta bust this move. I can't fight that charge O and me lookin' at."

"So, what chu lookin' at doin? Talk to me? I'm finna pour up this drank and listen…" Omar said as he journeyed out of his living room to just that.

"Alright, well…"

Tranay Adams

CHAPTER ELEVEN

Odette sat in the small interrogation room with her wrist handcuffed to a metal table. Detective Bradshaw had been drilling her for hours trying to get the full story on what happened down inside of the basement the night Nigeria was killed and the whereabouts of Kreon, but she wouldn't give him shit. Her lips were sealed. The way she saw it, she was already going up Shit's Creek, she wasn't about to have her man sailing up there with her. Fuck that! Her parents bred a better bitch than that.

Furious, Detective Bradshaw threatened to lock her under the fucking jail if she didn't cooperate. He then left the room and lowered the air conditioner, making it as cold as a meat freezer inside of the interview room. He left Odette inside of the room for four hours straight, hoping she'd crack under his neck round of questioning.

Hearing the door of the interview swinging open, Odette looked over her shoulder just in time to see Detective Bradshaw returning. He shut the door behind him and made his way over to Odette, scowling. A thick throbbing vein was at the center of his forehead and his face was rose pedal red. Odette had successfully pissed him off. He'd spent the past four hours talking shit to his colleagues about her and throwing darts at her mug shot.

Detective Bradshaw was in a button down shirt and a stained tie. He was scoffing down a salami sub with the works and mustard had splattered on his tie. He'd tried to scrub the stain out, but he'd only succeeded in making the stains worse than they already were. He didn't give a shit though. His main concern was getting Odette to tell him what he wanted to know.

Detective Bradshaw wasn't even within five feet of Odette, but she could smell the cheap cologne he'd sprayed on himself that morning. She couldn't figure out what made her sicker the scent of his fragrance or the time she was looking at in prison.

"Listen," Detective Bradshaw snatched up a chair and smacked it down on the side of Odette. He then straddled it backwards and continued with what he had to say, "We found traces of semen inside Forgit that belong to Kreon Williams. I take it he's your boyfriend or fuck-buddy, or whatever. Anyway, we know Williams was down there with you, so I tell you what. You gemme his whereabouts and I'll be sure to put in a good word with the D.A for you. Make 'em go easy on you when it comes time to sentence you. How's that, darling?" he went to caress her cheek and she snapped at him like a hungry dog. Startled, he jumped back and snatched his hand away. Feeling the heat of her breath near his hand and the edges of her teeth, he knew he'd almost lost a couple of fingers. "You fucking cunt, you almost bit my goddamn fingers off!" he said stun, looking back and forth between his hand and her scowling face.

Her head was tilted downwards and she was glaring up at him, clenching her jaws. The muscles in her jaws seemed to throb.

"You got me fucked up, pig. Kind of a bitch you take me for? I'd never sell out my mothafucking man." With that having been said, Odette harped up some phlegm and spat it in his face. A glob of sticky goo splattered on Detective Bradshaw's cheek and he frowned up. He wiped his cheek off with his tie and looked at Odette with a shit-eating-grin. He then leaned close to her, so close that she could smell the coffee and donuts on his breath.

"You little chocolate bitch, I'm gonna personally see to it that they bury you behind bars and concrete. You'll never see that kid of yours again." When he said this Odette stomach dropped and her heart started beating fast. The detective mentioning her baby boy struck a chord within her, but she had to keep her game face on. She couldn't have his punk ass thinking he'd rattled her fence.

Detective Bradshaw's head snapped up and he looked at something in the interrogation room that only he could see. He then straightened his hand as if he was about to karate chop a wooden board and brought it across his neck, signaling to whomever that was filming and recording the interview to turn everything off. After waiting a moment, he punched Odette in her stomach so hard that it knocked the wind out of her. Her eyes bugled and she gasped for air, doubling over holding her stomach. Right after, Bradshaw kicked the chair out from under her and she fell to the floor. Lying on the floor with her wrist still handcuffed to the metal table, the pissed off detective stomped her face a couple of times.

He then, for good measure, kicked her in the ribs. The final blow left her wincing and holding her side.

Bradshaw stood over Odette straightening out his shirt and then re-tucking it into his slacks. Afterwards, he whipped out a comb and combed his hair back in place, patting it in certain areas to make sure it was just right. Having slid his comb into his back pocket, he then adjusted his belt on his waistline and walked over to the door. Pulling it open, he looked back at Odette, mad dogging her, he said, "Smart mouth bitch!"

He slammed the door behind him and went about his business, leaving Odette on the floor withering in pain.

***

Not long ago Shonda had gotten off the jack with her sister, Odette. She told her what her charge was and that she didn't have bail. The best that she could do for her was get her an attorney for her defense. Although she already had someone in mind to get on her sister's case, she knew that more than likely she'd be sitting down for a long time with the evidence that the police had against her.

The conversation with Odette had left Shonda stressing like she was the one looking at time in prison. This was because she was the oldest and had always been told to look out for her sister. With her ending up in jail with a murder charge, she felt like she hadn't just let her down, but herself as well. This is what led her to her little wooden box which held the key to her personal utopia.

Shonda sat on the couch rolling up a blunt and occasionally glancing up at the television at Chopped which was a cooking show. She'd just finished preparing the blunt and was about to light it when she heard a knock at the front door. Still holding the blunt between her fingers, she looked to the front door and asked who was it?

"It's bruh-in-law, sis!" Kreon said from the opposite side of the door. He knew he was wanted by the law and he didn't want to say his name for fear of someone reporting his whereabouts to the authorities.

"Hold up." Shonda sat the blunt down in the ashtray and walked over to the door.

She opened the front door and embraced him lovingly.

Next, she shut and locked the door behind him.

"I gotta plan to get cho sista outta the can." Kreon said as he sat down on the couch.

"What kind of plan?" She sat down on the couch beside him.

"Neva mind alla that, just know I'm bustin' her up outta that bitch. I ain't lettin' lil' momma rot behind bars, you Griff me?"

"Yeah, I guess so."

"When I lay this shit down. We gone have to dip outta town...for good. You comin' with us or are you stayin' behind?"

Shonda picking her blunt back up and put a flame to the end of it. She took a deep pull and blew out a cloud of smoke into the air. She then crossed her legs and thought on it for a minute. "Missy is the only family I got besides my motha. I just found out about our father, but nobody means more to me than her," She took the time to take a drag from off her bleezy before continuing, "Where do you have in mind to relocate to?"

"Cuba."

"Cuba." She nodded as she thought on it some more, massaging her chin. "Count me in. Just lemme know when I should be ready and how we getting there."

"Alright," Kreon came and sat on the couch beside her. He then went on to fill her in on the plan he had in mind.

"Okay, bruh-in-law, I'm with it." Shonda told him. She'd just finished listening to his big plan.

"You sho'?"Kreon gave her a look like *be sure*.

"Yeah, gemme a hug, my nigga," Shonda sat her blunt in the ashtray and rose to her feet. She then gave him a sisterly hug.

"Cool. I'ma be gettin' mom's in a few days. I'll drop her off over here. Y'all can get to know one anotha until we make this move."

"Alright."

"Lil' dude in there knocked out, huh?

"Yeah."

"Lemme kiss 'em goodbye and I'ma gone get outta ya hair." Kreon went on to kiss Marquise goodbye. While he was gone, Shonda picked her bleezy back up and lay back on the couch. Smoking, she thought about whether or not if there was any good weed out there in Cuba.

***

When Odette was un-cuffed and released inside of the bullpen, she took in her surrounding while rubbing her aching wrists. There was a quartet of women talking amongst themselves, a woman lying sleep beside the toilet while another woman sat on it, a couple of chicks telling one another what they were locked up for, and the rest of the broads there were just occupying the benches wearing sadden looks on their faces.

Spotting an empty space on the bench against the wall to her left, Odette made her way over and sat down. As soon as her ass graced the scarred up, graffiti sprawled oak wood bench, she looked up to find a mean ass looking broad heading in her direction. She had a head the shape of a volley ball and short hair. Her hair was slicked down with so much grease that it looked like it had been painted onto her scalp. She also had a big mole by her top lip and a faint mustache. Her hefty body filled out a pocket T-shirt and baggy jeans.

The heavy set woman stop before Odette and pressed her boot against the bench, right beside Odette. Odette looked at the woman's boot beside her. She scowled and looked up at the bigger woman scrunching up her nose.

"Excuse you." Odette told the big bitch. There wasn't a trace of fear in her eyes.

"Nah, excuse you, lil' momma," the big woman told her. "My name's Leslie, and you sittin' on private property. If you wanna sit here then you gone have to come up off somethin'." She held up her meaty hand and wiggled her chubby fingers, expecting rent for the space on the bench she was claiming.

"It's like that?" Odette asked disbelievingly.

"This is America, baby girl. Ain't shit here for free."

"Well, here's my first down payment!" With a grunt, Odette threw her fist into Leslie's face. The blow caused the bigger woman to wince and everyone in the cell eyes bulged. Silent engulfed the entire stable, as everyone wondered what was to come next.

A scowling Leslie touched her beneath her nose and her fingers came away bloody. Seeing the blood seemed to enrage her, her nostrils flared and she gritted her teeth.

She looked at Odette with pupils of burning fire, resembling to flaming balls. Odette looked at the fist she'd thrown and then back up at her opponent. She damn near put everything she had behind that punch, so she was surprised that it didn't drop her big ass.

With a grunt, Leslie swung on Odette twice, missing her, thanks to her ducking. Having just missed the large fists that were meant to knock her off her feet, Odette threw two bon rattling blow into the huge woman's gut. She followed up by firing on her jaw, her fist whipped Leslie head around but it didn't seem to harm her. Nah, the punch only succeeded in pissing homegirl off. Madder than ever Leslie slowly turned her head back around to Odette, blood running from the corner of her mouth.

When she gritted her teeth, Odette could see that they were stained bloody. The big bitch spat blood on the floor and fired twice on Odette's face. The might behind the punches made it feel like Odette's teeth had been loosened and she felt light headed. She started swinging on Leslie, but her big ass backed back, avoiding the assault and laughing manically. Odette was too dizzy from the head shots she'd taken from her much stronger opponent to connect any punches, so she was as helpless as a baby now.

"Unh huh, bitch, hold this!" Leslie called out and fired on her again.

Bwap!

"And this!"

Bwhrack!

"And these, too!"

Bop! Leslie fired on Odette's face.

Bwop!

She kicked her in her stomach and sent her flying backwards into the cement wall. The impact caused debris to fall from the ceiling onto the floor.

"Uhhhhhhhhh," A grimacing Odette slowly tried to get to her feet, holding her stomach. She looked around seeing double with blurred vision. She saw all of the women on their feet pumping their fists in the air and egging on the fight. Seeing someone approaching through the corner of her eye, she looked to them and found an enormous woman coming at her. It wasn't until her vision had returned to normal that see realized it was Leslie. Seeing her coming she knew that she was about to get put in the Hurt Locker, so she scrambled to her feet, ready to get it on again.

By the time Odette had gotten to her feet and thrown up her fists, Leslie was stopping directly in front of her. The bigger woman looked at her with admiration. Odette was wincing, and from the way she was standing Leslie could tell her ribcage was giving her hell.

"Come on, bitch...bring...bring your big ass on." Odette continuously winced while holding up her fists. Although she wasn't in any shape to continue the brawl, her bruised ego wouldn't let her throw in the towel.

Leslie chuckled and said, "I gotta give it to you, lil' momma, you've got balls bigga than most niggaz." Suddenly, she scowled and lifted her sledge hammer like fist, about to crush her adversary with one devastating blow.

Clang! Clang! Clang!

The metal bar of the holding cell resonated as something equally as hard tapped against it.

"Aye, aye, you bitches knock that shit off in there!" A tall, slender African American sheriff said irately, tapping his nightstick up against one of the bars. Instantly, the cell went silent and the women surrounding Odette and Leslie returned to the areas of the holding cell they'd been before the drama popped off.

"You one lucky ass bitch, you know that?" Leslie told Odette as she dropped her arm at her side. She then looked her up and down, disgusted. Afterwards, she walked away from Odette and headed back to where she was chopping it up with the other women.

Odette took a deep breath and sighed with relief. She looked to the bars and saw the sheriff sheathing his nightstick as he walked away. Once the sound of his leather boots mashing against the floor had disappeared, she carried herself over to the bench she was sitting at and sat down. Laying her head back against the wall, she stared across the cell at Leslie. Leslie made her hand into a knife and pretended to slit her own throat. This was her way of letting Odette know that she was a dead woman.

Odette shut her eyelids briefly and took a deep breath. When she peeled her eyelids back open she watched as Leslie continued to chop it up with the women she was earlier.

Whenever you decide to bring it, I'll be waiting for your big fat-ass bitch. My momma ain't raise no punks. I got a pussy but I ain't one. Best believe that!

A few days later Odette and the rest of the women were bussed out to the county jail. It was there that she'd await trail and find out her fate.

****

Carlos sat on his bed watching television with his leg elevated on a stack of pillows. He tossed back cashew nuts and cackled at the antics of the Family Guy animated show playing before his eyes. Hearing someone knocking at the door, he picked up the remote and lowered the volume. He asked who was it and the person answered but he couldn't quite hear them. Figuring that it was best to be safe than sorry, he picked up his gun and tucked it at the front of his pants. He then grabbed his crutches and hopped to his good leg. Making his way towards the door, he asked who it was again as the knocking continued.

"Kreon!" the person that had rapped at the door responded.

Hearing who it was at his door caused Carlos' forehead to crinkle. He wondered what the fuck Kreon wanted with him. Whatever it was it couldn't have been good, which was why since what had went down between them back at the motel he had his gun with him twenty-four-hours a day seven days a week. Carlos stopped at the front door and said, "What chu won't, homeboy?"

"Can I come in for a minute? I needa holla at chu, big dawg." He responded.

Carlos took a deep breath thinking the request over. Having come to a conclusion, he leaned his crutches against the wall, beside the door, and unlocked it. He pulled the door open and allowed Kreon in over the threshold. As soon as he was inside of the house, Kreon took a look around the house his girlfriend's ex husband had rented in approval. A moment later, he heard the door behind him being shut and locked. Before he knew it, Carlos was grabbing him by the back of his collar and pushing him up against the wall, shoving his gun into his right eye socket.

"What the fuck do you want with me?" Carlos sneered.

"Ain't no secret that me and O are on fire, we all over the news."

"Yeah, I saw all of the reports." He admitted. "Now what exactly does that have to do with me."

"I'm gonna bust her outta prison, and I need your help to do it."

For a minute Carlos stared into his eyes and then he suddenly started laughing his ass off. He literally doubled over holding the hand that held his gun across his stomach cracking the fuck up. He laughed so goddamn hard that tears formed at the corners of his eyes.

"Wait a minute, wait a minute," he said coming down from his laughter. "You mean to tell me that you gonna bust my baby momma outta jail and you want my help in doin' it?"

Staring at Carlos with a dead serious face, Kreon smoothened out the wrinkles in his shirt that Carlos had put in it when he forced him up against the wall. "That's right. I'm gonna bust O up outta there with or without yo' help. I figured you'd want to help.

I mean, figurin' she's your son's mother and all." With that having been said, Kreon turned his back and headed for the door. He had grabbed the doorknob and was about to pull the door open when Carlos called him back.

"Hold on, bruh." Carlos called after him, causing him to turn around. The Dominican wore an expression on his face just as serious as the one that Kreon was wearing.

"Are you serious about ridin' out on this thang, man?" Kreon nodded yes. "Alright, you can count me in on it." He switched hands with his gun and extended his free hand.

Kreon looked down at his hand wondering if he was trying to trick him or some shit. Reluctantly, he went on and shook his hand.

Team work makes the dream work, baby.

CHAPTER TWELVE
Three nights later

Kreon pulled his L.A fitted cap low over his brows and threw his hood over his head. It was the best he could do with so little time to properly disguise himself. He wasn't worried about his mother blowing his cover because his uncle had went to go see her at the hospital the day prior and let her know that more than likely that he'd be the one picking her up since he hadn't seen her in quite some time.

Kreon pulled up at the front entrance of the hospital to find his mother, Ella, sitting in a wheel chair. An orderly stood behind her with his hands on the handles of the chair. As soon as he saw the patient's ride pull to a stop before them, he locked the wheel chair into place and helped her get up out of the chair. Once he passed Ella her cane, he opened the front passenger door for her and helped her inside. After that, he shut the door behind her and bid her a farewell. Once Kreon had pulled off, the orderly unlocked the wheel chair and rolled it back inside of the hospital, whistling.

How you doin', ma?" Kreon asked, making a right out of the hospital's parking lot.

"I'm okay; son.You got something to drink so I can pop one of these pain killers? The gunshot wound is kicking my natural black ass." She said, opening her white paper bag with RX on it and pulling out a dark orange bottle. She looked over the label and then popped the lid on it. While she was removing the lid on the pill bottle, Kreon was taking the can of Coca Cola he'd been drinking on the way over from out of the cup-holder and passing it to her. "Thanks." She used the cold beverage to wash the pills down and sat the can back down inside of the cup-holder.

"Mom, we movin' outta state?" Kreon told his mother, looking back and forth between her and the windshield.

"We? Who is we?" Ella's forehead wrinkled.

"You, me, O, unc...shit, everybody. We goin' to Cuba, ma."

"Cuba?" He nodded yes.

With the confirmation having been given, Ella stared out of the window massaging her chin as she gave the idea some thought. Taking a breath, she turned to her son and gave him a nod of approval. Getting his mother's approval made Kreon smile. When he pulled up to a red stop-light, he leaned over and kissed her on the side of her face, multiple times. She smiled and giggled.

"I love you, ma." Kreon told the woman whose womb he'd came from.

"I love you too, baby boy."

"You get my cigarettes?"

"Yeah, I got chu a pack." He grinned, thinking of how his mother stayed blowing cancer sticks. "Look inside of the glove-box."

Kreon glanced at his mother as she popped open the glove-box and took out the pack of Newport's he' purchased for her on the way over. He hated that she smoked cigarettes, but he'd rather she indulged in them instead of crack. Besides, the way he saw it if she was going to get off crack then she'd need some other vice to take its place.

Ella stuck a square between her lips and lit it up. Taking the Joe from out of her mouth, she blew smoke out and polluted the interior of the compact vehicle. As she smoked, Kreon went on to fill her in on the plan that he had in mind to bust Odette out of the prison bus. Although she didn't like it and made a big fuss about it, she knew that there wasn't any way to change her son's mind, because once his mind was made up, there wasn't any way that someone could change it...ever.

"Yeah, it's safe to say you love this girl. I mean, really, really love her." She said, looking over at him. "You got to if you willing to risk it all for her."

"Not just for her, but *our* baby."

When he dropped the bomb on her, her eyes bulged and her jaw slacked. She dropped the cigarette on her lap and went wild, trying to smack it off of her lap. Her smacking at her lap caused embers to fly everywhere and the cigarette eventually fell on the floor, between her sneakers.

"Wait a minute, you mean to tell me I'm going to be a grandmother?" She asked him, grasping the sleeve of his hood and smiling excitedly.

"Yes, ma, you're gonna be a grandma." He smirked.

"Ooooh," she unbuckled herself and threw her arms around him, kissing him on his cheek. Next, she settled down in her seat and buckled up. She took the time to wipe the tears that slid down her cheeks. She was truly happy about the new addition that would be entering their family. "I can't believe it. I'm going to be a grandmother. Y'all know what she's gonna have yet?"

"Nah, not yet, ma, O just found out to tell you the truth."

"Ok. It doesn't matter, long as the baby is healthy."

"That's what I said."

"Well, this changes everything. You do what chu have to, Kreon," she grasped her son's hand. "You do what you gotta do to make sure your family stays together, you hear me?"

"Yes, ma'am, that's why I came up with this plan. And I'm gonna follow through with it come hell or high water." He said with a dead serious expression.

"Well, I just want you to know that I commend you, and I support your decision whole heartedly." she patted his hand affectionately.

"Thanks, mom."

The car was silent for a minute as Kreon drove through the streets. His mother could tell that he had something on his mind and it caused her brows to wrinkle. Her curiosity got the best of her and she decided to ask him what was eating him.

"Is there something you want to say, son? If so, put it out there. You know you can tell me anything." She rubbed his shoulder soothingly, trying her best to put him at ease so that he'd feel comfortable to express whatever was on his mind.

Kreon could already feel himself getting emotional about the subject that he was about to present to his mother, so he took the time to compose himself before he went on with what he wanted to ask. Once he found that he was in a better state of mind than he was previously, he went on to talk with his mother. "Ma, I'm gonna ask you somethin' and I want chu to be completely honest with me, okay?"

Ella's heart started beating fast. She had an idea of what her son was about to ask her but she hoped it wasn't what she had in mind. If it was, she already had her mind made up to tell him the truth in its entirety. She wasn't going to bullshit him or sugar coat things. They were both of blunt nature so she knew that he could take it.

"Okay. Shoot."

"Who is my father, ma?"

The car was pregnant with an awkward silence as Kreon continued to drive and his mother pondered things. His question was the one she knew that he was going to ask. She had hoped to delay giving him an answer so soon, but fate didn't see things happening that way. So she was left with giving him an answer to a question that all children deserved to know. It was his right, and she had no right to deny him it.

Ella bowed her head and took a deep breath. Once she looked back up at her son, she had teary eyes and was on the verge of crying. "Okay, I guess it's time I told you the truth. I just hope that you can handle it." Teardrops fell from her eyes and she sniffled, wiping her eyes with the back of her hand. "Your father is…"

Kreon's eyes bulged and his next breath got caught in his throat. He couldn't believe what he had just been told. Taking the time to gather himself as best as he could, he focused his attention back on the streets. "Are you sure? How…how did this happen?"

He inquired as he looked for somewhere that he could pull over to park. The news was overwhelming for him and he didn't want to risk a car accident due to his devastation.

Ella bowed her head and more teardrops fell, splashing down on the table top. When she looked back up at him this time her face was soaked and snot was threatening to drip from her left nostril. Clearing her throat as best as she could, she went on to address his question, "…After that, it happened a few more times, but I never told anyone. I was ashamed, and I was afraid how people would look at me. More importantly, I was afraid of how the news would affect your grandfather. I thought my father would have a heart attack and die should he have found out what had happened. I didn't want to risk it so I kept everything to myself." Ella watched her son pop open the glove-box and take out a few napkins, passing them to her. She used them to wipe her face and blow her nose. "Around the time I was dating Khadafi. I told him the news and it broke his heart. He wanted to kill him, but I stopped him. To be honest, that's what drove him to start drinking, and then later on, crack. He was physically and mentally abusing you because he hated what you represented every time he looked at you. Khadafi couldn't accept the fact that he was help raising a child that wasn't his, or how he'd like to put it…a rape baby." She broke down sobbing and Kreon embraced her. Teardrops fell from his eyes as he swept his hand up and down his mother's back, trying to comfort her as best as he could.

"It's alright, mom, it's okay." He assured her as he continued to shed tears. "We're gonna be fine. We're gonna get through this as a family." He kissed her on top of the head and continued to comfort her.

Poor Kreon, life seemed like it wasn't ever going to give him a break.

***

The next day

Omar, Candy and Kreon sat at the dining room table smoking hookahs and waiting for the last person's arrival. Omar probed his nephew about the last man that he'd gotten to come along on the mission, but he didn't tell him who it was. He only insisted that he'd know just as soon as he'd gotten there, and that he didn't want any shit once he came. Kreon tried to make his uncle promise him that he wasn't going to do anything should he not favor the person that he'd gotten to roll out with them, but he wouldn't agree to any such thing. By this time, Omar had poured himself up a glass of liquor to take the edge off but that didn't help. Liquor only made that nigga irate and more confrontational, than he already was.

A rap at the door stole everyone's attention. Kreon motioned for Omar and Candy to stay seated while he went to open the door. He hadn't notice his uncle sit down his drink and rise to his feet to follow him to the front door. Omar stood a few feet away from his nephew, watching as he removed the chain and locks of the door. Kreon pulled the door open and Carlos crossed the threshold on crutches.

As soon as Omar's eyes met him, his eyebrows arched and his nose scrunched up. Carlos acknowledged this as Kreon was shutting and locking the door behind him. The Dominican's eyebrows arched and he clenched his jaws, feeling threatened by the man standing before his menacing eyes. Kreon had just turned around from locking the door when Carlos threw down his right crutch. In a flash, he was drawing his gun and pointing it at Omar, and Omar was doing the same. The two men stood there in the middle of the kitchen with their bangas pointed at one another, mad dogging each other. A vein throbbed at their temples and their nostrils pulsated. Their trigger fingers were itching, and someone was bound to come up dead any second.

"Hold up! Hold up!" Kreon's head snapped between Carlos and Omar, as he stood between them, both arms outstretched. Should they dare to pull the triggers then he'd most likely be a casualty of their firefight. "Aye, y'all niggaz needa chill the fuck out, man!"

"Fucka chill, nephew! This punk-ass nigga and his bitch-ass cousin shot at chu, dawg! They tried to lay you down! Now, move out the way so I can make sure the next words he say, he'll be sayin' 'em to God."

"If I'm seein' God then yo' black ass gone be seein' 'em, too." Carlos threatened.

"Y'all wait a minute goddamn it," Kreon roared, looking between the two men. "Now, I called y'all here because I need y'all to help me bust O outta the slamma. Not 'cause I wanna turn this mothafuckin' house into a goddamn shootin' range."

"Fuck this!" Carlos went to bust his gun.

"Wait!" Kreon turned to the Dominican which made his gun be pointed at his chest. He found himself staring into the merciless eyes of Marquise's father and Odette's ex-husband.

"Move out the way, nephew, I'ma blast on this nigga!" Omar swore with the same merciless eyes as the man who had his gun pointed at his sister's only son.

"No, unc, I need 'em, I need you too…both of you." Kreon said over his shoulder. "Lower yo' banga, man."

"Boy, have you lost yo' fuckin' marbles?" Omar questioned his sanity.

"Yeah," He turned around to face his uncle. "I have lost my marbles when it comes to O and the baby, 'cause I'm willin' to do any and everything there is to bust them outta that bus, no matta how crazy it may seem to anyone."

As Kreon stared into his uncle's eyes, he swallow the excess spit in his throat and continued, "I'm beggin' you, please, please, lower yo'gun so I can go ova this plan with everybody, and get my girl and my unborn baby back."

Kreon stared into Omar's eyes pleadingly. His uncle, who still had his banga pointed at Carlos, eyes darted back and forth between Kreon's eyes and those of the opposing man. His thoughts raced as he tried to make a decision. Having made up his mind, he shut his eyelids briefly and took a deep breath. He then reluctantly lowered his gun at his side and wiped the perspiration from off his forehead with the back of his hand. Seeing that Omar had lowered his banga, Carlos lowered his and tucked it at the small of his back. Seeing someone at the corner of his eye, he looked over his shoulder and saw Candy. She was lower her .357 Magnum revolver, which she was clutching with both hands. Little momma had drawn that thang as soon as Omar had pulled his piece. The man that Kreon affectionately called 'Unc' was her lover and friend, and she was down for him no matter what the odds were. *Now that's love!*

After seeing that Candy had lowered her pistol and was no longer a threat to him, Carlos focused his attention on Kreon.

"So, my boy's gonna have a younga brotha or sista, huh?" Carlos inquired.

"Yeah." Kreon nodded slowly.

"Congrats."

"Thanks." Kreon placed his hands on Carlos's and Omar's shoulders. "Y'all come on. We needa chop it up 'bout this move we 'bouta bust."

Kreon led Carlos and Omar inside of the dining room. Candy, Omar and Carlos smoked hookahs as they listened to the plan Kreon had put together. The threesome gave the young man their undivided attention as he gave them the rundown on what he believed was a foolproof plan.

They nodded their heads and continued to indulge in their vices, smoke wafting around them. They were all eyes and ears when Kreon showed them how they were going to reach the prison bus on a map he'd drawn up himself. He had two black Hot Wheel toys that he used to symbolize the vehicles that they would be driving in. And he had a toy bus that symbolized the prison bus that Odette was going to be driving in. He moved the toys around showing which route the prison bus was going to take and what route they were going to take to catch up with it.

Kreon appeared to be very confident in the plan he'd orchestrated. He could tell that all the listening ears in the room believed in what he was telling them and he loved that. But he had to keep it real with them, because he knew that what they were about to attempt was very dangerous and causalities were a possibility.

"Look, I'ma keep it a buck and some change with y'all. There's a good chance some of us won't make it out to Cuba. Some of us could wind up dead or on lock for the rest of our life, but my goal is for all of us to make it out there." Kreon looked around at everyone to see any hesitation about going through with his plan. There wasn't any hesitation written on any of their faces. They all seemed to be down for the mission, but he had to be sure. "If anyone doesn't want to follow through with this shit, then say so now. There won't be any hard feelings, I assure you. I mean, I ain't askin' y'all to knock over a liquor store. I'm askin' you mothafuckaz to help me bust my girl outta fuckin' prison bus. That's a tall order, so I wouldn't blame any of you for bowin' out at this moment." Again, he looked around at everyone trying to see if they had hesitations about coming along with him on the mission. They all appeared to be set on rolling with him and that was fine by him. "Okay, then, that's what I'm talkin' 'bout."

Kreon stuck out his hand; Omar walked over and laid his hand on top of his nephew's hand. Candy walked over and laid her hand on top of her man's hand. Everyone else looked to Carlos. He just sat there for a minute staring at them, and taking pulls from his hookah. Having taken one last pull from his hookah, he rose from the chair and walked over to the threesome with the assistance of his crutch. Stopping beside Kreon, he outstretched his hand and laid it on top of Candy's hand.

"Alright then, let's get it." Kreon said, sounding like he was in a huddle of his team mates on a football field. With that having been said, everyone took their hands away from the pile. Kreon went on to fill everyone in a little more about his plan. Afterwards, he saw Carlos to the door and locked it behind him.

"Yo', unc, make sure you get up with yo' people about them Hondas. We gone need them shits, fa sho." Kreon told his uncle upon returning back to the dining room.

"Don't worry about nothin', nephew. I got everything covered."

"What about the money?"

"Boy, yo' uncle paper'd up, I'm sittin' onna lil' ova a mill, we straight once we get out there to Cuba. You ain't got nothin' to worry about, I assure you."

"Alright, cool. Thanks for ridin' with me, man."

"You ain't gotta thank me, we family. You know I always got cho back." He dapped his nephew up and gave him a hug. With that love having been shown, Omar and Kreon sat back at the table with Candy to finish smoking on the hookahs.

CHAPTER THIRTEEN

Odette sat at the lunch table hunched over her tray of food. The meal before her looked less than desirable, but considering she was starving she'd have to make due with what she'd been given. Odette ate a spoonful of mashed potatoes and discovered that they didn't taste so bad. Seeing her indulging in her food and having finished eating her own, Leslie found herself still hungry. Some of the ladies sitting at her table offered her some of the food on her trays but she declined their offerings. Fuck those bitches food! She wanted whatever that bitch, Odette, had on her tray.

Leslie wiped her mouth and then her hands off with her napkin. She then balled it up and dropped it into her tray. All eyes were on her inside of the chow hall as she made her way down the asile towards Odette. She'd just reached Odette as she was about to take a bite out of her apple. Before little momma could sink her teeth into the ripe juicy fruit she snatched it out of her hands. Leslie bobbed off like she didn't have a care in the world as she took a bite out of the apple.

"Bitch, you got me fucked up!" An angered Odette hopped up from the bench and punched Leslie in the back of her head, causing her to drop the apple. The moment that little momma's fist connected with the back of her skull, the entire chow hall went silent. Bitches stopped munching their food and others stopped their forks and cartons of milk at their mouths. Even the correctional officers were stun because no one dared lifted a hand against Leslie. Bitches feared her big ass like the wrath of God.

Odette mad dogged Leslie and clenched her fists causing her knuckles to bulge in her hands. Leslie spat out the hunk of peach she was eating and slowly turned around, letting the peach drop from her hand. Her eyebrows were arched and wrinkled formed between her eyes. Her nostrils expanded and shrunk as she breathed heavily. She squared her jaws and swung on Odette.

Little momma ducked the wild swings of her opponent and gave her two swift stomach blows. She then fired on her mouth which threw her head back. When Leslie brought her head back down, she smiled and showcased a grill of bloody teeth. She then spat blood on the linoleum and wiped her dripping lip with the back of her fist.

"Fuck!" Odette looked up at the enormous woman towering over her. The lesbian's shadow left her in the shade. Before she knew it big bad momma was cocking her fist back and punching her in the face. The punch sent Odette flying backwards and leaving a shoe behind. Her face was covered in wrinkles from frowning having taken a powerful blow. Seeing Leslie fist land flush on Odette's face caused the convicts to cringe. Odette landed on the floor and slid up against the wall. When she looked up, she saw half moons, stars and birds circling her crown. Once her vision did come back into place, she saw Leslie charging in her direction like a pissed off bull.

"Aww, shiiit, here this big bitch come; the bigger they are, the harder they fall, my little chocolate ass," Odette grimaced as she slowly got to her feet. She was slightly dizzy, but she wasn't going to take a beating lying down. Nah, fuck that, she was going to give homegirl all of the fight she had left in her. Leslie threw three haymakers at Odette, all of which she ducked and maneuvered around. She countered with body shots and an upper cut. The uppercut sent a spray of blood into the air and Leslie stumbling backwards. Seeing that she hadn't dropped the hefty lesbian, Odette jumped upon the bench and then the lunch table.

She then interlocked her fingers, creating one large fist, and leaped off the table. Flying towards Leslie she swung her fist into her jaw. The impact from the devastating blow caused Leslie to crash into the lunch table on the left side, spilling the trays of food sitting there. Beverages and food splattered on the linoleum, coming behind them was Odette. She landed on her bending knees and went charging after Leslie. Seeing the wild cat coming for her, Leslie scooped up a handful of mashed potatoes from off the floor and hurled it at her.

Splat!

The mash potatoes splattered against Odette's eyes and blinded her. She winced and went staggering backwards, swiping the food from out of her eyes. Seeing that she was at her mercy, Leslie hurriedly got to her feet, running at her. Reaching her, with a grunt, she lifted her high above her head and slammed her down upon the lunch table. Beverages spilled and trays of food splattered on the floor.

Nose and mouth bleeding, nostrils flaring, chest heaving, Leslie looked around the chow hall. All of the female inmates were pumping their fists, cheering and egging her brutality on. This seemed to inflate her monster size ego.

"This bitch ain't got shit on me!" Leslie screamed at the top of her lungs and pounded on her chest, like she was King Kong. In a flash, the correctional officers rushed in. A riled up Leslie was able to knock a few of them on their asses out but eventually she was overpowered and slammed to the floor, hard. The correctional officers mashed the side of her face into the cold dirty floor, cuffed her and battered her back with their nightsticks. Some of them even took the liberty to kick, punch and stomp her big ass.

Crack! Whack! Wop! Bop!

Leslie's forehead wrinkled and she clenched her jaws as her back was assaulted by the black steel rods.

"Ahhhh! Fuck you! Fuck you!" She bellowed over and over until a sharp blow to the back of her skull put her hostile black ass out cold.

Odette was roughly pulled upon her feet and her wrists were handcuffed behind her back. While the metal bracelets were being snapped around her wrists, she watched as an unconscious Leslie was drug on her needs out of the chow hall. It wasn't long before Odette found herself being escorted out of the chow hall as well.

Girl fight!

***

That night

Dr. Fonzworth sat at his desk sipping coffee and filling out paperwork. Hearing a noise outside in the hall, he suddenly stopped and rose to his feet. His forehead creased and his curiosity got the best of him. Wondering who or what it was that had disturbed him, he headed out of his office and into the corridor. He looked up and down the hallway but he didn't see anyone. Feeling movement at his back, he whipped around in a flash but there wasn't anyone there. Dumbfounded, he scratched his head and shrugged his shoulders. He then headed back into his office and shut the door behind him, locking. When he turned around he was startled to find Kreon sitting in his chair. He was dressed in a trench coat and holding a shotgun at his side. At the moment he was sucking on an apple Tootsie Roll pop and smiling having laid eyes on the psychologist.

"What's up, doc?" Kreon said like he was Bugs Bunny.

"Holy shit! What're you doing here, Kreon?"

"Well, you don't sound to happy to see me."

"Do you know you and some woman are all over the news? I can't change a channel without seeing y'all faces."

"I know. Ain't I handsome?" he smiled hard and turned his face from side to side so that he could get a better look at him.

"What, what are you doing here?" Fonzworth kept looking down at the shotgun and up into his eyes. He had a feeling that he'd come there to kill him but he couldn't be too sure.

"I'm sorry, this lil' lady has you uptight? Don't mind her." Kreon racked the shotgun and sat it on the desk. "This isn't really for you. Like you said, my face is all ova the news... for all I know I could have ran into The Boys comin' and goin' here. Should that had happen; I woulda held court in the streets. I ain't neva gone see the inside of a cell, you Griff me?"

"Yeah, I, uh, Griff you, whatever that's supposed to mean," Fonzworth relaxed a little. He pointed to the cup of coffee. This was his way of asking Kreon could he pick it up. Once the young man gave him the go-ahead, he picked up the cup and took a sip. "Tell me...If you haven't come here to kill me, what is it that you want from me?"

"The last message I got from you, you said that..."

"Oh, so you have been receiving my messages. I was wondering why you haven't contacted me."

"My fault, doc, I couldn't find the time to holla back at chu. Besides, did you really expect me to chance it? I'm hot. For all I knew, you coulda answered yo' jack and kept me on the line long enough for them people to find my ass. I coulda go out like a straight up sucka."

"Smart man, but I wouldn't have ratted you out," Fonzworth took another sip of his coffee.

"Oh, yeah, why is that?" Kreon frowned up.

"Not my style," he sat his cup down on the desk. "Besides, I like to think of us as friends, although it isn't professional for me to do so."

"Thanks, doc; that means a lot to me. There aren't many people I can trust these days. It's nice to know now that you one of 'em."

"No problem." he leaned back against the desk and folded his arms across his chest. Placing his fist to his mouth, he cleared his throat and proceeded with what he had to say. "Now, what is it that I can do for you?"

"I needa 'script, and anything you can get me on the DBT program and managing my emotions."

"Ahhhh, the DBT program, you have been listening to my messages." He smiled.

"I told you I been keepin' up with yo' messages. You musta thought I was bullshittin' you." Kreon told him. "I don't know if they have the program where I'm goin', but just in case they do I want some info on the program. But just in case they don't have the program there, I at least want some documents on how to manage my emotions. That way I can hold it together until I figure out my next move."

"Okay. Let me get that info on managing your emotions for you." Fonzworth did a little research on his computer and found the information that Kreon was looking for. He printed it out and handed it to him. The young man folded up the paperwork and slid it into his backpocket.

"Thanks for this." Kreon said of the paperwork.

"You're welcome. Now, about your medication, there's this new technology we're using," Fonzworth told Kreon. "We can swab your saliva and narrow it down to medications that'll work for you."

"If that's the case, why the fuck haven't you been told me about this shit, then?" Kreon frowned up.

"Like I said, Kreon, this technology is fairly new. It's been out a year, tops. I didn't have any idea it existed until a few weeks ago." He told him. "As soon as I found out about it I tried to get in touch with you, but you never answered any of my calls."

Fonzworth looked at him as he waited for his explanation as to why he didn't answer his calls.

"What?" he shrugged.

"I think you owe me an explanation."

"Oh, my fuckin' God, dude." Kreon threw his head back and took a deep breath, rubbing his hand down his face. He then looked to Fonzworth. "I been busy, nigga, damn! Why you on my bumpa?"

"I was just fucking with ya, Kreon." He playfully punched him in the arm.

He then pulled opened his drawer and took out the items he'd need to swab Kreon's jawfor his saliva.

Afterwards, he motioned the young man over and collected a sample of his DNA with a Q-tip. He slid the Q-tip into a small bottle and slipped it inside of a thick Ziploc bag, which he sealed and wrote a fictitious name on it, Dallas Winston.

"Alright, now, I drop this baby off at the boys at the lab and they work their magic. Then we'll find out exactly what medication will help you with your illness."

"When are you gonna find this out?" Kreon inquired.

"Tomorrow."

"Nah," he shook his head no. "That ain't gone work for me, homie. I needa know what's up pronto. I ain't tryna stick around in L.A no longa than I have to. You know I'ma wanted man out here."

"Right," Fonzworth folded his arms across his chest and lay back in his executive chair, massaging his chin as he thought on it. He then glanced at his watch, seeing what time it was and snatching up the Ziploc. "Well, look, the boys down at the lab should still be down the hill, I'll run this over to them and see about getting that info tonight for you, how's that?"

"Sounds like a plan."

Without saying another word, Fonzworth snatched his coat from off the back of the door and slipped it on. He pulled open the door and was about to head out of it when Kreon called him back.

"Thanks, man, I really appreciate it." Kreon said sincerely.

Fonzworth looked back at him and smiled before heading out of the door.

***

Fonzworth stayed down at the lab for an hour. When he returned he was able to look the data up on the computer. He came up with several medications that matched perfectly for Kreon. Grabbing a sheet of paper and an ink pen, he looked back and forth between the computer screen and the sheet of paper, jotting down the names of the medications that were best suited for his patient. Once he was done, he passed the sheet of paper to Kreon and he looked them over. Having done this, he folded the paper up and slipped it into his back pocket.

Kreon pulled out a roll of duct-tape and held it up. "It's best if I do it this way. You can tell 'em I jacked you for the info, 'cause should they find out you helped me, you stand to lose yo' career. You Griff me?

"Yeah, I Griff you. Smart man," He cracked a smirk.

"Thanks. Goodnight."

"Huh?" A look of confusion crossed Fonzworth's face.

Wap!

Kreon smacked Fonzworth across the head with his banga and his tall, lanky ass fell out to the floor. He lay there eyelids shut, mouth closed, with a lump forming on the side of his head. Kreon tucked his gun waistline and duct-taped his mouth, wrists and ankles. Next, he sat the duct-tape on Fonzworth's desk top and fled the scenery.

***

The medications that Fonzworth had written down were Depakote and Hydroxyzine. He knew that he couldn't walk into the pharmacy and pick the shit up now that he was wanted man. He would either have to stick the place up or have someone steal it for him. Figuring that he was already on the run for a charge anyway, he decided to stickup CVS for the medication he'd need. He did just that, too, making off with a year's worth of the drugs he'd need to have his mind right.

CHAPTER FOURTEEN

Doom! Doom! Doom!

The iron door resonated as it was rapped upon. The noise startled Odette from where she was lying. When she looked to the door, the square slot was being opened and a pink, hairy hand was sticking a cellular phone inside of her cell. She stayed where she was for a while trying to see if it was a trick or if she was dreaming. It wasn't until the hand wagged the cell phone that she cautiously approached the slot and took it. As soon as she took the device, the hand shut the slot and she heard the sound of leather boots making their way down the corridor. Odette sat down on her bunk wondering what she was given the cell phone for. She opened it, and the blow of its screen shined it in her face. The first thing she did was go to the contacts in it. She didn't find a name in it, but she did find a letter, a capital *P*. Looking at the number, she didn't know who it belonged to, but something told her that it was Kreon, and he used the letter P for his nickname, Papi.

Odette went to dial the number stored inside when her cell began to vibrate with a call through Skype, from *Anonymous*. Her brows furrowed as she wondered who it was, but she didn't dare answer it. The vibrating of the cell phone stopped and a missed call came on the screen.

A moment later, the cellular was vibrating again with a video call from *Anonymous*. Odette's brows furrowed further and her thumb hovered over the accept button, but she still didn't answer the call. The vibrating stopped and the cell began vibrating again with a third call from the same caller. By this time, Odette's curiosity had gotten the best of her and she answered the call. A smile stretched across her battered face once she saw her boo, Kreon, before her eyes. He smiled at her as she traced his face with her finger.

"Hey, baby?" she waved as she continued to smile.

"'Sup, slim? You good?"

"Yeah, I just caught a fade as you would say, with some big bull-dyke bitch in her. Hoe tried to do me, you know yo' girl wasn't about to have that."

"It looks like she tagged you pretty good there. I told old boy to make sure ol' girl went easy on you."

Odette frowned and said, "Wait a minute, you mean to tell me that you set that up? You paid that fat bitch to whoop my ass?"

"Yeah, I had to, or I wouldn't be able to talk to you how I am now." He confessed. "I didn't wanna chance you gettin' the phone the cell phone when you gotta celly. For all I know the punk bitch could run and tell The Ones up in there, you Griff me?"

"Yeah, I Griff you," She nodded.

"Good."

For a while, Odette didn't say a word, she just sat there smiling and staring into the face of the love of her life, and wishing she could kiss and hug him.

"I love you, bae."

"I love you, too, slim. I miss you like crazy, too, that's why I came up with a plan to bust you outta that shit-hole."

"Bust me out?" she lay back on the mattress and stared at her phone, light illuminating her face.

"How are you gonna do that? You're a hot boy out there; the police are looking for you, too. It will be hard for you to make some moves out there. Not only that, babe, but that's a dangerous move you're talking about making. You could get chu and who every else you plan on taking for the ride killed. And that's the last thing I want to happen, for real for real, boo. I ain't worth the risk. You want to do something? Well then, save yourself, get as far away from Cali as you can."

"Stop with all that bullshit with you ain't worth the risk, you worth the risk and then some. I ain't tryna live the rest of my life without chu and the baby. I'm not leavin' y'all behind, fuck that. It's not up for debate."

Hearing this caused Odette to smile and tears to run down her face. She was smiling because she never felt more love from anyone in the entire world. She could see in Kreon's eyes how madly in love with her he was and it warmed her heart. She wanted to do nothing more than hug and kiss him. Oh, how she wished she could come through the screen of her cell phone right then.

Odette wiped the excess tears from her eyes and sniffled. "I love you, fat head."

"I love you even more, Mocha Brown," he replied. "Now, listen up. This is how things are gonna go..."

Odette listened closely to Kreon as he ran down the plan he had came up with to break her out. It seemed simple enough, but she knew that there was sure to be casualties. Now, she didn't want anyone to die, but if some niggaz had to die in order for her and her family to be together, then so be it.

"You think you up for it?" Kreon asked of her participation in the prison break.

"Yep," She nodded.

"Team Four."

"Team Four?" his brows creased wondering what she was referring to.

"You, me, Marquise, and the one in the oven," she touched her stomach.

"Team Four."

"Oh, that's so cute, babe. Team Four. Ride or Die." He tapped his fist to his chest.

"Ride or Die." She kissed him through the cellular and he did the same.

As soon as the Skype call with Kreon ended, another Skype call was coming in from someone known as Daddy

Dearest. Confusion etched across Odette's face and her forehead creased. She figured it was her father trying to reach out to her, but she had to be sure. Taking a deep breath, Odette pressed the button that accepted the call. Instantly, the upper half of her father filled up the screen. Homie had ear-buds in his ears so only he could hear what was being said to him. The last thing he wanted was to get busted and end up in segregation.

Drennen was smiling from ear to ear and so was Odette when she laid eyes on him.

"Daddyyyy." She said excited, jumping up and down.

"Hey, baby girl. How are you?" He smiled harder. He was very pleased to see his youngest, and quiet as it's kept, his favorite daughter.

"You look mighty handsome." She complimented him.

"Thank you, baby, you look beautiful, as usual."

"Awww, daddy, you really think so?" she looked at him with hopeful eyes. Besides Kreon, her father was the only man that told her that she was beautiful and she believed it. All the other times she had heard it she was sure niggaz were just saying that shit to get in her pants.

"I don't think anything, darlin'. I know so." He assured her, looking her straight in her eyes.

"Thank you, daddy." She beamed brightly.

There was silence as they both cleared their throats and tried to find something to say.

"Baby girl, I already know you have a lotta questions. In fact, that's the reason I called you," he admitted to his last born child. "So lemme begin with the day you and yo' sister ran into me outside of McDonald's." He bowed his head and took a deep breath, throwing his head back up and looking Odette in the face.

He brought his hand down his face and began, "The day you and yo' sister ran into me outside of McDonald's...I found myself starin' at my reflection in the window's glass of that fast food place. I was ashamed at what I saw starin' back at me. And you know what that was, baby girl, huh? Well, I tell ya. A no good goddamn junkie...I could only think about what must have went through your minds when y'all saw me that day." Drennen's eyes misted and his bottom lip slightly trembled. Thinking back to the day on Flatbush Avenue he'd bumped into his daughters outside of McDonald's brought tears to his eyes.

"Daddy, me and Shonda were just happy to see you. We didn't care what you looked like...we were just happy to be in the presence of our father. But it broke our hearts all over again when you ran away. That opened our wounds all over again. That day we relived the very first day you left us and we were running after your Cadillac." Tears jetted down Odette's cheeks and threatened to drip off her chin.

"I know, baby girl, and I'm sorry. I'm sorry, I'm sorry, I'm sorry." He cried, tears sliding down his cheeks. "Knowin' that I hurt chu girls like that hurts my heart."

"It's okay, daddy." She sniffled and pinched her shirt, using it to wipe her eyes.

"Now, if my memory serves me correctly, you asked what had happened to me since y'all bumped into me that day at McDonald's. Like I was sayin' earlier, I saw what I had become and I wasn't alright with it. So I ran from y'all that day, I ran as far and as fast as I could to get away. I knew I'd see y'all again, and when I did I wanted to be clean and doin' damn good for myself. Now if I was goin' to do this than it was goin' to take some time, and money. I sure as shit wasn't goin' to work a 9-5 for the shit, so I did the next best thing..."

"Where the money at, nigga?" Drennen said from behind a bandana, which he was wearing on the lower half of his face. He was standing over one of the most infamous dopemen in East Hartford, Connecticut and his

old, beat-up dusty .38 revolver with the tape around its handle was pointed at the back of his head.

"I ain't tellin' you shit, yo! You may as well go head and pop me, nigga!" Valentino said from the floor. His wrists were duct taped behind his back and so were his ankles. A lump the size of a golf ball was on his forehead. He'd gotten it when Drennen broke up into his spot and busted him in his shit, knocking him out cold.

"Oh, you must think it's a game, huh? Old pussy ass nigga! Lemme show you what time it is with me, youngsta!

Bop!

"Ahhh! Ahhhh! Ahhhhh!" Valentino screamed over and over again, like a little bitch. The bullet ripped through his thigh and ignited a fire inside of his leg. Tears came bursting through his eyes and he gritted his teeth, trying not to scream again.

"Now, let's try this again, Mr. Drug Dealer, where the money at? Choose yo' words wisely, lil' nigga!"

"Grrrrrrrr," Valentino gritted and squeezed his eye-lids tighter, combating the pain in his thigh. Tears slid down his cheeks and dripped off his chin. "Okay, alright, alright..." he took a deep breath and said, "It's inside of my bedroom inside of the mattress."

"Inside of the mattress?" Drennen frowned up and said, "Nigga, them old hidin' tactics for the loot." He shook his head as he looked down at homie pitifully. He then fled to the bedroom and grabbed the money. He came back inside of the living room with a hefty pillowcase slung over his shoulder.

"Sssss, ahhh, fuck! My gotdamn leg, man," Valentino squirmed in agony.

Drennen listened to his victim's pained cries as he approached him, whistling. He used to have mad love for the young hustler. The nigga used to work for him. In fact, when homie wanted to part ways and do his own thing, he gave him his blessing and even turned him on to connect on some blow. Now, although the nigga supplying him didn't have heroin as good as he had in his possession, the way he saw it, he had still looked out for him. Before Drennen, Valentino was sleeping in the streets and snatching old ladies purses to eat.

Drennen's ill will towards Valentino came when he started treating him like he was shit stuck at the bottom of his shoe. Drennen remembered one particular incident where his stomach was aching and he was throwing up everywhere. He was in dire need for some dope and he needed money badly. He spotted Valentino shooting hoops up at the park and asked him for a couple of dollars so he could get right. Valentino acted annoyed by his presence and made jokes of him smelling like baby shit.

He then called timeout and fished a knot of dead presidents out of his jeans, which were lying on the basket ball court where he could see them. He took all of the ones out of the money, folded them and stuck them inside of his basketball shorts. Valentino smiled devilishly and rubbed the money on his sweaty nut sack, staring Drennen in his eyes. He then pulled out the money which was covered in his stench and tried to hand it to his former father figure and mentor.

Drennen stared at Valentino with a look that could kill. Although he was strung out he still had his pride, and he wasn't about to let Valentino play him like that. With that mind, Drennen walked off the basketball court with his stomach giving him grief all of the way. He got his medicine that day by stealing a couple of pit bull puppies and selling them to a dope boy who was known around the hood to raise pure bred pits. That night, while preparing tying his belt around his arm to shoot up heroin, he promised himself that he'd get even with Valentino for the disrespect.

Drennen kneeled down to Valentino and pulled the bandana down from over the lower half of his face. He smacked him across the face viciously so he could have his undivided attention. Once he saw that his attention was focus on him, he began to speak, "I bet chu never seen me robbin' yo' old punk ass, did ya? Well, surprise, youngin'." Drennen smiled devilishly at Valentino just like he had that day he humiliated him on the basketball court. He stared into the younger man's eyes, seeing the fury that was written all over his face. He knew without a shadow of a doubt that if the young nigga could, he'd blow his brains out, but fortunately for him, he wasn't in any position to act on those thoughts in his head.

"I'ma kill you, yo! I swear 'fore God, youa dead man!" Valentino swore. His nostrils were flaring and he was clenching his jaws so tight that they throbbed.

"Oh, you mad?" Drennen angled his head to the side and looked at him like he was surprised that he was upset. "Well, you 'bouta be big mad, son." He stood up straight and drew his .38 again, popping Valentino in his head. He then headed towards the door whistling all the way.

Drennen had decided to use the money to get high one last time before he entered rehab. He stashed the money where he was sure no one could find it besides him. He knew that he'd be gone for at least three months and didn't want anyone getting their hands on it. He was going to use the hundred G's to get himself a nice place to stay and invest the rest back in the streets. That's right. He was going to get back to where he was in the drug game before he fell off.

After his stint in rehab Drennen found himself back on the streets a clean man. The money was right where he'd stashed it. He got himself a nice little apartment over in West Hartford in a middle class area. Next, he got himself a clean ass ride. It wasn't as flashy as he wanted, but it would get him to point A to point B, without any trouble.

Afterwards, he got up with his old plug and got a few of them thangs from him. Shit was cool and he was slowly creeping back to the top where he was before in the game, but he was missing two things...his daughters, Shonda and Odette. With his baby girls on his mind, Drennen set out to look for them. They weren't staying in the same house that they grew up in. Nah, someone else was staying there now.

After his discovery, he hired a private investigator to dig them up, but before he could get word back from the P.I he'd employed, his past came back to bite him in the ass.

Blocka! Blocka! Blocka! Blocka!

A nigga in black sunglasses and a black bandana over the lower half of his face, hung halfway out of the passenger window of an old ass Cougar, blasting at Drennen with a Glock.

"Haa! Haa! Haa! Haa! Haa!" Drennen ran for his life with sweat droplets falling from his brow. He constantly looked over his shoulder as he retreated from his house's porch. Homeboy dumping at him had popped up out of the bushes firing at him. He'd managed to hit him in the shoulder and caused him to drop his gun. He was on Drennen like stink on shit, so he couldn't recover his gun to defend himself. At the mercy of the gunman, he figured it was best he took the flight instead of the fight approach to the situation. And here he was now, hauling ass down the avenue and holding his bleeding shoulder

Blocka! Blocka!

"Ahhh

"Ahhh!"

A couple advancing in Drennen's direction caught the bullets that were meant to take him out. They fell to the ground and Drennen kept on running. The Cougar pulled up on him just as he rounded the corner of a bodega. As soon as it stopped, the front passenger door opened and the gunman hopped out. He ran after Drennen, but once he'd gotten within shooting distance of him, he kneeled, took aim, and opened fire.

A fire ripped through Drennen's calf and he crashed to the sidewalk, burgundy blood littering the ground. He turned over wincing and looked at his feet, seeing the gunman casually walking up on him, gun at his side. The gunman stopped at Drennen. He pulled the hood from over his head and revealed an old bullet wound on his forehead. He then pulled the black bandana from the lower half of his face, exposing his true identity.

"I thought...I thought I bodied yo' ass," Drennen's eyelids stretched wide open. He couldn't believe it was dude he'd popped some time ago standing before him in the flesh. He blinked his eyes three times thinking that his mind was playing tricks on him.

"'Sup, yo? You look like you seen a ghost." Valentino smiled wickedly.

"You know, old head, since you gave me that head-shot. A nigga feel different, my body be feelin' mad funny, yo. On top of that...I lost my sense of smell. I can't smell shit, but I can still taste though. And right now, I gotta taste for blood, mothafucka!" his eyebrows arched and his nose scrunched up.

He lifted his gun and pointed it at Drennen.

Drennen stared his killer in the eyes though, he wasn't afraid of death and he'd be damned if he gave this nigga the satisfaction of him being shaken.

Valentino pulled the trigger of his gun and it clicked. He frowned up and popped the magazine out of the bottom of his gun. He looked at it and saw that it was empty. Hearing something he looked up. His eyes bulged and his jaw dropped. Drennen brought a discarded Crooked I's 40 ounce bottle down on his head. The bottle exploded, sending broken glass and beer washing over him. Valentino fell to the ground groaning in pain and Drennen dropped what was left of the bottle. He then took off running as fast as he could on one good leg.

When he rounded the corner of the block, he ran into an approaching police car, which he flagged down. Seeing that he'd been shot, the cops stopped their cars and hopped out, with their guns drawn. The called an ambulance for Drennen and tried questioning him, but he stuck to the code of the streets. He didn't rat.

For the next few days Drennen was confined to the hospital. He tried to organize an attack on Valentino, but the hittas on his payroll didn't want any static with homie. They reasoned that he had more guns and more money than Drennen, and that he could easily wipe them all out of existence. Drennen's ego was brushed but he knew he didn't stand a chance against a nigga the caliber of Valentino. Hell, the young nigga was what he used to be when he was in the streets getting money and shit.

Acknowledging that he didn't stand a snowball's chance in hell against Valentino, Drennen got together the money he'd made on the streets and caught a train out Los Angeles, California. He'd always wanted to go there having heard so much about their sunny weather, beautiful women and bomb ass weed. He figured he could see what kind of hustles the streets had to offer once he'd gotten there.

Drennen got himself a $2,200 dollar apartment in Downtown L.A. It was a nice spacious place, and more than enough room for him. He spent his days tricking off on high-end escorts and alcohol. When night claimed the streets, he was up in the strip clubs throwing dollars and popping champagne bottles. One night in particularly, at this gentlemen's club called Starz, he found himself chopping it up with this blood nigga named, Omar. Omar was a mid-level crack dealer from the eastside of Los Angeles. They talked about everything from pussy to politics. Once the night was over, the two had exchanged *numbers so they could kick it again. They dapped up and went their separate ways.*

When Drennen had pulled open his car's door, he saw two jack boys creeping on Omar. Instantly, he drew his gun and started busted at them niggaz. A small shootout ensued between him and the jack boys.

Boc! Boc! Boc!

Splocka! Splocka! Splocka! Splocka!

"Get down, Omar, I gotcho back, yo!" Drennen called out to his new acquaintance, as he brought war to the fools that had came to do make him a victim. Hastily, Omar crawled around to the other side of his car with bullets flying over his head and broken glass peppering him. He stayed where he was until the gunfire ceased. A moment later, he looked up to see Drennen reloading his gun. As soon as he finished, he looked up to see where the jack boys were. He spotted them hopping inside of their getaway car and speeding out of the parking lot.

Police car sirens filled the air as Drennen tucked his banga and jogged over to Omar. He pulled him to his feet and the nigga thanked him for having his back.

"Don't mention it, man. We can chop it about this shit later, Jake is on the way. Let's get up outta here." He tapped him and jogged back to his vehicle. He hopped in behind the wheel and slammed the door shut. Drennen cranked his car up and pulled out of the parking lot. Shortly thereafter, Omar was pulling out behind him into traffic.

Every since then Omar and Drennen had been like brothers. Eventually Drennen gave up his dopeman aspirations and became his right-hand man's enforcer. Any nigga that needed to be got, Drennen was the one that got him.

"Daddy, I had no idea you'd came back for us," Odette wiped her dripping eyes with her curled finger.

"Well, now you know." He responded with tearing eyes.

"Listen, baby girl, I gotta go. I'll talk to you later, okay?"

"Okay, daddy, I love you."

"I love you, too, princess."

Odette kissed her father through the cellular and he returned the gesture. She then disconnected the call. Afterwards, she knocked on the iron door. A moment later, the slot inside of the door opened and she passed the cell phone out to the correctional officer. Next, she lay on her bed on her side. She held tucked one hand behind her head and held her stomach in the other. She shut her eyelids and a smile etched across her lips. Her thoughts drifted off to the happily ever after Kreon had promised her, and she couldn't wait to be free to experience it. There weren't any doubts in her mind that he was going to deliver.

***

Two months later

Odette was found guilty and given a fifteen year sentence. It wasn't long before she found herself being ushered onto a prison bus along with the other female prisoners. The next time the transporting bus stopped she'd find herself at her new home…at least for the time being.

When Odette stepped upon the bus she made eye contact with the driver. He was a white man with baby blue eyes and a bushy, dirty blonde mustache. He gave her a look that she quickly picked up on and then a slight nod, that she was sure no one had noticed besides herself. Although she'd thought about returning the gesture, she used her better judgment. She didn't want anyone picking up on what was about to pop off and foil her plans of escape. Walking down the aisle of the bus, Odette watched the women that had boarded the bus before her take their respective seats. She then sat down on the seat she was assigned beside Leslie.

Odette glanced out of the gated window and watched as one of the correctional officers walked down the length of the bus. He held a long rod that curved at its end and had a round mirror attached to it. He held the mirror underneath the bus as it walked down the entire length of it. Once he'd disappeared from out of her sight, she was sure he was checking underneath the bus from the opposite side.

A minute later, she saw the man that had been inspecting the bus step back from the enormous vehicle, having finished examining it. He looked ahead at the driver and gave him a thumb up. A moment later, the driver cranked the bus up and the gate of the facility came sliding back, leaving a clear path to the outside.

As the bus crossed the threshold Odette placed her hands on her stomach, talking to the life growing inside of her.

"Hang in there, Logan; in a minute daddy's gonna come to our rescue." She smiled as she continued to hold her stomach, looking down at it.

CHAPTER FIFTEEN

Kreon was as hot as a firecracker in the streets thanks to him and Odette's faces being plastered on every news channel. There wouldn't be a soul in the streets that didn't know his face so he knew it was best that he donned a disguise. With that in mind, he fitted himself with a wig made of cornrows and a thick goatee. He also wore glasses and slipped on a fat suit, which made him look all of three-hundred and fifty pounds. His clothing was a black P fitted cap, a white T-shirt, a black leather jacket and heavy gold jewelry.

When Omar and Candy saw his duds and disguise they gave it a thumb up, approving of his appearance. Afterwards, they left Omar's apartment and headed out to Gizmo's shop out in Los Angeles. It took them about 40 minutes to get there being that they were driving out from Paramount and there was a little traffic on the 105 freeway.

As soon as Candy pulled up outside of Gizmo's she murdered the engine. Right after, the doors were coming open and everyone was hopping out. Omar was on his cellular heading for the entrance of the auto shop, with Candy and Kreon flanking him.

"'Sup, Giz? We here, man." He spoke into his cell phone, then listened to what the person he called had to say. "You'll meet us inside of the garage? Alright, bet." He disconnected the call and told his crew exactly where they were headed.

As they made their way towards the garage, Kreon was looking all around suspiciously. For some strange reason he got the feeling that the cops were going to pounce out on him and arrest him. If they did, he had no plans on going down quietly. Nah, he was going to grab that tool off his waist and sing all of their asses a lullaby. He was just paranoid at the moment though. With the getup and wig he was wearing, no one could tell who the hell he was. Shit, if it wasn't for him getting dressed at Omar's crib, Candy and Omar wouldn't be able to tell who he was.

Entering the garage of the auto shop, Omar, Candy and Kreon saw sparks flying as a crew of Mexican men in oily jumpsuits were hard at work. They were wielding parts onto cars, adding tires, sunroofs, sound systems, spoiler kits and a host of other things. The threesome moved through the garage taking in their surroundings. They were so engrossed in the scenery that they didn't notice the tall, slender dude standing ahead of them. Homie was rocking short twisties, a thin goatee, and thick eyeglasses. He was dressed in a navy blue Dickie jumpsuit and steel-toe boots. Right then, he was rubbing the oil from off his hands with an oily rag. Once he was done, he tucked the rag into his right back pocket.

"Finally came by to pick up ya toys, huh?" Gizmo said, taking the time to shake everyone's hands.

"Yeah, they ready, right?" Omar asked as he took his hand back from shaking Gizmo's hand.

"Yep, they're ready and waiting. They got clean plates and everything."

"Let's see 'em then." Omar replied.

"Right this way." Gizmo motioned for them to follow him. He headed towards the shutter of an even larger garage, whistling Dixie. Reaching the garage, he stepped over to the digital panel which was on the left hand side of the shutter. Still whistling, he placed his palm on the flat screen which had the imprint of a hand. A blue laser ran up and down the screen. He placed his palm down on top of the hand impression and the laser turned red. *Access Denied* showed up on the screen.

Gizmo whipped out his rag and wiped his hand off thoroughly. He then placed his palm back down on the hand impression. A second sweep of the laser caused it to turn green, and *Access Granted* appeared on the screen.

Gizmo pulled out his cellular and used its flashlight to find the control panel on the inside of the second garage. Locating it, he pressed the button that lowered the shutter. Once the shutter had shut, and they were left in darkness, he found the light switch with the help of his cell phone's flashlight.

He flipped on six light switches. Each switch turned on a light that lit up a different section of the enormous storage space. Once the space was well lit, there were two sports cars at the center of the floor. Both of the vehicles were Hondas. One was a turbo charged Honda Del Sol and the other was a turbo charged Honda Accord V6. The automobiles were black on black. They had black leather seats and matching tinted windows. They were complete with spoiler kits, chrome exhaust pipes, and other equipment that would allow them to go faster than they normally would.

"That's them?" Omar looked back at Gizmo.

"That's them." He nodded the confirmation.

"Good," Omar responded and then turned to Kreon. "Come on, nephew, let's check these bitches out. See what they workin' with."

"The keys are already in the ignitions." Gizmo called out to the threesome as they fled towards the Honda race cars.

After sliding his cellular back inside of his pocket, he folded his arms across his chest, watching them fire up the Hondas and speed around the spacious garage. The vehicles ripped back and forth, around in circles, vertically, horizontally and diagonally on the shiny waxed floor of the garage.

The scene looked like some shit out of the Fast and the Furious movies. Suddenly, the Hondas stopped and everyone hopped out. They were dapping one another up and giving each other high fives as they made their way in Gizmo's direction. They were discussing the speed of the cars excitedly.

"So what chu think, Omar? You fucking with me or naw, dawg?" Gizmo smiled and opened his arms. He knew that they loved the Hondas and he was glad that he could deliver vehicles to them that they adored.

"Most def', my nigga," Omar dapped him up.

"What's up with the fire power though?" Kreon asked, rubbing his hands together in anticipation. He knew with the move that they were about to bust that the police would more than likely be on them like stink on shit, so they'd definitely need some shit that would lay their asses down.

Gizmo snapped his fingers as if he'd just recalled something and said, "Them bitches are in the trunk of the Del Sol, man. I forgot. Follow me," he motioned for them to follow him and proceeded towards the vehicle he'd stashed the weaponry inside of.

Gizmo popped the trunk on the Honda Del Sol and revealed to low black boxes. He took them both out and sat them down on the floor. Shutting the trunk, he sat the boxes on top of the trunk and popped the locks on them. Opening their lids, he revealed the AK-47s assault rifles with the two drums that they came with, which were embedded in the charcoal gray cushioning inside of the gun cases.

Omar and Kreon stepped forth and grabbed the AKs out of their gun cases. They hoisted the sticks up and looked through their sightings, aiming them across the garage at imaginary threats. Once they were done doing this, they placed the assault rifles back inside of their respective gun cases and shut them, snapping their locks closed. Afterwards, they placed the gun cases back inside of the trunk and Omar slammed it shut.

"Alright, that's everything." Omar began smacking imaginary dirt from off his hands. "Pay the man, baby."

With that having been said, Candy stepped forth with a worn brown leather bowling bag. She handed it to Gizmo and he unzipped it. Peering inside the bag, he saw several stacks of wrinkled dead presidents secured by rubber bands. He smiled from ear to ear and then zipped the bag back up. He shook the hands of the threesome and told Omar how it was a pleasure doing business with him.

Omar and Kreon drove the Hondas back to the rally point while Candy drove back the Excursion. On the way back Kreon sent out a group text to everyone letting them know that they had the cars they'd need to break Odette out of the prison bus. He then told them to meet him at the low key spot that they had before when he called a meeting with them. With that out of the way, he hit up Drennen to let him know that everything was going as planned and that he'd hit him with another text once everyone was airborne

"...It's like I told you before, OG. I got this." Kreon assured him, speaking into the Blu-tooth headset as he drove through the streets, bringing up Omar's rear.

"I really do hope so, youngin'. 'Cause it's not only my daughter's life that rests in your hands, but the life of my grand baby." Drennen said as he spoke into his contraband cell phone, pacing back and forth across his cells floor.

His celly was sitting on the top bunk flipping through the pages of Smooth magazine. He didn't even appeared to be paying the conversation at hand any mind, and he actually wasn't. Homie was too busy thinking about fucking the half naked women in the magazine.

"I know. Believe you and me, it's a lot on my plate, OG. But a young nigga gone rise to the occasion, just have faith in me."

"I got all of the faith in the world in you, youngsta. I like to think I had a hand in raisin' you." He lay down on the bottom bunk and looked at the picture of Odette that was being held upon the wall by a piece of chewed up gum.

"You did," Kreon made a right at the corner, still following behind Omar. "I look at you and unc as father figures, you Griff me?"

'Yeah. Just be sure to lemme know once y'all up in the sky in that bird. You hear me?" he asked, still staring at the picture of Odette.

"Fa sho'. I got chu faded."

"I love you, man."

"I love you too, OG." He disconnected the call and tossed his cellular onto the passenger seat.

***

Omar, Carlos, Candy and Kreon stood inside of the living room with their heads bowed, holding one another's hands. They were all dressed for the day's mission. Omar had decided to say a prayer for them before they set out to execute the task they had in mind.

"Dear, Lord," Omar began the prayer, "We're gathered here today to ask that you cover us in yo' blood, and shield us from our enemies fire, as we embark on our mission to save Odette from her impending doom. In Jesus' name, we pray. Amen."

With that having been said, everyone crossed themselves in the sign of the crucifix.

"Hold up y'all, I gotta take a piss 'fore we get up outta here." Kreon announced before he headed for the bathroom.

He shut the door behind him and lifted up the lid of the commode, unzipping his Dickie's. As soon as he pulled out his meat he started pissing.

Once he was done, he flushed the toilet and shut the lid. He then stepped to the sink and turned the dials. Instantly, the faucet ran with warm water. Having lathered his hands with soap, he held them under the flow of water and rinsed them clean.

Afterwards, he cupped his hands under the water and splashed some onto his face. When he looked back up, he met the evil reflection of himself again. It was the same reflection of him he'd seen in the men's rest room at the gas station.

"What the fuck?" Kreon's forehead wrinkled, startled by the presence of his evil reflection

I can't believe it, you really finna go through with yo' dumbass plan of bustin' this broad outta that prison bus? Damn, man, is the pussy that good?

"Shut the fuck up and watch cha bitch-ass mouth." Kreon scowled. "O ain't just some broad to me. She's the love of my life and she's carryin' my seed."

Unh, huh, how you know that mothafucka yours? It's probably that nigga, Donald's baby. You rememba the situation with Donald, right? What makes you so special that it can't happen to you?

"I'm not Carlos, I'm Kreon. What she had goin' on with that man is between her and him. Ain't got shit to do with me," Kreon said confidently. "What me and O got is on an entirely different level. I ain't never felt this way before about anyone, and neither has she."

She told you that lame ass shit and you fell for it? Soft-ass nigga, bein' led by his emotions. You may as well cut cho nut sack off and...

Crack! Crackk! Crackkk!

Kreon slammed the butt of his banga into the medicine cabinet's mirror. Broken glass and particles fell inside of the sink, looking like crushed diamonds. After wiping the butt of his gun off on his Dickie's, he tucked it on his waistline where he'd drawn it from and laid his shirt over it.

Knock! Knock! Knock!

"You okay in there, Kreon?" Candy called out from the opposite side of the door.

"Yeah, I'm straight. I'll be out in a minute," Kreon looked to the door as he talked to her.

Once he heard her footsteps receding, he focused his attention back to the conversation he was having with his thoughts.

"I'm tired of hearin' yo' dick suckas, nigga, you always got somethin' negative to say out cha lips. From now on, fuck what chu got to say. I'ma ignore that shit 'cause I gotta family that's dependin' on me to come through for 'em. I can't let chu fuck up this mission. I gotta pull this one off; O and the baby are countin' on me. I'm all in. Win, lose or draw, so fuck you all in yo' mothafuckin' ass. And I mean that with the utmost disrespect. Now, if you'll excuse me, I gotta young lady that needs to be saved."

When Kreon came out of the bathroom he saw Omar and Candy surrounding Carlos, as he was removing the blanket off of something that looked like it would be used in the military. Not only was Kreon surprised to see the deadly weapon, but Omar and Candy appeared to be also.

"My nigga, what the hell you plan on doin' with that?" Kreon inquired as he stepped between Candy and Omar, observing the weapon along with them.

"Just in case we go to bust baby momma out and one of them helicopters get on our asses. I can blow that bitch straight outta the sky." A smiling Carlos pointed his deadly weapon at different furniture in the room, before lowering it down to the floor at his side. He then patted it like it was an obedient dog. "Great idea," Kreon smiled and dapped him up, "Now come

CHAPTER SIXTEEN

A police car sat parked on the side of a 7-11 occupied by two cops. They stuffed their faces with Big Bite hotdogs topped with the works and slurped mixed Icee's.

The day seemed to crawl by so they found themselves bored, just hoping some sort of drama would arise to keep them busy until it was time to clock out.

"Ahhh, fuck, man!" O' Reilly looked down at the mustard and ketchup stain on his uniform.

"Yeah, that's a beaut!" Bennette whistled seeming the stain on his partner's shirt. He then tossed what was left of the hotdog into his mouth and munched it down. Afterwards, he wiped his mouth with a napkin and balled it up.

"Gemme a couple of those napkins, will ya?"

"Sure thing," Bennette passed his partner a few napkins. For a moment he watched as he tried to rub the stain out of his shirt, before partaking in his Icee again. Looking up, he saw a prison bus drive pass them. His partner looked up shortly after he did. A minute later, two black Hondas raced behind the transporting bus, back to back

Vrooooooom! Vrooooooom!

The speeding race cars left debris in their wake.

"You thinking what I'm thinking?" O'Reilly asked Bennette.

"Those cars are going to bust some one outta that bus?" Bennette inquired.

"Fucking aye, call it in!" he balled up the napkin and threw it out of the window. Right after, Bennette was cranking up the vehicle and radioing in for help.

Bennette made a right out of the parking lot and followed behind the speeding Hondas. A few minutes later, three more police cars joined in on the pursuit. They raced after the police car that Bennette and O'Reilly where occupying. Loose trash and debris rose into the air as the respective automobile ripped up the road.

***

Omar adjusted the rearview mirror and saw several police cars speeding up behind them. Candy glanced into the side view mirror and saw them hot on their trail also. Realizing that she had to get them off of their ass, she reached into the backseat and drew the blanket back from off one of the AK-47s with the hundred round drums they'd purchased from Gizmo. Taking hold of the deadly weapon, she let down her window and oozed out of it. She sat on the pane and turned around, pointing the stick over the roof of the Honda. Gripping the weapon firmly, she took aim at the police car's windshield that was directly behind them.

Blatatatatatatatatatatatatat! Blatatatatatatatatatatatat!

Empty shell casings flew from out of the slot on the side of the AK as it spat rapid fire. It jerked in Candy's arms as she held it as steady as she could. The stick blew thirty holes through the windshield of the police car and made just as many cobwebs. The police officers' blood splattered against the inside of the ruin windshield.

The vehicle lost control and slammed into the police car on the side of it. The vehicle's driver tried his best to regain control of it, and he did. It was too late though, because Candy had just turned the fury of her AK on his vehicle as well

Blatatatatatatatatatatatatat! Blatatatatatatatatatatatat!

Both of the police cars went flying off the side of the road and crashing into a ditch.

"Whoooooo, that's what I'm talkin' 'bout, baby. Way to go!" Omar took his hand off the steering wheel and smacked Candy on her ample buttocks, giving her a slight squeezed. "Gemme some," he said, holding out his fist. She dapped him up.

Meanwhile...

Kreon glanced back and forth between the windshield and the rearview mirror, seeing the police cars speeding up on either side of him. He scowled and looked to Carlos. He told him to grab the shotgun from out of the backseat. The Dominican obliged him, racking the powerful weapon and passing it to him.

"Grab the wheel," Kreon switched hands with the shotgun and eased his foot off the gas pedal. Seeing that his Honda was decreasing in speed and was about to align it's self with either police car, he hung halfway out of the window, pointing his shotgun at the front passenger wheel of the vehicle.

He pulled the trigger of the shotgun and the front tire exploded, sending the police car swerving out of control, flipping over. The police car tumbled down the road, coming apart as it went along.

Seeing something in his peripheral, Kreon looked over his shoulder and saw the last police car. He switched hands with the shotgun and turned around, pointing his weapon at the front driver side wheel of the police car. He shut one eyelid as he took aim and pulled the trigger. The shotgun jerked in his hand and the tire exploded, sending the police car high up into the air. The vehicle plummeted back towards the ground, its shadow eclipsing Kreon's Honda. Seeing that it was about to come crashing down upon them, Kreon passed the shotgun back to Carlos and plopped back down into the driver's seat.

As soon as he sat down, he grabbed the steering wheel and floored the gas pedal. The Honda went flying down the road and the falling police car crashed to the ground hard. The impact from its fall sent one of its wheels rolling down the street so fast that it looked like a blur.

***

Odette sat on the side of Leslie staring out of the metal gate that covered the window. She had a solemn face as she watched car after car drive by her transporting bus. Abruptly, she perked up and looked alive seeing the black Honda racing car speeding alongside her. The window rolled down just enough for her to see Kreon's serious eyes. Instantly, a smirk formed across her lips and her heart filled with joy. She'd never been so happy to see him in her life.

Kreon nodded to Odette and she nodded back. It was from this that they let one another know that it was time to get the show on the road. After successfully communicating with her man that she was ready to execute the plan, Odette took in her surroundings. All of the women seemed to be either wrapped in their own thoughts or dozing off. Glancing ahead and over her shoulder, she saw the two transporting guard, who were armed with shotguns. They seemed to have their eyes and ears open, watching everyone carefully. It was because of this that Odette knew she had to be quick.

Leslie, who was also in on the prison break, watched as Odette stuck her fingers down her throat. She watched as she gagged and eventually spat the small, duplicate handcuff key out into her hand. The silver key gleamed in her palm, lying where it was in a pool of thick saliva. Odette wiped the handcuff key off on the leg of her jumpsuit. She then hurriedly unlocked the cuffs around her wrists and ankles. Afterwards, she passed the key off to Leslie. Once Leslie started freeing the cuffs from around her wrists and ankles, Odette went on to retrieve the items that had been secured underneath the seat in front of them.

Reaching underneath the seat in front of them, Odette pulled out a Glock .40 and a small can of spray, which didn't have a label on it to distinguish exactly what its contents were. Having seen the women moving around, the transporting guard at the back of the bus frowned. Hostile, he went to approach cradling his shotgun.

"Hey, what the fuck you bitchez doin'?" he called out from where he was.

Seeing Odette with the Glock in her hand, he went to draw a bead on her, but it was too late, she sprung into action. Odette dropped the small can of spray and dove out into the aisle. Narrowing her eyelids into slits, she gripped her gun with both hands, and pointed it up at the transporting guard. He's just trained his shotgun on her when she was pulling the trigger of her banga.

Blocka! Blocka! Blocka!

Bullets ripped through the transporting guard's side, thigh and hip, causing him to drop his shotgun. Wincing and crawling on his knees, he tried to grab his shotgun but one of the Mexican female prisoners, who wore her hair in short cornrows, had grabbed it before he could recover it. She pointed the shotgun in his face and told him in Spanish, *If you move, I'll blow your fucking head off, bitch.*

"Okay, okay." the transporting guard held up his hands in submission.

"Good boy." She slammed the butt of the shotgun into his chin and knocked him out cold. The mothafucka fell flat on his face snoring aloud.

By this time, the entire bus was in pandemonium with the women hollering, hooting and egging Odette and Leslie on with their mission.

Feeling someone running up behind her after she'd just taken out the transporting guard at the back of the bus, Odette swung her gun over her head, leaving herself looking at the approaching man, upside down. Still holding the Glock with both hands, she squeezed rapidly.

Blocka! Blocka! Blocka!

He took three to the chest and fell over dead, leaving his shotgun just out of his reach. Still looking in his direction, Odette saw the driver of the bus looking back and forth between the windshield and the rearview mirror.

She didn't have to worry about him busting a move because he was in on the whole thing. He'd been the one that had secured the gun and the can of spray she'd need for her escape.

A shadow loomed over Odette and she brought her gun back around to open fire again. That's when she saw Leslie towering over her and outstretched her hand.

"Come on, girl, let's get outta here." Leslie said.

Odette lowered her gun and grabbed Leslie hand. The bigger woman pulled her up to her feet and they ran to the back of the bus. Leslie shook up the small can and sprayed around the rectangle shaped metal gate that covered the window.

The areas of the metal gate that had been sprayed with the contents of the can turned to ice. Throwing the can down, Leslie stuck her fingers into the openings of the gate and gave it three strong tugs. On the last tug the metal gate broke free and particles of the frozen gate fell to the floor. Leslie threw the remnants of the gate to the surface. When she looked back up she was face to face with a black tinted window, which she could see out of, but outsiders couldn't see through.

"Stand back!" Odette ordered Leslie. She then pointed her Glock at the window and pulled the trigger, twice. Bullets ripped through the window and particles of broken black glass fell. Squeezing her eyelids shut, she turned her head and whacked the window with her Glock, repeatedly. The window cracked further but it didn't give. Seeing this,

Leslie looked around for something that could break the window completely.

"Hey!" someone called out to Leslie. She looked up and saw the Mexican chick that had knocked out the transporting guard with his own shotgun. She tossed the shotgun over to her. The shotgun went high up into the air, twisting in turning while en route to the bigger woman.

Leslie caught the shotgun. She then tossed the duplicate handcuff key down the aisle. The key gleamed like a diamond as it flew across the air. The Mexican chick caught it. She then gave her a thumb up and went about the task of unlocking her shackles. Next, she passed the key to the next woman in shackles. And once she was done, she passed the key to the next woman. This went on for a minute, as the women in the shackles were freeing themselves from their restraints one by one.

"Gemme some room, lil' momma." Leslie got into a shooting stance and lifted the shotgun, bracing the stock of the weapon against her shoulder. Odette stood off to the side, still holding her Glock as she watched the woman fire the shotgun on the ruined window.

Bloom! Bloom! Bloom! Bloom!

The report from the shotgun was loud and angry. The firing of the powerful weapon blew out most of the window, but left jagged black shards around the window's frame.

This didn't stop Leslie though. Flipping the shotgun around, Leslie used it to remove as much of the jagged shards outlining the window frame as she could. The sound of gunfire and roaring engines filled the air.

Looking out of the shattered window, Odette and Leslie saw the black Hondas blazing at the police cars. Once the police cars were out of the way, the Honda that Kreon was driving flew up to the rear of the bus. He stuck himself halfway out of the window and told Odette to jump out onto the hood of the car. She gave him a nod. She then ran back as far as she could to the opposite end of the bus. Looking ahead, she took a deep breath and took off running towards the window.

When she felt that the time was right she leaped through the window, soaring across the air in what seemed like slow motion and landing on the hood of Kreon's car. The impact from the collision caused her to drop her

Glock. The gun clacked on the streets and went tumbling down the road.

"I got chu, I got chu, babe. Hold on, just hold on." Kreon called out to her. He watched her grasp onto the opening at the beginning of the hood, holding on for dear life. She squeezed her eyelids shut and clenched her jaws, lying the side of her face against the car.

Looking up, Kreon gave Leslie a nod to let her know that she was next to be saved. He then glanced behind him and gave Omar a hand signal for him to take his place behind the bus. Having done this, he flew into the next lane and Omar zoomed up behind the bus, taking his place. Leslie passed the Mexican girl the shotgun. She then disappeared out of the window, running to the back of the bus. A moment later, she came running forward and leaping through the window. She landed on the hood of Omar's Honda, making a loud thud. Once Omar made sure that she had a firm grasp on the hood, he zoomed out of the lane to catch up with Kreon.

***

Vrooom!

Kreon's Honda ripped up the street with a police helicopter following high above him.

"Fuck, man, a goddamn police helicopter is on our asses," Kreon heard the spinning propeller of the ghetto bird above. He shook his head because he knew that once the ghetto bird was on you that you didn't have a snow ball's chance in hell of getting away. "Ain't no escapin' this bitch, fuck it, if I'm goin' out then I'm goin' out bangin'." He dipped his hand underneath the driver seat and his hand came back out with a banga.

"Not as long as I have a say about it." Carlos told Kreon. He then turned around to Odette who was occupying the backseat, "Odette, gemme that thang underneath that blanket back there."

Odette looked to her right and found a blanket covering something. When she drew the blanket back she found a rocket launcher underneath it. She passed the rocket launcher up front to Carlos. He grasped the deadly weapon with both hands and turned back around in his seat. When Kreon glanced over and saw the rocket launcher, a big smile stretched across his face. He remembered the Dominican showing him the weapon back at Omar's house, but he'd forgotten he had it.

"Yeahhhh, that's what I'm talkin' bout." Kreon nodded his head in approval as he feasted his eyes on the rocket launcher.

"Carlos, what are you about to do with that?" Odette inquired.

"Save the fuckin' day," Carlos answered. He held the rocket launcher with one hand and gripped the window pane with the other, pulling himself out of the window. He sat on the pane and prepared the rocket launcher, placing it on his shoulder and adjusting the sight on it. As he tried to draw a bead on the helicopter, the Honda swerved a little, dipping in and out of lanes of traffic. "Say, bruh, you gone have to keep this bitch steady if you want me to get this bird off our asses."

"I got chu." Kreon said, ripping up the street down an empty lane.

"Okay, there you go…beautiful." Carlos smiled. He'd just gotten the helicopter in his sight. His forehead was wrinkled and his nose was scrunched up. He rested his finger on the trigger of the rocket launcher and waited for the perfect time. Finding it, he pulled the trigger. The launcher jerked a little as it sent the rocket flying through the sky, with smoke trailing behind it. The rocket slowly twisted through the air as it hurled towards its target. Before Carlos knew it, the helicopter was exploding into burning wreckage. Flaming debris came falling down from the sky. Some of it stabbed into the roofs of the cars below while others landed in the street, causing other vehicles to swerve out of the way.

"Yeeeeehaaaa!" Carlos called out like an excited cowboy before ducking back inside of the Honda. Odette gave him a high-five and Kreon dapped him up, giving him his props.

"That's it, that's what I'm talkin' 'bout! That's how you handle yo' mothafuckin' shit!" Kreon said, mashing down on the gas pedal. The Honda ripped up the road, swerving out of the way of the way of the burning wreckage of the helicopter that landed before it from out of the sky.

Kreon glanced into the side view mirror and saw his uncle swerving out of the way of the burning wreckage as well, before joining the same lane that he was in, hastily approaching him from behind.

"Y'all good?" Kreon asked Omar through the walkie talkie.

"Yeah, we good, nephew."

"Yep, we takin' it to the next destination now."

"Smooth."

Vrooom! Vrooom!

The two black Hondas flew up the road and left debris in the air. Everyone, in both foreign cars, were hooting and hollering while pumping their fists, except for Kreon. The young man wore a slight scowl on his face. This was because he knew that his job was far from done. You see, he had a few more loose end to tie up before it was all said and done.

****

The Hondas pulled off of the road into the woods. They drove until they came upon an ambulance and a hearse. Candy and Leslie hopped out of their Honda while Omar took his time to wipe down everything inside that they'd touched with his red bandana. He then hopped out and walked over to the hearse, opening up its hatch. Once he climbed inside he opened the coffin and took out the suits that were inside. He kept one for himself and passed the other to Candy to get dressed.

Meanwhile, Carlos and Odette had jumped out of their Honda, leaving Kreon to wipe their fingerprints off of everything that they'd touched. Once he was done, he tucked his rag into his back pocket and approached the rear of the ambulance. Odette had opened it up and was handing out EMT uniforms. She kept one for herself and gave Kreon one for him to put on.

"Carlos, you hop into the back on the gurney, I'll fix you up. It'll look like Kreon and I are transporting you to a hospital should we get pulled over." Odette informed her son's father.

"Good idea." Carlos buried his crutches in the leaves on the ground and crawled into the back of the ambulance.

"What about me?" Leslie asked Odette, wondering what role she'd play in the getaway.

"Here," Odette tossed her one of the EMT uniforms. She then went ahead and got Carlos ready in the back of the ambulance. Once she was done, she began putting on the uniform she'd taken for herself.

Everyone besides Omar was looping their respective belts around their waist and buckling them. He'd already gotten dressed and reached inside of the hearse for something inside of the glove-box. While he was busy doing God only knew what, Leslie was stripping down to her bra and panties. Holding the pants to her uniform, Leslie had just stuck one leg inside of her pants when she saw a shadow emerge behind her.

Wait a minute. If Odette and her dude are going to masquerade as EMTs, how the hell is there gonna be a third? That doesn't make any sense.

Leslie frowned as she came to the realization that there was a flaw in the plan. She went to turn around and a bullet ripped through her left eye socket, leaving a black, bloody gaping hole behind where her eye used to be.

Horror etched across her face as she had her one good eye stretched open and her mouth hanging open. She fell face-first onto the dirt and brittle leaves on the ground, revealing Omar standing behind her. He was dressed in a suit and black leather gloves, his hand clutching his smoking gun at his side.

The shot that Omar put into the back of Leslie's skull didn't bother everyone else. They went right along getting dressed, and once they were done they climbed into their respective vehicles. Omar took the time to admire his handiwork before dropping the murder weapon beside his victim's dead body. He then peeled off the gloves and tucked them inside of his suit's jacket. He gave Leslie's lifeless body one last look before retreating back to the hearse and peeling off.

Leslie was facing life without the possibility of parole. She had gotten high of PCP and drowned all three of her children. The nigga that Omar was plugged in with had hollered at her while she was on lock with Odette. They promised her freedom if she would assist in breaking Odette out of the prison bus. All she had to do was make sure little momma made it off the bus in one piece and she could board the plane with everyone else to Cuba. Needless to say, she agreed to the deal. The way she saw it the choice was a no brainer. She could either help Odette escape or spend the rest of her days behind steel and concrete.

Once Leslie had served her purpose Omar went ahead and put her out of her misery. There wasn't any chance in hell he was letting her catch that flight with them. He didn't trust her as far as he could throw her, so he wasn't taking any chances whatsoever. She had to go, so he set her free, like she was a caged pigeon.

Vrooom! Vrooom!

The ambulance and the hearse flew in one after another, stopping not too far from a jet. Everyone hopped out of their respective vehicles, dapping one another up and giving props on a job well done.

Once the pleasantries were exchanged, Candy grabbed a duffle bag out of the hearse that she and Omar came in. Kreon grabbed a duffle bag out of the back of the ambulance he, Carlos and Odette had driven there in. After Carlos had hopped out with a cane that had been stashed inside for him, Kreon slammed the doors of the emergency vehicle. Right after, he passed Odette the duffle bag and kissed her.

"Go on up to the jet, baby." Kreon cracked a smile and smacked her on her ass as she sauntered towards the ladder that led up to the jet that was waiting to fly them to Cuba.

Odette stopped at the bottom step of the ladder that led up to the jet. She turned around and ran over to Carlos. She then thanked him and pecked him on the cheek which caused him to blush.

"You welcome, take care of our boy." Carlos cracked a one sided smile, as he walked his child's mother back towards the ladder. When he looked up, he saw Ella and Shonda standing at the entrance of the jet. Shonda and Ella were smiling and waving as she held Marquise in her arms.

"Hey, momma, daddy, and Kreon." the little dude waved to them and they returned the gesture.

"I love you, son. I'll be out there to see you once you get settled." Carlos kissed his palm and blew his baby boy a kiss. Right after, Marquise returned the gesture.

"Okay." Marquise replied.

"Hey, sis, you ready for this move?" Omar called up to Ella.

For a time Ella was silent, looking between her brother and son, trying to figure out how she should respond. "Yeah, it's time for a change."

"Ma, we'll be up there in a minute, y'all gone and get strapped in." Kreon called up to his mother.

"Okay. I love you." Ella said to her only son.

"I love you more." He smiled up at his mother. She smiled back and headed back inside of the jet along with Odette and Shonda. Once they were out of sight, Omar turned around and addressed his uncle.

"What's up, nephew? Somethin' you wanna holla at us about before we hop on this jet?" Omar asked with a creased forehead.

"The only nigga I wanna holla at is you...*Uncle Daddy*'

The words that came out of Kreon's mouth caused Omar's forehead to wrinkle. A confused expression came across his face and he looked out the corners of his eyes. He appeared to be thinking about something, when suddenly a smile spread across his face.

Omar chuckled and said, "Oh, you got jokes? Very funny, come on, nephew. We gotta flight to catch," he motioned for Kreon and the others to follow him, but when he didn't hear their footsteps behind him, he turned around with a look of wonderment across his face. Looking around at everyone, all he could see were their scowling faces and clenched jaws. Everyone was mean mugging him, even his bitch, Candy. "Fuck is y'all so hostile about?"

"Nigga, don't play stupid, you know exactly what the fuck we hostile about!" A teary eyed Kreon spat, as he pointing his gun at Omar. He never thought he'd see the day that he'd be turning his banga on his own uncle. But life was funny like that sometimes; you never knew what kind of situation it would put you in.

"Boy, is you crazy, pointin' a mothafuckin' strap at me, I'm yo' uncle?" Omar's brows wrinkled, and as soon as he took a step forward, he saw movement at the corner of his left eye. When he looked, Candy had tears in her eyes and she was pointing her gun at him, too. "Candy?"

"You're a sick, sick man," she shook her head like it was a crying shame. "the things you've done to yo' own people."

Seeing movement at the right of his eye, Omar looked and found Carlos pointing his gun at him too.

"Yo, Kreon, what the fuck is up?" Omar inquired. He was nervous now and his heart was thudding inside of his chest.

"You know exactly what the fuck is up." Kreon, still pointing his gun at his uncle, took the time to wipe the tears that slid down his cheeks.

"No, I don't, talk to me, nephew, lemme know what's up."

"The fact that you standin' there actin' as if you don't have the slightest idea of what I'm talkin' about is an insult within its self. But fine, I'll humor you…"

An eighteen year old Ella was lying in bed asleep when her bedroom door slowly opened. Once the door was ajar, the hallway light shined on Omar's back as he stood in the doorway. He shut the door quietly behind him and made his way in Ella's direction, groping himself. He slowly peeled the covers off of Ella and exposed what she was wearing. She had on a bra that was straining against to hold her enormous breasts and panties that struggled to contain her meaty buttocks. Seeing his half naked sister caused lust to fill his eyes and his dick hardened inside of his Dickie's. He groped himself roughly and licked his lips. The sick bastard could wait to be between his sister legs.

"Damn, Blood, sis thick as a mothafucka. Onna gang," Omar looked around for anything that he could find that would keep his sister's wrists and ankles bound. He knew that she wouldn't willfully let him fuck her, she'd most definitely put up a fight. So he knew that it was in his

best interest that she could move her hands and legs to fight him off.

The ends of Omar's lips curled and made a wicked smile. His eyes landed on the items he could use to keep Ella's wrists and ankles bound. Having pulled the pillowcases from off the pillows on the bed, he used them to tie his sister's wrists behind the headboard. He then snatched the sheet from off the bed and used it to tie her ankles to the bed rail. Having done this, he let his red Dickie's drop around his ankles. Doing this, he revealed the nest of nappy hair above her hardened dick as well as his hairy legs. He switched hands with the red bandana he had and stepped out of his pants. Sneakily, he crawled into bed and positioned himself in between his sister's legs. Spitting a glob of saliva into his palm, he then lubricated his manhood and pushed himself inside of Ella.

Feeling the walls of her vagina opening up, her eyelids popped open and she stared at her brother accusingly. When she tried to scream, he shoved his bandana inside of her mouth and clamped his hand around it. Ella's muffled screams filled the air and she thrashed violently, trying desperately to get away. It didn't matter though. Her efforts were useless because her restraints held her in place.

"Uh! Uh! Uh! Uh!" Omar pumped feverishly inside of Ella, jumping up and down inside of her womb. "Awwww, fuck, Blood, you got...you got some bomb ass pussy! Shiiiit!" his eyes rolled back into his head and a silly smile etched across his face. He licks as ecstasy consumed his entire body.

"MmmmmMmmmm!" Ella screamed and screamed as her brother's sweat droplets pelted her face. Her eyes accumulated tears which came running down her cheeks. She threw her head from left to right, and continued to try to break free of her bondages. Realizing that her struggles were in vain, she gave up and went limp right then. At that

moment, she squeezed her eyelids shut and tears jetted down her cheeks.

Ella lay in bed like she was lifeless. She listened to Omar's grunts and moans as he continued to sex her against her will. All she could do was pray that he'd finished soon. She just wanted the nightmare to be over with as soon as possible.

Omar went on violating his sister. It wasn't long before his body was wet and sticky. He started humping Ella faster and harder, feeling himself about to drop his load. The faster and harder he humped her, the quicker the tears flooded her cheeks over and over again.

"Awww, shit, I'm 'bouta cum, I'm 'bouta bust all in yo' pussy!" Omar threw himself into Ella three more times, causing the headboard to smack up against the wall. His last thrust made him bust deep inside of Ella. Omar's warm semen painted his sister's internal walls. A second later, his clear goo oozed out of Ella's pussy and slithered between the crack of her buttocks.

Omar collapsed on top of Ella. He lay with the side of his face against her chest, breathing hard. Having gathered himself, he peeled the side of his face from off his sister's check. Looking down into her face, he saw her staring blankly up at the ceiling. She breathed easily, lying as still as a statue. Seeing this, Omar removed her restraints and took the bandana out of her mouth. Keeping his eyes on her, he put his Dickies back on and fastened them on his waistline. He then tucked his bandana inside of his back pocket.

Omar walked over to the bedroom door and pulled it open. Looking back, he saw her staring at him with fresh tears in her eyes. She watched as he smiled evilly and placed his finger to his lips, telling her not to tell anyone. With that gesture given, Omar shut the door behind him, leaving Ella behind in bed. Ella's head dropped back down onto the pillow and she continued to stare up at the *ceiling. Her pussy felt as if it had been ripped open. It was aching, and she was sure that it was bleeding.*

Ella managed to get herself out of bed. Sitting up on the side of the bed, she leaned over and placed her face into the palms of her hands. Having gathered herself, she shuffled over to the bathroom and opened it. Closing the door behind her, she turned the dials of the shower and instantly the water sprayed out. She then adjusted the dials to she found a temperature for the water that was just right for her. Once she done this, she reached between her legs and rubbed her hand up her pussy.

When she looked at her palm it was smeared with blood and semen. Staggering over to the commode, she plopped down on the toilet and pissed out as much of her brother's semen as she could.

"God," Ella began, looking up at the ceiling. "Please, don't let me be pregnant. I don't believe in abortions, Lord, but, damn, could I really have my brother's own child."

Ella got up from off the toilet's seat, wiping herself and flushing the soiled toilet tissue down.

Afterwards, she took off her bra and climbed inside of the tub. She felt a slight calm come over her body as soon as she felt the hot water hit her. She bowed her head and placed her hands upon the tiled wall. Ella's entire form shuddered as she dropped teardrops that couldn't be seen within the spraying water from the showerhead.

Ella found out she was pregnant a couple of days later. At the time she was only having sex with her boyfriend, Khadafi, unprotected so she didn't know whether the baby was his or Omar's. She told Khadafi what happened and he loaded up his gun, vowing revenge. She was able to stop him though.

Although Omar was a raping bastard he was still Ella's brother, and she didn't want to see him dead. Once the baby was born and she found out that it was her brother's, Khadafi was mad with rage but he vowed to raise the child as his own.

Khadafi turned to drinking and later on crack to deal with the fact that he was helping raise his girlfriend's and her brother's child. The wretched mothafucka hated Kreon. He abused him verbally and physically every chance he got. His neglect caused the boy severe psychological problems that he was still suffering from today. The only reason why Ella had broken up with Khadafi was because he'd turned his alcohol fueled rage onto her, and she'd almost killed him. Realizing that if she kept fucking with homeboy that she'd eventually kill him or he'd fuck around and kill her or her son, she severed ties with him.

Sometime later Khadafi gave his life to the Lord and became a Catholic priest. He delivered the word of God to anyone willing to listen, and ushered misguided souls into the direction of the religion he believed would be their salvation. Still, he was willing and dealing in drugs on the side which was how he found himself in Omar's clutches.

Kreon had told Omar all the wicked things that Khadafi had done to him growing up. Angry, the gangsta/drug dealer lured the crooked priest into a trap with promises of big money for transporting drugs for him. When Khadafi showed up at the location that they were suppose to meet, Kreon murdered him, and sent him to the very God that he worshipped and served.

Realizing that he wasn't going to be able to talk himself out of his impending doom, Omar cautiously pulled his red bandana from out of his back pocket. He went on to tie the bandana around his head Tupac Shakur style. Next, he took out a pair of black sunglasses and slid them on his face. Afterwards, he held his hands at his back and lifted his head high to accept the fate awaiting him

"Not in the face, alright? I wanna at least have an opened cask…"

"Nigga, fuck you!" Tears spilled down Kreon's face as he opened fire on Omar, sending muscle and broken bone flying from out of his face. Candy and Carlos were right behind him. They squeezed the triggers of their guns rapidly and they slightly jumped as they spat fire. The bullets from the three guns went through Omar's body and splattered blood at his feet. He danced in place for a minute before falling face first, and landing on the surface like a fish out of water.

The smell of gun smoke and blood lingered in the air. Everyone that had been busting on Omar lowered their guns at their sides. Kreon, still mean mugging his uncle, strolled over to him and put two more into his face. *Fuck an open casket funeral!* Standing over him, he kicked him in his side and spat on him.

"Punk-ass mothafucka...rest in shit!"

Hearing whimpering at his back, Kreon turned around to find a crying Candy. Still holding her warm gun, she wiped the wetness from her cheeks with the back of her fist. Feeling for her, he walked over to her and gave her a hug. She wept in his arms for a while as Carlos stared at them. Once they broke their embrace, Kreon thanked her and kissed her tenderly on the forehead.

"We good here, my nigga?" Carlos asked Kreon from where he was standing with his gun at his side. He turned around to him glassy eyed and serious. His heart ached having had to kill his uncle/father, he was hurt that he'd molested his mother and added to his internal pain. Now here he was with another reason to hate himself and not trust anyone. He wasn't going to use these situations as excuses to go on living how he was though. Nah, he was going to start his life from scratch in a new place with his new family.

"Yeah, we good here," Kreon held out his fist for dap.

Carlos looked down at Kreon's hand like it was holding a poisonous snake. His forehead crinkled and so did his nose. He sucked his teeth and said, "Don't get it fucked up, we ain't friends. I'll neva forgive you for the shit you had me do."

"Fair enough," Kreon nodded, understanding where homeboy was coming from. "Well, listen, we gone get outta here; I left yo' slice of the pie inside of the glove-box in the Challenger over there." He nodded to the car behind Carlos. When the Dominican man looked he discovered a yellow 2015 Dodge Challenger with black racing stripes on it. It had a V-12 hemi engine and shiny alloy rims.

When Carlos turned back around Kreon was tossing him the keys to the sports car. He caught them at the last minute. Looking down at his fist, he opened it and saw the keys in it. Seeing them, he looked back up at Kreon.

"She's all yours, my nigga. Salute," Kreon saluted him. He then motioned for Candy to follow him. Together, they grabbed two gas-cans and doused the ambulance and hearse with gasoline. They splashed the smelly, flammable liquid on the inside and the outside of the getaway vehicles. They poured the last of the gasoline out around the cars and tossed them aside. Afterwards, they climbed the ladder inside of the jet and shut the hatch behind them.

Carlos pushed the ladder out of the way as best as he could on one good leg. He then looked up at the jet. A smile etched across his lips as he saw Marquise's face pressed against the window, looking down at him and waving. He returned the gesture as the jet slowly made its rounds before lifting off into the air. Once the jet was in the sky Carlos made his way over to the Dodge Challenger. En route, he pointed the small remote on his car key chain at the vehicle and pressed a button that unlocked it.

Carlos opened the driver door and plopped down on the seat, slamming the door shut behind him. He tossed his cane into the backseat and popped open the glove-box.

This caused several stacks of money to come spilling out onto the floor.

Carlos smiled. He picked up one of the stacks of money and ran his finger over the top of it, watching the cash flicker before his eyes. Afterwards, he kissed the money and tossed it inside of the glove-box. Right after, he tossed the rest of the stacks of money inside of the glove-box and smacked it closed. Adjusting himself in the driver's seat, he strapped his safety belt across him and stuck his key into the ignition. As soon as he turned the key the vehicle came to life and triggered the explosive that was underneath it.

The Challenger exploded instantly and sent burning debris flying. Embers went up into the air and landed on the gasoline that the Hondas had been soaked with. As soon as the embers met with the flammable liquid a fire was ignited. Blue flames swept over the ground and spread towards the getaway cars, engulfing them in flames. It wasn't long before the Honda and the Challenger exploded.

***

Twenty feet into the air, Kreon stared down at the Challenger as Carlos made his way towards it. He watched him jump behind the wheel of the vehicle and slam the door shut. He continued to watch him for a minute as he waited for the precise time to press the button on his detonator.

"See ya, wouldn't wanna be ya," Kreon smiled devilishly and pressed the button on his detonator. Instantly, the Challenger exploded and embers went flying everywhere. Before he knew it flames were sweeping over the ground and engulfing the Hondas. A few minutes later all three of the cars exploded into flames, sending wreckage rocketing everywhere.

Kreon watched as the driver's door swung open and Carlos fell out on the ground. The flames cooked him alive as he crawled forward without a destination. He got about five feet before his movements ceased. He laid where he was dead and the fire continued to cook his corpse.

"Babe, what're you looking at?" Odette asked curiously as she tried to look over his shoulder and peer out of the window. Hearing her at his side startled Kreon. Swiftly, he pulled the window shade down and looked to his curious girlfriend.

"Nothing, baby, I was just admiring the city from up here." He looked to her, smiling.

"It's beautiful, huh?" she asked.

"Not as beautiful as you." He answered her

"Awwww, baby, gemme kiss." She shut her eyelids and puckered up, sticking out her thick, succulent lips. He leaned forward and kissed her 'plumpers'. Before they knew it they were French kissing. Once Kreon pulled away, he rested his back against the seat and she laid her head on his shoulder. She shut her lids and interlocked his fingers with hers. He kissed her again on the forehead and looked to his right. He found his mother, Shonda and Marquise nodding off to sleep, and he smiled.

"Family," he said to no one in particular, no louder than a whisper.

Afterwards, he laid his head back against the headrest and shut his eyelids, smiling. It wasn't long before he'd drifted off to sleep.

The End

Submission Guideline

Submit the first three chapters of your completed manuscript to ldpsubmissions@gmail.com, subject line: Your book's title. The manuscript must be in a .doc file and sent as an attachment. Document should be in Times New Roman, double spaced and in size 12 font. Also, provide your synopsis and full contact information. If sending multiple submissions, they must each be in a separate email.

Have a story but no way to send it electronically? You can still submit to LDP/Ca$h Presents. Send in the first three chapters, written or typed, of your completed manuscript to:

LDP: Submissions Dept
Po Box 870494
Mesquite, Tx 75187

DO NOT send original manuscript. Must be a duplicate.

Provide your synopsis and a cover letter containing your full contact information.

Thanks for considering LDP and Ca$h Presents.

<u>Coming Soon from Lock Down Publications/Ca$h Presents</u>

BOW DOWN TO MY GANGSTA

By **Ca$h**

TORN BETWEEN TWO

By **Coffee**

BLOOD STAINS OF A SHOTTA **III**

By **Jamaica**

STEADY MOBBIN **III**

By **Marcellus Allen**

BLOOD OF A BOSS **V**

By **Askari**

LOYAL TO THE GAME **IV**

LIFE OF SIN

By **T.J. & Jelissa**

A DOPEBOY'S PRAYER **II**

By **Eddie "Wolf" Lee**

IF LOVING YOU IS WRONG… **III**

LOVE ME EVEN WHEN IT HURTS **II**

By **Jelissa**

TRUE SAVAGE **VI**

By **Chris Green**

BLAST FOR ME **III**

A BRONX TALE

By **Ghost**

ADDICTIED TO THE DRAMA **III**

By **Jamila Mathis**

Tranay Adams

LIPSTICK KILLAH **III**

CRIME OF PASSION **II**

By **Mimi**

WHAT BAD BITCHES DO **III**

KILL ZONE **II**

By **Aryanna**

THE COST OF LOYALTY **II**

By **Kweli**

SHE FELL IN LOVE WITH A REAL ONE **II**

By **Tamara Butler**

LOVE SHOULDN'T HURT **III**

RENEGADE BOYS **II**

By **Meesha**

CORRUPTED BY A GANGSTA **IV**

By **Destiny Skai**

A GANGSTER'S CODE **III**

By **J-Blunt**

KING OF NEW YORK III

By **T.J. Edwards**

CUM FOR ME **IV**

By **Ca$h & Company**

GORILLAS IN THE BAY

De'Kari

THE STREETS ARE CALLING

Duquie Wilson

KINGPIN KILLAZ II

Hood Rich

STEADY MOBBIN' **III**
Marcellus Allen
SINS OF A HUSTLA II
ASAD
HER MAN, MINE'S TOO **II**
Nicole Goosby
GORILLAZ IN THE BAY **II**
DE'KARI
TRIGGADALE II
Elijah R. Freeman
THE STREETS ARE CALLING **II**
Duquie Wilson

Available Now
RESTRAINING ORDER **I & II**
By **CA$H & Coffee**
LOVE KNOWS NO BOUNDARIES **I II & III**
By **Coffee**
RAISED AS A GOON I, II, III & IV
BRED BY THE SLUMS I, II, III
BLAST FOR ME I & II
ROTTEN TO THE CORE I III
By **Ghost**
LAY IT DOWN **I & II**
LAST OF A DYING BREED
BLOOD STAINS OF A SHOTTA I & II

Tranay Adams

By **Jamaica**

LOYAL TO THE GAME

LOYAL TO THE GAME II

LOYAL TO THE GAME III

By **TJ & Jelissa**

BLOODY COMMAS I & II

SKI MASK CARTEL I II & III

KING OF NEW YORK I II

By **T.J. Edwards**

IF LOVING HIM IS WRONG…I & II

LOVE ME EVEN WHEN IT HURTS

By **Jelissa**

WHEN THE STREETS CLAP BACK I & II III

By **Jibril Williams**

A DISTINGUISHED THUG STOLE MY HEART I II & III

LOVE SHOULDN'T HURT I II

RENEGADE BOYS

By **Meesha**

A GANGSTER'S CODE I & II

By **J-Blunt**

PUSH IT TO THE LIMIT

By **Bre' Hayes**

BLOOD OF A BOSS **I, II, III & IV**

By **Askari**

THE STREETS BLEED MURDER **I, II & III**

THE HEART OF A GANGSTA I II& III

By **Jerry Jackson**

CUM FOR ME

CUM FOR ME 2

CUM FOR ME 3

An **LDP Erotica Collaboration**

BRIDE OF A HUSTLA **I II & II**

THE FETTI GIRLS **I, II& III**

CORRUPTED BY A GANGSTA I, II & III

By **Destiny Skai**

WHEN A GOOD GIRL GOES BAD

By **Adrienne**

A GANGSTER'S REVENGE **I II III & IV**

THE BOSS MAN'S DAUGHTERS

THE BOSS MAN'S DAUGHTERS II

THE BOSSMAN'S DAUGHTERS III

THE BOSSMAN'S DAUGHTERS IV

THE BOSS MAN'S DAUGHTERS **V**

A SAVAGE LOVE **I & II**

BAE BELONGS TO ME

A HUSTLER'S DECEIT I, II

WHAT BAD BITCHES DO I, II

By **Aryanna**

A KINGPIN'S AMBITON

A KINGPIN'S AMBITION **II**

I MURDER FOR THE DOUGH

By **Ambitious**

TRUE SAVAGE

TRUE SAVAGE II

TRUE SAVAGE **III**

TRUE SAVAGE **IV**

TRUE SAVAGE **V**

By **Chris Green**

A DOPEBOY'S PRAYER

By **Eddie "Wolf" Lee**

THE KING CARTEL **I, II & III**

By **Frank Gresham**

THESE NIGGAS AIN'T LOYAL **I, II & III**

By **Nikki Tee**

GANGSTA SHYT **I II &III**

By **CATO**

THE ULTIMATE BETRAYAL

By **Phoenix**

BOSS'N UP **I , II & III**

By **Royal Nicole**

I LOVE YOU TO DEATH

By Destiny J

I RIDE FOR MY HITTA

I STILL RIDE FOR MY HITTA

By **Misty Holt**

LOVE & CHASIN' PAPER

By **Qay Crockett**

TO DIE IN VAIN

By **ASAD**

BROOKLYN HUSTLAZ

By **Boogsy Morina**

BROOKLYN ON LOCK I & II

By **Sonovia**

GANGSTA CITY

By **Teddy Duke**

A DRUG KING AND HIS DIAMOND I & II III

A DOPEMAN'S RICHES

HER MAN, MINE'S TOO

By Nicole Goosby

TRAPHOUSE KING **I II & III**

KINGPIN KILLAZ

By **Hood Rich**

LIPSTICK KILLAH **I, II**

CRIME OF PASSION

By **Mimi**

STEADY MOBBN' **I, II**

By **Marcellus Allen**

WHO SHOT YA **I, II**

Renta

GORILLAZ IN THE BAY

DE'KARI

TRIGGADALE

Elijah R. Freeman

GOD BLESS THE TRAPPERS I, II, III

THESE SCANDALOUS STREETS I, II, III

FEAR MY GANGSTA I, II

THESE STREETS DON'T LOVE NOBODY I, II

Tranay Adams

Tranay Adams

THE STREETS ARE CALLING

Duquie Wilson

SINS OF A HUSTLA

ASAD

BOOKS BY LDP'S CEO, CA$H

TRUST IN NO MAN

TRUST IN NO MAN 2

TRUST IN NO MAN 3

BONDED BY BLOOD

SHORTY GOT A THUG

THUGS CRY

THUGS CRY 2

THUGS CRY 3

TRUST NO BITCH

TRUST NO BITCH 2

TRUST NO BITCH 3

TIL MY CASKET DROPS

RESTRAINING ORDER

RESTRAINING ORDER 2

IN LOVE WITH A CONVICT

Coming Soon

BONDED BY BLOOD 2

BOW DOWN TO MY GANGSTA

www.ingramcontent.com/pod-product-compliance
Lightning Source LLC
Chambersburg PA
CBHW071252250626
47159CB00004B/1150